R.L. CARROLL

In Too Deep

Book One in the Idolverse Series

R.L. Books
Stories Against The Tide

First published by R.L. Books 2024

Copyright © 2024 by R.L. Carroll

This novel is entirely a work of fiction. The names, characters and incidents portrayed in it are the work of the author's imagination. Any resemblance to actual persons, living or dead, events or localities is entirely coincidental.

Designations used by companies to distinguish their products are often claimed as trademarks. All brand names and product names used in this book and on its cover are trade names, service marks, trademarks and registered trademarks of their respective owners. The publishers and the book are not associated with any product or vendor mentioned in this book. None of the companies referenced within the book have endorsed the book.

First edition

ISBN: 978-1-7382543-0-9

*This book was professionally typeset on Reedsy.
Find out more at reedsy.com*

Three cheers for delulu pills and throwing them out the window.
Keep daydreaming.

This one is for my kpopies.
Thank you for helping me find a home.

Contents

Acknowledgement

Thank you to my beta readers and editors. You polish my writing into the gem it is. Thank you to the readers who found and loved my story in it's chaotic fic version, your words and praises are fully to blame for this books creation.

Another thank you to my partner, who encourages me and spoils me in my delusions. Thanks for being my grass to touch when I lose myself, and for motivating me to keep working on this project when I started to lose sight of my goal.

Finally, thank you to those of you who read this. I wrote something that normally stays on AO3. It's "unpopular" and doesn't fit a genre mold, especially not the cookie cutter romance one. But that's okay, because neither do we. So I hope you find amusement, escape, or even love when you read this.

Intro and Glossary

Omegaverse: an alternate universe in fiction where human biology evolved to have sub-genders that follow the wolf hierarchy. In my fictitious world there are no physical differences in the human body except for the secretion of pheromones, or scent.

1. **Alpha:** the 'top' dog, dominant, aggressive, providers. They are typically well built and have strong physical features, as well as instincts and scents.
2. **Beta:** middle ground, often the peacemakers. They typically are most 'human' in that they don't have strong scents or instincts.
3. **Omega:** the bottom, or 'submissive'. Often treated as 'breeders' or lesser than. Highly sexualized, yet also the homemakers. Their scents can be as strong as an Alpha, however tend to be sweeter.
4. **Scent/pheromones:** much like our sweat, but coated in pheromones that can affect others emotionally and physically. A person's scent smells different to everyone, usually invoking some emotion or memory associated with it. Strong scents can be used to calm someone down, and emotions can affect, and be smelled, through the pheromones.
5. **Mate:** a partner within a pack.
6. **Pack:** a found or made family pod. Oftentimes mated to each other in a romantic capacity. Modern packs are usually family units, however sometimes include platonic members as well.

KPop: Korean Popular Music. Unlike western pop, it can be a multitude of musical genres, as well as be made by non-ethnic Koreans.

Idol: a musician in the KPop industry.

Trainee: someone being trained to be an idol by one of the entertainment companies. Average length is under 3 years, where they will go through rigorous training in music, dancing, press, languages and more.

Debut: when a group releases their first album and debuts to the world. Hierarchy within the industry depends on debut date, therefore a group who debuts in 2018 will be seniors to a group who debuts the following year, regardless of the ages of the members.

Comeback: period when a group releases a new album and promotes it on music shows, reality programs, and social media.

Entertainment Companies: unlike western music, these companies have a strong hold over their idols and trainees, imposing strict rules and guidelines like diets, dating bans, whether they can change hairstyle, when to talk to fans etc.

Dorms: groups, and trainees, live together in dormitory style apartments, monitored by the companies and managers.

Maknae: the youngest member, often doted upon by the

older members.

Aegyo: the act of making cute faces or expressions, used on reality programs or in content to make fans/others laugh.

Bias: someone's favourite member.
 Bias wrecker: the second favourite who threatens the favourite's spot.

Sasaeng: a crazed fan, or stalker, who can range from disrespecting personal space, to acts of violence.

Korean Honorifics: a very complex subject but integral to understanding Korean culture. Generally, speaking to someone in a higher position, or who is older, than you requires a polite form.

'**Nim**' or 'ssi': attached to names or titles to show respect. There are levels of honorifics, with friends of the same age being the most casual polite form. Which is why age is often brought up in early introductions to decide how they should address you. If you are close to someone you can use other titles as a casual show of respect:

1. **Hyung:** what a younger male calls an older male whom they are close to.
2. **Eonnie:** the female version of Hyung, from a younger female to older female.
3. **Oppa:** from a younger female to an older male.

4. **Noona:** from a younger male to an older female.

One

Panic and Petunias

Where the hell is this restaurant? I swear to God I've
passed this park three times already. That's the same
old lady sitting on the bench! Ugh. Stupid Google
maps and stupid me for thinking I could go to a foreign fucking
country and not know the language.

You looked at your phone for the umpteenth time. The map
said you were in the right place, but the area was so dense,
and the roads were more like alleys and sidewalks. You knew
basic Korean, could read the Hangul letters, but that didn't
mean squat when you had no idea what you were reading.

You sighed, thinking you should have hired a translator. Or
taken the car the company had offered you. At least that came
with a chauffeur who wouldn't get lost like you.

"I just wanted some dumplings. Is that a crime?" You mumbled out to the universe. Your feet were starting to hurt, so you walked over to a bench in front of a beautiful array of flowers. You turned your back to the park, deciding to face them to take some pictures. There were some that were the most beautiful purple ombre.

It was only your second day in Seoul, and finding you're lost and staring at flowers would surprise no one who knows you. You have a bad habit of wandering off and getting yourself into weird situations. There was that one day you wanted to go for a hike and ended up stumbling into a secluded cult in the middle of the forest. They had been really nice though, and the grilled tofu and tomato salad was still one of your go-to barbecue recipes. It wasn't always such an agreeable situation, though. Once you got lost in Mexico City and stumbled into a drug sting operation. You really wanted a coffee, and you were also naturally clumsy. The silver lining with that one was that it gave you a great plot point for one of your books.

Which, in a roundabout way, was kind of why you were in your position today. Not the lost part, that was solely on your need for dumplings. Rather, it was why you were in Seoul to begin with. You were meeting with publishing companies who wanted to bid on the Korean translation of your newest book. Luckily, being the witty and overconfident youngster you were, you had retained your rights for translations in your contract. Score one for the underdog. Kinda. It meant you had to decide on who was going to publish and translate your work, and you were very picky.

With the last installment of your series set to come out in a few months in English, you should have already decided on this. But, being the procrastinator that you were, you'd put it off. And now, your company had all but buckled your ass in the plane themselves. Seriously, agents were so pushy.

You have three meetings set up over the next two weeks. Korea had always been somewhere you wanted to visit, so you made sure to leave yourself lots of time to play tourist. Your first meeting wasn't for another three days. Your manager hadn't loved the idea of you spending your days exploring on your own, but you hated being "guarded". Look, you'll admit, their logic is sound. It's not the safest for an unmarked Omega to be walking around alone. Especially one that could possibly be recognized. Very bold underline on the possibly, because who really remembered what their favorite author looks like? No one.

Still. You're not a complete idiot. You bought one of those self-defense key chains, with the sharp pointy things and mace. And you also took self-defense classes for a couple years. For a bookworm, you were pretty athletic, which isn't saying much. Although, right now all you wanted was a hot bath and your kindle.

And dumplings. Your stomach rumbled angrily at you. Sighing, you stood up to restart your search.

"I hear you, gosh. You're so needy, you know that? It's been like… Three hours. You can wait and digest some of this baby fat while you're at it." You rattled off to yourself. Probably a weird habit, but you found yourself talking aloud often. Chalk it up to the antisocial life you led.

Taking out your phone to pull up the map again, you began walking without looking up. But before you could go further you stopped dead in your tracks, body frozen. The wind had picked up, gusting around you and changing directions. Underneath the smells of fall leaves, fragrant flowers and dirt, was the scent of salt and ocean and sun. It smelled like sun kissed skin and salt caked hair.

It smelled like Alpha. And more than that, it smelled like Mate.

Mate. Your head spun, it was like all the lights in your brain turned off, and instead of walking into a familiarly lit room you fell off a cliff. The word mate echoed in your head over and over. After what seemed like a millennia, but was really only a few seconds, your head snapped up. The owner of the scent was standing five feet away, phone in hand and just as frozen in shock as you.

You couldn't see much of his face, the bottom half being covered by a black mask and a beanie covering his hair. But his eyes, his striking brown eyes, were wide and boring into you. He was dressed in a plain black T-shirt, black pants and white sneakers. Nothing special about any of it, and yet something inside of you screamed out at how special he was. Not something, your omega, she was the one doing the screaming and you wished now more than ever you could get her to shut up.

4

Instead of doing that, or moving or doing anything else moderately helpful, your gaze traveled and took in every tiny detail it could. He was muscular, but not in an overt way, his arms defined and his shoulders wide. His skin was pale, like really pale, but marbled beautifully with azure veins across his hands and arms. And up his -

You fell off a cliff again. Except this time, you turned and jumped off it willingly. On your supposed Mate's neck were overlapping silver bite marks. You couldn't tell how many from here, only seeing them because the light fell through the leaves just right to hit the scars.

He was bonded. With a pack. A sizable pack. Fuck.

No, you couldn't stay here. He's got a pack, clearly this is a mistake. Yep, good old mother nature playing tricks, you try and reason with yourself.

Either way, you've adequately shocked yourself into motion. And that motion is running in the opposite direction and not looking back.

* * *

DAMON

On the other end of Seoul, earlier that day...

Across the mountain across the mountain
  Across the river across the river

He blindly reached for his phone that was blaring out the beginning verses of his alarm. He wasn't exactly awake, but it was loud and aggressive enough that it got stuck in his head, keeping him from completely drifting back to sleep.

He turned over on his stomach, letting the thin black blanket flip off him. It was 6 am, which meant he'd gotten about four hours of sleep. His head was spinning, and his body felt like it was weighed down by bags of sand. He was slow to wake up, but as his snooze went off, he finally sat up, running his hands through his hair and rubbing the sleep from his eyes.

Last night he'd stayed up later than he intended, no surprise there. He tried this time, he went to the gym to tire himself out, which kind of worked. But an hour after he'd laid down for bed he got antsy, staring up at the purple and blue hues reflected on his white walls from his lights. The anxiety always got worse at night, and the surefire way of shutting it up was to throw himself into work. So, work he did. Which led to many more hours until he was struggling to stay upright and eventually collapsed into his bed. He was impressed he even made it in the bed, with the blanket on and everything. Four hours was fine, he'd be fine. That was the mantra he repeated until he believed it.

The morning had them in the practice room, working on new choreo for next spring. Bright fluorescent lighting lit the wide space, reflecting off light wood floors and the wall of shining mirrors. They were having trouble with one section, the moves just didn't match up with the transition after the second verse. Minju was working on it with the choreography team, and while the routine was awesome, really, it was just… missing something. It was probably his perfectionist tendency since no one else shared his feelings.

They still had three months until they were scheduled to start shooting material for it, which is plenty of time. Still, it left him in a bad mood when they finally called it and everyone left for their own schedules.

"Dae-Hyung, can you hold up for a second?" He stopped where he was bent over picking up his bag. He shrugged it on and faced Hansung, who had spoken.

"What's up Sung?"

Hansung raised his hand and pushed back his sweat-soaked bangs. His hair was growing out, the tips lighter than brown roots and hanging over his face. It made his round cheeks appear smaller. "Do you have a schedule tonight?"

Damon shrugged, taking his phone out to check his calendar, despite knowing his schedule by heart. "I have some tracks to work on, and the costume department sent over some sketches. Besides the gym, I think I'll be pretty free. Why?"

Hansung was studiously watching his feet twitch together. His grey t-shirt was stained with sweat, but he still looked and smelled great to him. "Uhmmm. I know it's kinda out of the way, but well, I was watching this video on street foods and it was really cool how they prepared things. Like in Mexico there's these drinks that are beer but then have a bunch of food on them like one place puts a whole burger on top-"

Damon rolled his eyes and reached out to grab his omega's shoulder, shaking him a little. "Sung, I love you. I do. But I am too tired to speak Sungie okay? Use less words please."

"Ah, Hyung, can you pick up some dumplings from that place I like please?" He looks up now, his eyes wide and lower lip stuck between his teeth. He was really pulling out all the stops today, Damon thought as he instantly melted. Hansung was their one Omega, but at times you couldn't tell. He was broad shouldered, with a tiny waist, his chest muscles well defined and arms chiselled though still lean. He carried himself with the cockiness of an alpha half the time. The other half...

"Yeah sure baby, whatever my perfect omega wants, yeah?" He ruffled the younger man's hair. Looking at the smile that spread across Hansung's face instantly lifted the cloud over his head. Leave it to his pack to wash away any worries or bad moods.

He only mildly regrets his weakness for Sung as he has to trek uphill further into the winding neighbourhood. He was anxious to just get the damn dumplings and go home, he was exhausted and he could feel the sweat from the late summer day sticking to his back. Wearing all black, with a beanie in the summer was a terrible idea, but he didn't want to deal with being recognized.

Where the fuck is this place again? I swear to god that kid finds the most random fucking places. Who doesn't deliver?

Damon was busy on his phone, texting Sung to ask for directions. If he wasn't back soon he wasn't sure what state the house would be in. An omega with a craving could be a dangerous thing, especially a bratty one like Sung. A couple months ago, before his last heat, he got a random craving for hot Cheetos. At 3 am. Obviously, the timing sucked, and despite convincing him that there was no way to get them at the time, Sung had taken his frustration out on them. Damon had never seen his pack mates run so fast. Hyunbin stayed at the gym for hours, and Minju stayed the night with friends. They were the lucky ones. The remaining two were tortured by a whiny, passive aggressive omega. He pushed so many of Leo's buttons the maknae locked himself in his room. Yeah, not having that happen again, he shivered as he walked faster.

He had reached a small park, and he finally recognized a landmark, happy to be on the right track. Looking up from his phone he took in the small green space. It was a pocket of nature surrounded by buildings on all sides. It looked so out of place, and yet also like an oasis of peace. On the side closest to him was a sizable garden overflowing with flowers. He could see some bees flying in between the flower buds lazily. The wind sent the stalks swaying, almost as if the wind was music they were dancing to.

He inhaled through his nose, wanting to luxuriate in the moment of peace and scent of flowers and earth. Instead of the sweet floral and must of cement and rotten leaves he was expecting, he caught the scent of candied oranges. It was sweet, light with a sour bite of citrus he could almost taste. The smell set every one of his nerves alight, and a primal part of his brain roared. His alpha was scratching at its cage, screaming a word over and over, itching to get closer and claim that scent.

Mate. Protect. Mate. Claim. Mate.

Damon staggered as his head snapped around until it landed on a woman standing in front of him. Was she glowing? Was he losing his mind? Or hallucinating? His brain was whipping questions too quickly to answer, or even process. The rest of him was frozen in place, an internal battle between the eagerness of his wolf and the shock of the moment and urge to crumble in on himself.

He didn't have a mate. He couldn't. If he had a mate, surely it would be someone in his pack, someone he had loved fiercely for years. His pack had been set years ago, if he was to have a mate it would have happened then. No. It couldn't be. He had gotten over it, they all had.

And yet.

Standing in front of him was a woman who smelled like Christmas and homemade jam. She smelled like a comforting word from his mom, or a reassuring pat on the back. She was standing in front of the flowers, looking back at him with equal surprise. She was as beautiful as her scent, and as her eyes met his he lost his breath.

It could have been a year, a decade, an hour. He didn't know how long that moment of eye contact lasted, but as he was about to reach out, to give in to his Alpha and take a risk, she turned and fled.

His mate, his omega, turned and ran away. And suddenly he couldn't breathe for another reason. His heart constricted and his inner wolf howled in agony. He should have run after her, but he was too lost in shock and the pain of rejection.

Why... Why would she do that? She felt it, I saw it. But she... She ran away.

Looking back, he could swear he felt his heart crack, could see part of it falling to ashes and being blown away in the wind. The logical side of his brain, the human side, told him he should be relieved. That was a complete stranger, imagine the catastrophe it would have been if he had a mate that wasn't one of the boys. The scandals, the rumors, and the toll it would take on his pack.

But a bigger part of him, the primal wolf side, was in pieces. That was his true mate, the one who was meant to complete him, match him in every way. Finding a true mate was rare, and because of that it was cherished. Damon had already given up and made peace with not having one. But now he had another chance. Well, had had because she ran away and he has no idea who she is except what she looks like. Despair settled in his bones as he realized he'll likely never lay eyes on her again.

He was shaking, tears falling down his face, as he dialled a number on his phone. He was spiralling too fast, his intrusive thoughts taking control, that angry voice in his head telling him it was his fault, he wasn't good enough, not attractive enough. He needed help, and he needed it now.

"Hello?"

"Hyung. I need you."

His voice must be rougher than he thought, because the man on the other end didn't make a bad pun with his wording.

"Dae-yah. What's wrong? Where are you? I'm on my way. Talk to me." Minhyuk's tone was low and calming. Damon could hear him walking and doors slamming as he made his way out of wherever he was.

"Hyung. I.. Mate."

"What?! Mate what? Dae-yah... Did you find your mate?" Minhyuk was running now, his footsteps heavy and his voice wavering slightly.

"Yes. I did, but she. She ran away, Hyung. My mate took one look at me and ran the other way." He was choking on his words now, emotion clogging his throat and tears blurring his vision. How had the day taken such a turn? He wanted the ground to open up and swallow him whole.

"Fuck. Dae. I'm coming. Hyung's coming. We're going to figure this out, everything is going to be okay."

Damon zoned out, he could hear Minhyuk talking, doing his best to reassure him. But he was too far gone now. At some point he'd collapsed to his knees, still staring at where his mate had been standing. The flowers mocked him, their vibrant colours and sweet scent misplaced as he felt his chest constricting and his world falling apart.

She was just... Gone.

Two

Fickle Fate

Y ou'd gotten even more lost after running blindly away from the Eco-haven. You took turn after turn, not knowing how long you actually ran for, but your heart was beating like you'd just finished an iron-man. Your mind was clouded and your omega was howling in agony. It was fine, it was all fine because you were an expert at ignoring and suppressing her. It definitely didn't hurt like a bitch and tear at your soul. Nope.

Then why are you crying? Why run at all? That was so incredibly stupid and mean. That poor man. Alpha or not. Mate or not. He's a person and he's probably sad and confused. Likely in as much pain as you are.

You hated agreeing with your inner voice, in fact you took pride in arguing with it on a daily basis - your own built-in nemesis. But now, as you leaned against the side of a building to catch your breath, rough cement rubbing against your bare arms, you couldn't help but feel awful for what you'd done. Fuck, you'd just done a monstrous thing. Mates were rare, so so rare, and you'd just spat in fate's face. Fantastic, head hung in shame you wonder when this is going to bite you in the ass.

You were an adult, a somewhat capable adult, so you pulled up your big girl panties and scraped yourself away from the brick wall. Deep breath in, deep breath out, your therapist in your head telling you that everything is easier to face head on, and you were retracing your path. Except it was proving harder than you'd anticipated since you'd run off blindly.

Another dumb mistake I should have avoided. Who goes running around blindly when they were already lost to begin with? Well, I suppose I couldn't get more lost. I think.

Ten minutes and two sore calves later you finally spotted the park. You approached slowly, your head swivelling left and right in search of your mate. You made it over to the garden but no one was around. It felt like someone had poured cement down your throat. You wanted to throw up. You hunched over the once beautiful flowers, gasping and dry heaving. It was as if that moment had split your timeline. In another timeline you had been sitting here peacefully, smelling the flowers and bathing in their natural essence. In that timeline you had a container of dumplings, and were sitting alone and blissfully unaware.

15

It wasn't that timeline though, no, you were in a timeline where you were currently cursing the evil flowers and their sickly sweet smell. You tried to reason that if you hadn't stopped to admire them you wouldn't be in this situation to begin with. You tried, and you failed, because even if you weren't fate's most studious disciple, you knew deep in your gut that this was all fate's handiwork. There was no other timeline, not for you at least.

Maybe it was your storybook mind, or maybe it was the way you saw the world in words and make believe, but there was a flame (albeit a small one) that lit itself to wait for fate to intervene again. It had once, so surely it's possible for it to do it again. Right?

You shoved it down deep, letting that flame take the space furthest from your active brain that it could. It snuggled in tightly between your belief in karma and your hope that you get an apology from your mom. So, real far back there. You abandoned your search for dumplings, swearing you'll never eat another dumpling for as long as you live (it was an empty promise, you love them and couldn't fault the delicious envelopes of flavour for your own poor judgement).

* * *

The next morning was no kinder to you. As soon as you opened your eyes your head started pounding. Was it smart to drown your sorrows in the expensive complimentary champagne sitting in your suite? No. Did you regret it?

Also no. There was something both tragic and hilarious in drinking champagne while you cried in the bathtub. That bottle was probably meant to celebrate, shared between business partners or lovers, and there you were, a naked sobbing mess. That poor bottle.

It wasn't your first hangover, but they did get harder to rebound from with age. You groaned and pulled your protesting body to the kitchen to drink as much water as you could stomach while shoving ibuprofen down. This morning you were thankful for the built-in kitchen of the suite, a luxury coffee maker stacked with fresh beans taking place of pride on the marble counter top. There was a small sink, dark mahogany cabinets above it filled with everything you could need, along with a small fridge and stove.

You ordered the greasiest food on the room service menu. Sure, there were hundreds of supposed hangover cures, but you stuck with the tried and true: grease. It was times like this that you wished poutine was an international staple, because you could really go for some fries, cheese and gravy right about now.

By the time you'd eaten, showered and dressed, you felt more human. The two cups of coffee also helped. It wasn't as late as you'd assumed, you still had three hours before your meeting was scheduled. You checked your email and looked over the itinerary you had planned out with your literary assistant back home. Today was supposed to be a shopping day out in the city, since you had been roped into a dinner after the meeting. However, you weren't in the mood to deal with large crowds anymore.

All night you'd tossed and turned with the most vivid night-mares. You were used to normal nightmares, you know, needing help but never being able to call someone, or being held captive by your crazy family. What? That was only you? Ah, right, that's why you were in therapy. But last night they were different. It was almost as if you were living them through someone else, your body not your own. Every time you got close to getting out of danger something dark and unidentifiable would claw at you and drag you back into it. It was like fighting an endless battle, and you had this deep sensation of never being enough.

The ghost of it still lingered, adding to your upset stomach. It didn't help that you still felt like a piece of your soul had been ripped away and torn up before being stomped on and then lit on fire. Like you did with the pictures of your ex. It wasn't as bad as yesterday, but there was a constant empty feeling, and your omega was quieter than usual. Any other day you'd love that, you hated the primal and hormonal urges of your "secondary" gender. It really was a nightmare for a control freak like you.

Your phone pinged, dragging you out of your mental tangent.

Mel: Okay what the actual fuck were you on last night? Can you translate for drunk you please?

Your gut dropped and you smacked your forehead. Of course you'd drunk texted. Of course. At least it was Mel, while she was technically an ex, the two of you were still best friends. She'd probably understand, or at least you hoped she would. You scrolled up through the conversation, it was a mess and drunk you clearly couldn't type or make a sentence. Honestly, you didn't even know what you'd meant to say, so you figured it would just be quicker to call.

Mel picked up your video call after one ring. She was sat up in bed, glasses propped up on her head and long burgundy hair cascading in waves across her shoulders. Only she could manage to look so good so late at night. You weren't jealous.

"You look better than I expected. You even have make-up on. And it's not crooked."

"That was ONE time. I swear to - ugh. I don't have the energy to argue. I think I drank an entire bottle of champagne."

Mel laughed, her face breaking into a bright smile. You heard someone groan from beside her and you assumed it was her partner, Sara. Mel smiled down fondly at her wife and packmate. "Okay, so why exactly did you do that? At least it wasn't a bottle of tequila, I don't think your 29 year old body could take that."

You hated that she was right. "I'm a classy bitch, okay? Anyways. I, uh, did something. And before you interrupt or lecture or whatever you're planning on doing, just know that I'm well aware of the giant mess I've created. Well. Aware."

Mel nodded, her lips tight and eyes worried. She'd known

you since you were both freshmen in university. You'd been each other's first loves, and when the attraction faded you were both still so much in love you stayed best friends. She'd seen you through your hardest times, talked you down from metaphorical and literal ledges. She was the first one you told about your book deal, and was your date to every premier. You thought you were each other's soulmates. So she knew very well how you looked when you were about to spiral.

When she said nothing you continued, biting your lip and staring at everything but her. "Yesterday I wandered the city to find this one little hole in the wall restaurant. Of course I got lost, don't laugh! Anyway, I found this beautiful park and decided to sit and rest for a bit. And then… I met my true mate and may have turned around and run away before either of us could say anything. I tried to go back once I wasn't panicking so much but he was gone." You rushed out the last part, speaking all in one breath.

Saying it all out loud made it so much worse. They say it helps, but they lie. Mel was silent on the other end, staring at you with an open mouth and shocked gaze.

"You. Did. What? Holy shit, babe, are you okay?" She was in full crisis mode- assess damage, put out fire, patch up her best friend. Sara had woken up at her partner's raised voice and you could see Mel whispering what you just said to her. Soon it was two worried faces looking at you.

"Hun, are you okay? Seriously?" Sara asked. Her short silver hair was sleep ruffled, the light laugh lines around her blue eyes even more pronounced in the dim lighting of the room.

You sighed. You weren't okay but you also didn't want to worry anyone. This was your fault. "I'm fine. Well, I'll be fine eventually. My omega is… actually I don't even know. I've never felt this sad emptiness coming from her. It's like that part of me is just non-responsive. Whatever, it's not like I know the guy. It'll fade soon, right?" Honestly you had no idea. Mates were so rare that there wasn't much research on them, and there was even less on rejected mates. The only things you heard were more like ghost stories than reputable accounts.

Mel and Sara exchanged glances, and you knew that look. They were about to mother you. True to form and expectation Mel turned back to you. "Hun, I think you should come home. You can do your meetings over video, there's no need for you to actually be there."

Anger flared into you quickly and with heat. You knew this was going to be a fight. Neither of them, as well as your management team, had wanted to let you go on this trip alone. It's dangerous for an unmated Omega. You don't know the language. What if something happens and you can't defend yourself? It burned you up like you were soaked in kerosene. Your secondary gender didn't define who you were or what you were capable of. And you resented being treated like some frail, breakable thing. Someone who can't control boardrooms but rather should be controlling a brood.

"Stop. I know what you're going to say. I love you both but

I'm not going to come home just because of some hormone driven encounter. I will be fine." Your tone was sharper than you intended, but you weren't exactly in fighting shape right now.

Your friends seemed appropriately chastised as they dropped the subject, looking sad. "Okay, well if anything else happens you're coming home, okay? I don't give a shit what you think, this isn't about you being an omega, this is about you being my best friend."

You sighed and nodded, giving the pair a small smile that you hoped conveyed your apology and love. The conversation turned to less stressful topics, like how your cat Moon was terrorising their dogs. You were proud, he was a force to be reckoned with. Soon you were bidding them both goodnight, now in a much better mood than you'd started the call with.

There were still a couple hours left before your meeting, and with a new attitude you decided to go explore some of Seoul, close enough to the hotel you couldn't possibly get lost. Theoretically. You'd saved a tiktok of a cafe where you could decorate a custom phone case. They had walls of cute looking appliques. Coffee, cake and crafts, what better combo to detach from reality and calm your nerves before a big meeting?

* * *

DAMON

A hand was shaking him awake. He knew that he should wake up, address the person shaking him. You know, be polite. But his eyes were crusted closed with salt, and his body ached from being curled into a ball all night. He barely slept, because of course he couldn't. Instead, once Minhyuk had brought him to the elder's home and tucked him into bed, he cried until there was no liquid left. Then he just stared straight ahead, lost in his thoughts.

"Dae-yah, if you don't get up I won't be able to stop them from coming to get you. And I know you don't want them to see you like this." His friend tried to coax him, appealing to the inner leader in him. He knew though that the older man was only seconds away from ripping the blanket off and forcing him up. That wouldn't be pleasant, so he grumbled and flipped over.

Minhyuk was sitting on the edge of the bed, a sad smile on his face. Damon knew he hadn't exactly explained much last night. He meant to, but he just shut down, the stress of it was too much to handle. His hyung had a warm cup of tea in his hand and he passed it over once Damon sat himself up. He inhaled the herbaceous blend of peppermint and green tea, with just a hint of vanilla and honey.

"Thanks Hyung." He mumbled as he sipped from the hot cup. He kept his gaze down, studying the ripples in the liquid.

"Dae. Talk to me. What happened? I told Minju that you stayed over but he sounds worried. Your phone's been going off all night and morning." He laid a reassuring hand on

Damon's thigh.

Damon took a deep breath but it was shaky. "I don't really know. One minute I was on an errand to pick up Sung some dumplings, and the next thing the wind was shifting and the sweetest smell hit my nose. I don't even know how I knew what it was, but my Alpha immediately recognised it as my mate. Hyung, it was like time stopped. Every fibre of my being was on fire, but at the same time it was like I felt this completeness. That smell. And then I saw her. I've never… I've never seen someone so beautiful. It was like the entire universe collided and she was the walking embodiment. I know that sounds stupid and cheesy. But the pull I felt was unlike anything else. Even with the members, we have a pull, a bond, but this was like a culmination of all of those bonds together. My alpha wanted to claim her, and for some reason it felt like… Like the bond with her was a final missing piece." Damon scrubbed his face as an errant tear fell down it. He didn't want to cry anymore, he needed to get it together.

"And then she turned and ran away. She looked right at me. Why? What could she have seen in me that made her want to run away?"

Minhyuk rubbed his leg sympathetically. He didn't know what to say to the younger man. He'd never been in this situation. Being an idol, he'd never gotten to have a regular relationship, much like the younger. Having a true mate was something special, something everyone secretly longed or wished for. There was speculation about why they were so rare, the top theory right now was that true mates weren't biologically necessary anymore as people formed their own packs and our primal natures were pushed further and further away.

None of that would help his friend though. So he stayed quiet, lending his strength and his ear.

"It hurt so much. Like something being ripped away. I can't even feel my alpha properly right now. I'm so scared Hyung. What if the boys realise something is wrong? How do I tell them that I met my soulmate, and not only that but she ran away. What if they feel betrayed, or what if they think I don't love them? Fuck. I hadn't even thought of that yet. It's going to crush them." The tears had dried and been replaced by panic and distress. Minhyuk pulled away slightly, wrinkling his nose. Dae's pungent pheromones stinking up the room for the other.

"You definitely can't go around them smelling like that Dae. Your omega will freak out. You're basically pouring out distress and anger."

Damon tried to take in a steadying breath. He was right, going back to the house with his scent all messed up would do no one any good. He needed to put his game face on. He didn't want to lie to his pack though. And he didn't think his acting was good enough to get him through a conversation without suspicion. His hands were shaking, and he was one step away from a breakdown.

He was saved from making a decision, when Minju barged

in, much to Damon's dismay. His boyfriend sure did have fantastic timing. Minju knew the code to the apartment and made the executive decision to use it, marching into the room unannounced.

He didn't have to wonder where they were, as soon as Minju walked in he smelled Damon, his own scent spiking in worry. He was already coated in worry, his own and his three other boyfriends'. None of them had bought the flimsy excuse Minhyuk had called with last night. But they also knew Damon was in safe hands and would reach out when he was ready. Minju had spent the night calming their two sunshine twins. Missing their leader was wreaking havoc on them and they didn't handle it well. Leo slept in Damon's hoodie, while Hansung stole his comforter and cocooned himself in it.

"Damon Baek. What, the actual, fuck." It wasn't a question, Minju's unamused tone tinged with his emotions. Damon felt guilt gnaw at his stomach.

"Min... I'm so sorry, I should have called, I know. Something just came up. I'm sorry, truly. How is everyone?" He was almost afraid to ask, his mind was already berating him for abandoning his pack.

So selfish. Look at Min, I bet he barely slept. I left him alone to deal with a pack full of needy kids who were probably confused and worried and scared. Fuck Damon, you suck. No wonder she ran away, what kind of pack leader just disappears without even a second thought of looping his pack in?

Minju took his leader's face into his hands, rubbing away the stray tears. He could almost hear the thoughts he knew would be running through the older man's mind. "Dae-yah. Hey. Look at me. It's okay, everyone is fine." He sat down beside him, pulling him into his arms. Damon was shaking, tears streaming freely. Minhyuk gave Minju a look, quietly questioning if he was okay to deal with this. Minju nodded and the eldest left the room, shutting the door behind him.

Minju held Damon while he cried, letting out all the hurt and pain. He didn't try to calm him down, he just let him purge himself of his emotions. Minju carded his hands through Damon' hair, keeping his rhythm slow. He would never admit it, but he loved the way his leader's hair curled around his fingers. Eventually the sobs quieted and Damon's breathing evened out. He was so emotionally spent, he would be happy for a coma at this point.

"Better?" Damon nodded, laying his head more comfortably on Minju's chest. "Good. Now, explain please." And Damon did, he told Minju everything he'd just told Minhyuk. His voice was cracking and tired, but no more tears came. It was a sad numbness that took over now.

"Damon. You did nothing wrong. She didn't run away from you because you're not good enough, don't you dare think that again. You are caring, sweet, loyal, smart, talented, and the best leader our group could ever ask for. Not to mention attractive." Minju pinched his cheek when Damon blushed at the last compliment.

"Then why Min? Who would run from their mate? Honestly, I don't know how she did it. All my alpha wanted to do was run over and claim her. I barely kept myself in place. If her omega reacted anything like that, how did she fight against that?"

Minju shook his head, purple strands saying as his hair. "I don't know, but there's clearly a reason we don't know. You're right, people don't just run from their mates unless they have a pretty good reason. I just wish we knew what hers was."

Damon hummed, but a thought suddenly popped into his head. "Do you think… She looked shocked, and I thought it was because of the surprise and the chemical reaction, but maybe it was fear. Do you think maybe she was afraid? Of alphas?"

They both knew the prejudice that people still faced for their secondary genders. It wasn't as bad as it was a hundred years ago, or even fifty, but it still existed and they would be blind to not see it. Omegas got the worst of it, often treated as lesser than alphas or betas. They were denied important jobs with the excuse of their biology being inferior or a liability. And in worse cases, they were abused and hunted down. Every now and then they would catch stories on the news about an Omega trafficking ring, or an Omega who had been kidnapped or forcefully mated. It was a dark part of humanity people didn't want to shed light on.

Having an omega in their pack, a person they loved and respected dearly, they both had seen their fair share of the inequalities. Damon didn't want to think that his mate would be afraid of alphas, but it was a good possibility. It also eased some of his own self-hate; it was a reason to clutch onto that had nothing to do with him.

"Mmm. It's possible. It would make sense, fear can overpower our other functions or hormones. If her omega saw a threat it would make it easier to run away."

Damon sat up, hands tangling in his lap. He fidgeted as he thought over this new information. Even if it was true though... it didn't change anything. He didn't realise he'd said it out loud until Minju was grabbing his hands in his own, forcing his attention to him.

"Hey. It's not over yet. You forget who you are: Baek Dae, leader of an internationally famous K-Pop group with devoted fans. If anyone can find a needle in a haystack, it's you. And if anyone is going to play an obsessive amateur detective, well that's our lovely little Stars. You know they've won fandom awards for being nosy brats. Might as well use your power for good. Fate will be on your side."

Minju leaned in, capturing Damon's lips in a soft but sure kiss. Damon sighed into it, his body relaxing and hands coming up to cup behind Minju's neck and pull him forward. What started soft was now growing more passionate, mouths opening and tongues colliding. Damon moaned into Minju's open mouth as he pulled his bottom lip between his teeth and bit. Minju pulled back first, taking in the beautiful sight of his flushed boyfriend. This was his favourite view: a happy, kiss drunk Damon.

Then they made a plan. It was a guerrilla Hail Mary. There was no way they would get staff approval, and it needed to be done as soon as possible. They couldn't do it alone. They both reached out to friends that would back them up and spread their message. Finally, they sent a message to their group chat asking them to turn off their phones and not answer the door to anyone but them. He'd pay for that later, but he promised them all he would explain, and it really needed to come from him first.

Which is how Damon found himself logged into Jackson-Hyung's YouTube, pressing play on a live, while Minju filmed from his own phone on BTS' tiktok. They would cover as many bases as they could. They couldn't use their own channels because their staff could take them off air. Damon really hoped they wouldn't be in too much trouble.

Hi Stars! Hi Army! Hi Team Wang and Jacky! So... this is a surprise right? I bet none of you were expecting to see me. No, we didn't hack into anything. Actually, I want to thank our hyungs for helping us out and letting us use their platforms. I hope you don't mind. Because what I need to say today is beyond fandoms, and I hope whether you're a Star or not you'll help me out.

I see a lot of comments. Wow. Why aren't you on the Galaxy's channel? Oh, well, this isn't really a sanctioned live. And to be clear, manager hyungs and noonas, I'm sorry in advance. Don't blame the boys, I'm doing this alone.

(Hi Stars! It's Minju, I'm here too behind the camera. Dae-yah isn't alone.)

Anyways... Let's get to it then. I need your help. Yesterday, I found my true mate. Yes, it's true, and one day I'll share that story with you. But there wasn't a happy ending, yet. I hope to change that. So I need you to pass on this message, in the hopes that it finds them.

Hi there. I hope you remember me, we were in a park by some beautiful flowers. And then you ran away. I don't know why, but I think I have an idea now. I'm sorry if I scared you, and I'm sorry I didn't run after you. Generally, I'm sorry for a lot of things. But I'd like a second chance. Seeing you... it felt like a puzzle piece dropping into place. And when you left... well it hurt. So much. I understand you probably have a good reason, and I'll respect that. I just need to see you, to know your name. Can we do that?

Whew. Okay everyone, thank you for listening. If you know a foreigner who was in Seoul around that area please send them this. I'm trusting in you, in Stars, and Army, and Jacky, and every other person who believes in second chances and fate.

I need to go now. I love you all. Have a good day, bye!

* * *

The house was quiet when they got home, which gave them both a bad feeling. The house was never quiet. They found their other members curled up into each other on the large sofa in the living room, a movie playing on the TV. Everyone looked up as they walked in. There was a mix of expressions, happy, sad, and a little pissed off. Okay, a few pissed off expressions. Damon could understand that, he had a lot of explaining to do. Hansung and Leo were the first to react, jumping out of their cuddle pile and running over to him. They crushed him in a hug and he felt his chest constrict. He was most worried about how they would take the news, being the most sensitive members in the pack.

"Hi boys." He kissed the top of each of their heads and let them scent him all over. It was hard to not laugh as they rubbed their faces over every inch of skin that was showing.

"Damon, if you ever go AWOL again I'll cut off your balls." Leo threatened in English, his deep voice making a chill go down Damon's spine. He may be the sunshine, but he likely wasn't joking.

"Mmm I'll help." Hansung added, nipping at Damon's neck in retribution.

"Yah! Let him come in here and explain himself. You can threaten and scent him while he's explaining himself." Hyunbin levelled him with a look that said the excuse better be damn good.

Damon moved himself and his two new appendages to the couch and sat. The boys made themselves comfortable in his lap, curled around him and watching his face. He tried to soak it in before the bomb he was about to drop. He looked at Minju, who offered him a nod of encouragement from where he sat with Hyunbin on his lap.

He took a moment to soak in their presence. His mates were all gorgeous men; Minju with his sharp cheekbones and round eyes, his body toned and lithe from dancing. Hyunbin, though a smidge shorter, dominated his lap with his broad frame and bulky muscles, his dark black hair curly and puffed up making him look like a giant teddy bear. The two wrapped around him were their twins, born a day apart. Leo was all golden sunshine and smiles too big to recreate. He was classic beauty, sought after by every magazine and luxury brand to be their face. Hansung was darker, more emotional but cocky. Despite being the omega he exuded the aura of an alpha on stage. He let himself trace every one of their figures before taking a calming breath.

And then he told them. He told them of the mate who ran away, of how devastated he was, of how he didn't think he could be around them like that, and of his and Minju's impromptu live. And he waited.

The boys were slower to process than Minju had been, but that wasn't a surprise. Minju was quick to accept and move on in stride. However, the reactions that finally came weren't what he was expecting.

Leo was clutching onto his torso, crying. "Hyung, you must have been hurting so bad! I'm sorry we weren't there for you."

"Yeah, Hyung, why didn't you come home? You should have been with us, we should have been there for you." Bin calmly said like it made the most sense in the world. Which of course it did. He was an idiot to think that his boys would be anything but caring and supporting of him.

"So wait. You don't know who it is? We have to find her! Hyung, she's your mate but that makes her our pack too. I'm texting Wooyoung and the other group chat. Everyone of you better start doing the same." Hyunbin was already on his phone, a determined look in his eyes. The others were quick to follow, reaching out to everyone they knew who could help them.

Damon's heart was so full. They weren't devastated, they weren't mad, they were... helping him. He really was an idiot.

"Hyung, what was she like?" Leo asked, eyes wide and waiting to hear all about the mysterious person.

So he told them of you, well, of the one minute of you he got to see. He told them about how full he felt, and how beautiful you were.

"So she's a foreigner? That means she may just be a tourist..." Leo sounded worried. He was already attached to the woman. He could see the shine in his mate's eyes when he talked about you, and he knew that you were going to be amazing. After all, mates compliment each other perfectly, and Damon was amazing in every way.

"She is. But let's not think too much about it... we don't know if we'll even find her, Seoul is huge and filled with foreigners." Damon had to be realistic, he could see the light in all their eyes as they got excited and didn't want their hearts to break like his.

"Hyung's right. Plus, I know for a fact that Hyunbin didn't cook you lot any real food so let's eat." Minju teased, his retort earning a loud string of whines from his target.

That afternoon they cooked and ate together, watching movies and checking their phones. The lives were already trending, and the group had all been ignoring calls from their managers. The shit could hit the fan tomorrow, and they'd all deal with it together.

After all, they were a pack, so Damon's mate was their mate too.

* * *

Text Notification
   Mel: You really have a horseshoe up your ass or something. He's cute though.
   (link attached)

Galaxy's Baek Dae's Desperate Call for Help to Find His True Mate! - She ran away.

Well fuck. He was really cute.

Three

How I Met Your Father

F ucking fuckity fuck. This has to be a sign right? That stupid video was so sincere, how could I ignore it? But now I'm ass deep in stan twitter and I regret being alive. Seriously, what the hell is this place? If I see one more thirst post about being his soulmate I'm going to gouge my eyes out. It doesn't even seem like he thought this out. How the hell am I supposed to contact him and not come across as a stalker fan?

You hit your head on the desk for probably the tenth time. At this rate you'll be brain damaged by lunch. You'd watched the video Mel had sent, and you had to admit that it tugged at your heartstrings. As well as your guilt, which might be what's actually fuelling this search. Hearing the hurt in his voice broke a small part of you. You knew what you did was wrong, and selfish, but seeing it written all over his face... Well, you definitely didn't sleep after that.

You'd gotten up this morning with a new resolve. You'd make this better, find him and explain yourself. You owed him at least an explanation, even if you weren't sure you could give him anything else. Right, don't think about that, focus on your task.

It was starting to feel hopeless though. The video had indeed gone viral, and with it the trending hashtags were blowing up. Everyone and their mother had something to say about it. It kinda made sense you thought, mates were rare and celebrity mates always made the news. A celebrity mate rejection is completely novel. Unfortunately it meant you were also treated to everyone's opinions about you, which weren't great.

The consensus ranged from mild intrigue, to a downright witch hunt seeking your blood. Damn, those fans are scary. The silver lining was that no one had any idea of who you were, male or female, or your subgender. He'd kept that all out of it, you assumed in a way to weed out any fakers. The only people who knew were you and Mel. The latter had been just as focused on your task, currently tasking her pack mates into researching this Baek Dae.

You didn't recognize him that day, and still probably wouldn't recognize him on the street. Of course you knew about Kpop and Kculture, you'd be ignorant not to, but you weren't exactly a fan. You did a little googling on Dae and his group though, and they seemed like really great people. Their careers were soaring at the moment, and the articles you found always painted them in a good light. Yet still, you'd only skimmed the surface.

At least you were playing their music in the background. Music had always been better at speaking to you than people. Being a writer, you were a sucker for well written prose. Unfortunately, you didn't know Korean. The music was still catchy though, and you found yourself replaying their latest album and the vibe seemed very unique.

Your rise to fame in your own career was wrought with pitfalls and hardships. You fought against prejudice, both for your age and your two genders (the joy of being the two bottom rungs of the social ladder: female and omega), and poured your soul into your work. Many years later and you were a bestselling author, you had an impressive portfolio of investments and a budding new career in screenwriting.

And yet, as you translated the words of their music, you felt your hunger and desire for more reflected back at you. That feeling of constantly striving for better, for perfection, that lingering fear of it being taken away from you. It was a connection forging itself deep in your soul.

Your phone started ringing and you picked up the incoming video call. Mel's face popped on the screen. She looked tired but also excited, like she was surviving on caffeine and adrenaline. She probably was.

"Hey-"

"Yeah yeah. Kay so, I think I figured something out. First off,

their company KC is like freaking Fort Knox. I had no idea
how locked down these idols are, seriously. None of them
have their own socials, and everything goes through about
a million levels in their company. Anyways. I tried that, but
their company is either pissed at them or something because
they've shut down every thing I've found."

You sighed. It wasn't exactly motivating to hear. Mel had
connections everywhere, a perk of being in the entertainment
industry and owning shares in the biggest entertainment
company in the world. So if she couldn't get you in, well
the hope was slowly fading and being replaced by a bleak
darkness.

"Jeez, let me finish before you start planning your obituary,
God. I swear, you get more lost in your head than you do in a
corn maze. Anyways, I have good news."

"You couldn't have started with that Mel? I haven't slept, I'm
on edge and probably on the verge of a breakdown. And yet
you casually leave that to the end." You roll your eyes, if it was
any other time you'd hang up on her and pout for a few days.

"Over dramatic much? Fine, I'll get to the point. My assistant's
cousin is a makeup artist for a group there, and apparently
some of the members are friends with the ones in Dae's group.
I've already called her and had an interesting video chat with
someone named Wooyoung. Didn't understand anything
he said but he was very excitable. Sunmi, the cousin, said
Wooyoung is going to reach out to his friend and give them
your contact info."

The air left your lungs in an audible sigh. This was it. Task accomplished, sort of, and now it was too late to back out. The wheels of fate were rolling downhill. Mel must have seen the panicked look that crossed your face because she spent the next ten minutes talking you back into yourself, assuring you everything was okay and you could still just fly home if you changed your mind. It kind of worked, enough so that when you hung up and your phone pinged from an unknown number you didn't immediately yeet it across the room and hide.

Unknown number: Hi, this is Damon, or Baek Dae. My friend gave me this number and said you were the woman I was looking for.
    Wow, sorry, that sounded super cliché and cringy. Hi, I'm Damon.

                    You: Hi Damon, it's nice to meet you.
    Damon: Nice to meet you.
    Not to be rude, but I do have to ask you a couple things first, just to make sure I have the right person.
                    You: Oh, of course, go ahead.
    Damon: Thanks. So, first off, where did we meet? And what were you wearing?

You: It was in a little park, in a neighbourhood in the north end of the city. There was a large garden
    with a rainbow of flowers. I was wearing a teal blouse with black skinny jeans and white converse.

Damon: (typing…)

(typing…)

It's really you.

You: yeah.. I'm so sorry Damon.

I really never meant to hurt you, well either of us.

It was such a stupid decision.

Damon: It's alright.

I don't know why but I'm sure you had a good reason.

I'm just happy you reached out.

You: Well, you kinda put me on blast to the entire world

Damon: oh God, no that's not

I didn't mean for that.

Shit, I'm so sorry. I didn't even think.

You: Woah, it's okay!

I was just kidding.

Honestly I'm glad, I felt horrible but when I went back you were already gone.

I owe you an explanation and an apology.

Damon : You don't owe me anything, but I would love to actually meet you.

Can we meet for a drink? What area are you staying in?

You: Yeah, a coffee would be great. Are you free this afternoon?

Damon: Yes!

I mean, of course.

After you told him where you were staying Damon sent you the address of a cafe nearby. It was in a straight line down the block, which was perfect so you could walk and get some fresh air without getting lost again. Your meetup was set for two hours from now. Just enough time to have a mini breakdown about what to wear.

The cafe was tucked into the basement of an office building. It was just past lunch so the place looked pretty empty. You walked in, the bell above the door signalling your arrival and bowed your head at the barista who called out a greeting. The decor was modest, light wood colours and hanging industrial style lights were set off by the fresh flowers and well cared for plants. You scanned the empty tables, it seemed your obsessive earliness had won today and you were the first to arrive. You ordered yourself an iced coffee, extra shot, and made your way to a booth towards the back.

Now you just had… Fifteen minutes until you meet your mate. For the second time. This time you promised yourself you wouldn't run.

* * *

DAMON

"Are you sure you want to wear that?" Hansung asked from the doorway. He was looking him up and down, his brow raised questioningly. Damon sighed, what was wrong with his clothes now? He'd already changed three times. Which was three times more than he normally did.

"What now? This is all nice." Hansung just rolled his eyes and shrugged, walking away. Damon sighed in exasperation and followed.

"Hyung, you know there are other colours besides black right? You need to make a good impression. Why don't you wear that blue shirt I got you last month? It shows off your muscles really well." His eyebrows waggled and he giggled as Damon scoffed and tried to swat at him.

"Sungie, Dae-Hyung needs to keep a low profile. It's a public cafe and he's going alone. Which I still think is a bad idea." Hyunbin pipes up as they round the corner into the living room. He's lying across the couch, head in Leo's lap while they both play on their phones. Leo's head shot up, smiling widely when he noted their presence.

"Honestly, he's more recognizable in that outfit. It's like his uniform, everyone knows that." Leo smirked. He had a point though. Damon was dressed in a simple black T-shirt, black skinny jeans and his favourite black baseball cap. His hair was styled and he had on a bit of makeup, courtesy of Leo. He thought he looked as good as he could for a secret cafe date with his soulmate. But it was what he wore most days…

Before he could anxiously worry about whether he should change, a hand clamped down on his shoulder, jolting him back to the present. He looked over at Hansung, who was smiling at him warmly. He felt a bit of his unease melt away, taking comfort in his partner's big brown eyes and heart shaped smile. He was acutely aware of the sweet cinnamon that wrapped around him like a warm blanket, his omega pushing out his calming scent for him.

How did he get so lucky? He's off to meet his true mate, who isn't them, and they're doing everything they can to support him. Maybe he should just call it off, he already had four perfect mates that completed him. He'd be selfish for wanting another.

His scent must have changed because Hansung's hand left and instead his face was being pressed into his neck, scenting around his glands. Damon's arms wrapped around his slim waist, pulling his body into him gratefully. He let his instincts take over as his alpha inhaled his omega's scent. Sometimes he needed to step back and let biology take its course.

Soon he was being pulled from one set of arms to another, the action repeated until each of his pack had thoroughly scented him. He was going to go in there absolutely reeking of them, but he didn't care. They were the most important people to him, he should smell like them. A small voice worried about how it would affect you, but it was drowned in the hormones flooding his system. By the end he was calm and a smile was stuck on his face.

"Okay okay, you've all thoroughly marked your territory, it's time for Daedae to go. We're letting you go alone, but Leo and I will be shopping nearby. Just in case." Minju pulled the younger to his feet, both of them walking to the door with

Damon right behind. They waved off their members and headed out.

They decided to walk, since it wasn't that far, and the weather was nice. Damon held Leo's hand and they swung their joined arms back and forth.

"Hyung? If things go well, and she seems okay with it, do you think she would be up to meeting some of us today? I'm just so excited, I really want to meet her." Leo looked at him hopefully.

He ran his hand across the back of his neck, eyeing Minju on Leo's other side. They always kept the beta in between them, it wasn't ever discussed or planned, but he always ended up in the middle. It happened with Hansung too, but he always assumed it was his inner alpha tendencies where the omega was concerned. "I dunno Leo. But I'll ask, and if she says yes I'll text you. Alright?" Leo nodded happily.

All too soon they were separating, Damon continuing on by himself to the small cafe. He'd been there before, he liked the pastries they offered but mostly he liked the quiet ambience the cafe offered. He took in a deep breath before he opened the door. The bell jingled and he bowed to the staff before his head shot up and looked around.

It didn't take long to spot you, as you were the only one there. You were seated in the back, facing the front. His breath caught as you looked up to meet his eyes. His veins were on fire, his heart beating erratically. You were absolutely stunning. Even in the fluorescent lights, you still looked like you were glowing. Your eyes were wide, and your pupils blown wide. He expected he was probably looking at you the same way, like you were the last glass of water in a desert.

He dragged his eyes away enough to walk over to the counter to order. He noticed your almost empty drink so he asked the staff for a refill along with his own tea. He wasn't a coffee person, he didn't need anything else to keep him awake at night. The entire time he could feel your gaze on his back, like it was setting him on fire. He felt this tug in him, pulling him back towards you.

He approached the table and you stood up. He bowed low, a little awkward now that he was here. He was usually more confident, but it was like you sucked everything out of him and he was left bare in front of you.

"Uhm, hi Damon, it's nice to meet you in person." His eyes twitched, even your voice was sweet. You bowed your head but also extended your hand. That was when he realised he was still holding the drinks. He set them down before taking your hand, almost purring at the skin-to-skin contact. It didn't escape him that you flinched a little as he came closer, your nose wrinkling and body stiffening.

"Likewise. God, you're even more beautiful than I remember." He choked on his own words, eyes closing and face heating up as red crept its way across his cheeks. What the fuck did he just say? Has he lost his mind?

Thankfully you seemed just as embarrassed but managed to laugh it off before turning to sit down. It gave him a second to get himself together before sitting across from you. His leg bounced nervously as he fiddled with his drink.

"Well, this is super awkward. Thanks for the drink though, I can use all the caffeine I can get today. I'll probably be able to power the city grid by the end of the day." Your laugh was like twinkling lights, and your smile made his heart skip a beat. But he felt his nerves die down a little. Part of him wondered if that was because of the sweet orange he was smelling now.

"No problem. Did you not sleep well last night?" He asked, a tinge of worry he couldn't keep from leaking out.

You sighed a little, a sad smile playing over your mouth. "Ah, not really. I don't have a great sleep schedule. But last night... well, I was kind of a mess."

His face fell, he knew why. But before he could say anything you kept talking.

"It's my own fault though. I, uh, after I was sent your video I had a lot to think about. And I couldn't really do much but think. Oh, and watch some of your music videos." Your smirk was teasing and it warmed him.

"Oh god. I really hope you didn't find anything too embarrassing yet. Is it too late to delete my entire existence off the internet?" He cringed a little, knowing full well there was too much embarrassing content out there. It hadn't even crossed his mind as to whether you knew who he was, or that you might see the things his fans made about him.

"Wait, so, does that mean you've never heard of us before?" He asked.

You looked at him sheepishly. "Not until yesterday. I'm not really... into Kpop. Not that it isn't great! I know, uh, Blackpink and BTS? But that's mostly just when it plays on the radio or something." He nodded, that was fair, Kpop was only just starting to gain a real foothold in the western countries.

"But you listened to our stuff now? What did you think?" He couldn't help but ask. He wanted to know what you thought, completely unbiased.

"Oh! I actually really like it. I've been listening to your newest album a lot. You guys are really talented. I also watched a few videos of your group together, they all seem really great. Although.. If I'm honest, and this is super embarrassing, but the one guy, the blond one with the deep voice. Holy heck. I think his parts might be my favourite."

Damon's smile was huge and proud. Leo was their secret weapon, he always drew people in. He was so proud of his friend, and he agreed that Leo often had the killing part in their songs. "Leo will be so happy to hear that!" You smiled shyly, silently mouthing the name to yourself. His heart lit up in hope, but it also reminded him why you were both there.

"Not to change the topic. But I would love to know what happened the other day. I noticed today too, you seemed a little… afraid of me when I shook your hand."

Your smile fell and he could see the panic in your eyes. He kicked himself for even bringing it up, but he needed to know.

"Right. No, it's okay, you have every right to know. I don't… Really want to get into too many details but I'll try my best." You took a deep breath and looked right at him. He tried to school his expression, sitting on his hands to keep himself from wrapping his hand around yours.

"You didn't do anything wrong. And I'm not afraid of you, per se."

"Is it because I'm an alpha?" He asked, holding his breath until you vehemently shook your head and he exhaled.

"No! Oh no not at all. Well, I mean, any unknown alpha makes me a little uncomfortable, but honestly any stranger has the possibility of being harmful. I don't hold someone's secondary gender against them. And I know enough good alphas that I don't believe in the whole 'macho, toxic, primal' stereotypes."

He let out a little chuckle. "That's good. The alphas in my pack are the opposite of that." At the word 'pack' you twitched, and it didn't go unnoticed. His face held a concerned look, which encouraged you to continue.

"That day, I ran because I saw your pack bites." Your words were barely more than a whisper. A confession meant to blow away on the wind, but instead it tumbled into his chest and exploded like shrapnel.

"My.. pack? That's why you ran? But why... They're all very supportive if that's what you're worried about! They've been so happy for me, and would be more than welcoming." He trailed off.

"I... have a bad history with packs. I know a few, and logically I know that there's nothing wrong with packs. But, I saw all those marks and my brain just malfunctioned. I was running before I even knew what happened. It was a protective instinct."

His heart clenched in his chest. "Protective instinct?" There was a haunted look in your eyes, and his alpha reared up, wanting nothing more than to burn down the world for causing it. His scent spiked and he saw you flinch away, hands flying away from your glass.

"Fuck, I'm sorry. I'm not mad, not at you. I just... it hurts me to see that you were clearly very hurt. Especially because my pack is my everything. I would do anything to see them happy, and I would die before hurting them."

You took a few deep breaths, but he recognized the signs of a panic attack well enough. Your eyes were wide and darting around, hyper aware and searching for signs of danger. He reigned in his anger, instead trying to surround you in comforting alpha scent. It was a risk, but he had to do something.

"Hey, hey, look at me. Can you give me your hand, please?" You looked at him, hesitating. He put his hand face up on the table, face calm and open. Slowly you reached out, gently placing your palm in his. It was shaking as he closed his hand around it. His thumb gently rubbed circles on the back of your palm.

"Thank you, you're doing so well. Now, can you breathe for me sweetheart? That's right, deep breath in and deep breath out. Just focus on how warm my hand is. Can you tell me something you can hear right now?"

"Your.. voice. Music, from the speakers. Cars outside." He hummed his approval as you followed his deep breathing. The tension was slowly leaving you, and he could feel your hand stop shaking and tighten in his. A few more moments of speaking low praises and you were looking up at him, embarrassment evident in your eyes.

"Thanks.. I'm sorry. Gosh, we're saying that a lot to each other." He chuckled and squeezed your hand. You were joking, that had to mean you were okay. And you hadn't withdrawn your hand yet.

"Don't be. One of my members has bad anxiety. We've done a lot of work on it, so I'm used to it." He paused, thinking over how best to continue.

"You don't have to tell me anything else, it's okay. I understand more now." He decided on.

"Thank you. For what it's worth, you seem like a great alpha. Your pack is lucky to have you."

His cheeks lit up like a Christmas tree, he was never good at accepting praise. He figured a change of topic was in order, and he was still desperate to know more about you. So he told you about his life, his childhood in Australia and his teen years and career in Korea. He talked about his music and producing, and his hobbies of gaming and working out.

In turn you opened up, your face getting brighter as you talked about your life. You were a writer, but you wouldn't tell him your pseudonym. He didn't push, but he hoped you'd let him read some of your work one day, you seemed as passionate for your work as he was for his. You told him about your friends and your cat, who sounded like he and Minju would get along. You even told him funny stories about your adventures around the world. He was in awe, you'd seen and experienced so much. You talked animatedly, your one free hand flying up as you tried to explain something. But your other stayed snugly in his own.

Time had flown by, and by the time he looked at his phone two hours had passed. He couldn't remember the last time he'd laughed so much with someone outside of his pack. Everything felt easy with you. You hadn't even noticed the happy candied orange you were pushing out, and he felt like he could bathe in that scent forever.

"Tell me about your pack." The comment took him off guard. You wanted to hear about his pack? His heart jumped into his throat, and he looked into your eyes, searching for any discomfort. But all he found was open encouragement. You really wanted to know, and hope bloomed in his heart further.

* * *

Damon's face lit up as he talked about his packmates. His eyes looked so fond as he recounted how he'd met Hansung first. How the rest had followed, despite some of them not getting along at first. You'd been a little confused at him laughing as he talked about their fights, but it all made sense when he explained it was because they were terrible at feelings back then. It took locking them all together in a room to figure out that they all fought because they lived and breathed the same thing: music and performing.

You felt like you were getting to see a special side of Damon. He obviously held so much love for these men, and you believed it. Everything you'd seen about them or of them, they all got along so well. It made a pang of jealousy go through you, that was how packs were supposed to be. It was how Mel's pack was, so you shouldn't have been surprised. It just wasn't something you ever thought you were allowed to have, so your mate having it threw you for a loop. That was when you realised the real reason the pack marks set you off so much. You figured if you ever found a mate they would be alone, like you. But your mate had a whole pack of lovely people. Where did you fit?

Absentmindedly you started playing with Damon's fingers in your own. It was comfortable, the touch. His warm skin was soft, and even the scents coming from him were nice. It was mostly his ocean salt scent, but it held tinges of other scents, his pack you assumed. They all blended together so beautifully, like they were each made for each other. Maybe that's why you agreed when Damon asked if you'd be willing to meet one of his pack, their only beta.

"Really?! You don't have to, but Leo would be so happy." You just nodded before you could think about it. His smile was so wide, his cute dimples poking through. He'd taken off his hat, and his rich brown hair was pushed back in smooth waves. It was curling a bit on the ends, and as you stared at the beautiful man in front of you, you wondered if his hair was naturally curly.

Damon happily tapped away on his phone, almost vibrating in his seat. You decided it was a good time to go to the bathroom, so you reluctantly untangled your hands. It felt bad letting go, and Damon instinctively reached out to grab it again. You smiled and patted his hand before excusing yourself.

You can do this. It's just Leo, Damon assures you he's a ball of sunshine. And he's Australian too. Australians are great, they're so nice. Nothing to worry about. Splash some water on your face and get back out there.

You were surprisingly not that nervous. Damon put you at ease. You were starting to think that maybe you could have this, have him, have a mate. You two fit together, and it hurts your heart to think about leaving. So, if you wanted to see if you could work, you needed to see if you could be around his pack. You'd never make him choose, that was wrong on so many levels.

As you walked the few feet to your table you noticed a cute blond boy sitting beside Damon. His blond hair hung loosely around his face. He had cute, elfin, features and you thought he might be one of the prettiest people you'd ever met. His face was covered in freckles which made him look adorably innocent. When he heard you approaching he looked up, his mouth split in an impossibly large smile and his eyes were twinkling. He stood up, holding his hand out to you and you smiled back, stepping up to him to shake it.

That was when you were hit with his scent, the perfect balance of vanilla beans and the barest hint of sugar. It was like a hot vanilla latte on a cold day, or coming home to your mom's fresh baked sugar cookies cooling on the counter. It was sweet, pure, and wormed its way into your heart easily.

It also screamed at you, freezing your hand in mid air. Leo's eyes were blown wide, the galaxies on his face mirrored in his endless brown eyes. His mouth dropped open, nose twitching as he took in your scent.

Suddenly arms were flying around you, Leo wrapping you into his body. Your face fell into his neck, inhaling his scent deeply as your head swam at the intensity of the scent while your omega purred. It wasn't like the other day, your body felt calm and at ease, not throw into shock.

So when Leo murmured happily in your ear, loud enough for Damon to hear and react by grinning widely and opening his mouth like a fish, you didn't run away, you just clutched him tighter.

"Mate."

Four

And In Came A Lion

LEO

"Hyung, do you want to go get waffles? I'm done shopping, I think. There's a shop close by." Leo nudges Minju, who was sitting on a chaise in the corner of the dressing area looking at his phone. He was surrounded by bags of different sizes and colours. Leo had to admit, they might have gone a little overboard. Well, he may have gone overboard. He loved shopping, but he loved buying his loved ones gifts even more. One of the bags held a new set of marker pens for Hyunbin, they were watercolour and his packmate had been talking about getting them for a month now. He'd also found a cute buds case for Hansung. It had an NFC tag in it so Hansung could program it to ping it's location.

Needless to say, Leo was in a great mood.

"Sure of course Lele-yah." Minju smiled at him, his eyes becoming fond crescents. Leo didn't love the nickname, but it was that or some overly flowery mashup of three different berries. He had no idea what went on in his hyung's head, and he's fine keeping it that way. Minju grabbed the handful of bags, huffing out a laugh when Leo tried to take some from him. Leo shot him a pout, but it quickly disappeared as he got distracted thanking the staff as they left. Leo bounced with every step, darting in front of Minju every few steps to walk backwards as he rambled on about something until Minju would chastise him about not watching where he was going.

By the time they'd gotten to the waffle shop they were both giggling and clinging onto each other. They ambled up to the counter to order, Leo happily pointing out all the flavours and debating the merits of each one. Minju humoured him, staring at the beta with endearment. Once they'd ordered he left to grab a table and sit down while Leo waited for their order. He was watching one of the employees go through the process of filling the bubble waffle mold when he felt an intense stare burning into him.

He looked up and was startled to see the other employee openly checking him out. He wasn't unused to attention, that was the nature of his job. But the way the man unabashedly stared made him uncomfortable.

The man caught his gaze and a self-satisfied smirk drew his lips upwards. "A pretty thing like you would have a sugar daddy. You're pretty lucky, your sugar daddy over there is quite the looker too."

Leo's face turned red, from both mortification and an undercurrent of indignation. *Sugar daddy? Who the fuck does this bloke think he is to say something like that to someone? Even if he were, it's none of his damn business.* But Leo couldn't voice his thoughts, so instead he just ducked his head, hoping his lack of answer would be enough. Luckily their order was ready, and the woman making it gave him a sympathetic look as she handed it over. Clearly she'd heard the insensitive comments of her co-worker.

Leo tried to shake it off and regain some of his previous giddy excitement, but it was too difficult. The man's words kept repeating themselves over and over, like a skipping record of doom. It wasn't the first time and it wouldn't be the last. Although he was a beta, his delicate features and unusually sweet scent led people to believe he was an omega. It wasn't an excuse for their treatment of him, but he was privy to the underbelly of society's standards more than he'd like.

"Lele-yah. What's wrong? Why do you smell so sad?" Leo cursed inwardly, trying to force a smile on his face.

"It's nothing Hyung. I just remembered something I have to do later. Here!" He sits down and shoves Minju's strawberry waffle in his face, praying the older man would take the bait and just eat.

Minju eyed him suspiciously. But, thankfully, he wasn't the

prying type. It was something Leo loved about the man; you could always count on his support, but he would rather wait for you to open up to him than hound you. He just shrugged and bit into the waffle, a small moan of appreciation leaving his mouth.

They fell into quiet conversation as they ate, and soon Leo's mood was starting to lighten. He couldn't let these small blips affect him, they happened too often and most of the time the people saying those things had no idea how rude they were being. He was the type to give everyone the benefit of the doubt after all.

His phone pinged and he eagerly fished it out of his pocket.

Daeday: Hey baby, are you still close by with Minju?

Leo: Yeah mate, just finished shopping

Eating some waffles *nom*

Why?

Are you done already?

How'd it go?

What's she like?

Daeday: Yah!

Too many questions. Do you want to come meet her?

She said she would be okay meeting you.

Leo: YES!

IM COMING

RN

JUST ME?

Daeday: Leo, you need to calm down. If you come in here all rabid you're going to scare her away.

And yeah, just you for now. A beta would be easier than an alpha I think.

Leo could probably power a spaceship with his excitement. He relayed the texts to Minju, who had been very worried when Leo had shot up in his chair, but who was now laughing and packing up their things. Underneath the happiness he felt at watching Leo, Minju felt a refreshing wave of relief. This was a good step for Damon, and he was hopeful that Leo would help win you over for all their sakes.

* * *

Leo all but dragged the alpha out the door and down the street towards the little cafe. His gut was churning and he thought that his palms might even be sweating. Why was he nervous? It's Damon's mate. That's why. Whoever was his mate had to be an extraordinary person, just to match his own leader's worth. Some small part of his heart felt like, since Damon was his soulmate and other half, that maybe you'd be like his pseudo-mate too. Maybe you would learn to love him just as much. It was a tiny flame of hope he held onto tightly.

He spotted Damon sitting in a booth, back facing him. His

smile couldn't be helped, he always smiled when he was close to Damon, it was subconscious at this point. He walked over, sliding in beside Damon. Looking around briefly, he wondered where you were. For a split second he thought you had left, and the disappointment was about to set in when Damon grabbed his hand under the table.

"She just went to the bathroom." Leo exhaled, leaning into Damon's side. He shouldn't be surprised Damon had read his mind. Soulmates and all that. Truly two parts of the same being.

It wasn't long until you walked out. Leo's first thought was that you were so beautiful. You looked cute in your fitted jeans and he had an intrusive thought that he wanted to pet your hair. His grin grew wider, eyes shining, as he stood up to greet you properly. He already knew you were a foreigner, so he held out his hand instead of bowing.

It was then that his nose was filled with the tart sweetness of citrus and candy. His mind whirred and time slowed. He could see the same thing happening to you as your pupils dilated and you froze in place. You smelled like fairground sweets, impossibly long nights laughing with friends, wind blowing through the air carrying the scent of candy and citrus. His body acted before his mind could tell it to stop. His rational brain was screaming at him that you had already run once, that you needed space.

His beta disagreed. It knew you wouldn't run from him as much as it knew you were his mate, his safety, his home. He enveloped you in his arms, holding you tightly to his body as his head dipped into the crook of your neck. Your body fit against his perfectly, every curve slotting into his frame like you were two puzzle pieces from the same set. He felt warmth bloom in his chest, your body so soft and warm against him. Where he was all toned muscles and hard planes, you were soft and supple, a perfect counterbalance.

"Mate." He whispered. To you. To the world. To Damon, who in the back of his mind he had heard take in a sharp inhale but whose scent had only bloomed in happiness.

He felt you took in a sharp inhale, your own face pressed into his scent glands, breathing in his own content scent. He had a mate. Who was a beautiful Omega. And also his best friend's mate. His heart was so full and happy he thought he might die of a heart attack.

Worth it.

He wasn't sure how long he stayed like that, but at some point he felt another pair of arms circle him from behind. He could tell Damon just by the feel of his arms alone, but his scent was so potent he could probably have smelled him from outside. The salty sea preened in happiness, wrapping around them, tugging the three scents together into the perfect salted vanilla orange cookies. If scents were a food, he would die eating this one.

He pulled his head away from your neck. You followed him but made no move to slip out of his arms, which he tightened happily. His smile was softer now as he gazed into your eyes, faces only a few inches apart. "Hey."

You chuckled and he thought about making a song about how beautiful of a sound it was. "Hi." Your smile matched his, your chest rumbling underneath him in a purr.

"I'm Leo. It's nice to meet you."

"I think we're a smidge past pleasantries." He laughed at your joke, Damon chuckling into his shoulder on his other side. The three of you must make quite the sight, smushed together.

Damon was the first to let go, squeezing Leo's shoulder so he would do the same. He did, but he kept one of your hands in his, unable to part with you completely.

"This isn't how I imagined this going." Damon was smiling at you both. But Leo felt your hand tense in his. Looking over he could see the panic starting to seep into your eyes. Damon must have sensed it too because he was quick to grab your other hand in his, holding it tightly as he looked at you sincerely.

"Hey, no. It's a good thing, I promise. I'm not mad, or jealous, or anything. I'm... I'm so fucking elated right now." Damon tried to calm you down, reassuring you that this miracle was the best kind.

"Seriously. We're both over the moon. I was nervous coming in because I really wanted you to like me. Damon is my other half, the person I love and trust the most. And. Ha! It's funny now. But I was thinking that maybe you'd be like my pseudo-mate." His confession had his ears turning red and Damon pinching his cheeks and cooing at him. But it was worth it as you huffed out an amused laugh. He'd make a fool of himself a thousand times over to make you laugh.

"Honestly. One mate was… a lot to consider. But two. Two very attractive, successful, and sweet mates. Honestly, this feels like the plot of some terrible story. Maybe I'll wake up to a romcom still playing on the TV, inducing this crazy dream." Your voice belied the sadness and unsurety behind your light banter.

Leo knows the cheeky look that crosses Damon's face, but before he can clamp a hand over his mouth Damon is already speaking. "Oh, you think we're attractive, eh?" Leo facepalms, shooting daggers at Damon. Not the first impression he would have liked to have made, you needed a slow introduction to Demon Damon or Daddy Dae as they had started to call him within the pack. It started as a joke, what with him calling Stars his baby girls, but unfortunately for them it had unlocked a particular kink in the older Australian.

You take it in stride though, even as your own cheeks flush a light pink. "I'm not blind am I? I know good looks when I see them. And, even though I only really had a little time, I managed to see some very interesting tiktoks."

Leo cackled as it was Damon's turn to groan now, hiding his

face in Leo's back. "The tiktoks eh? What's your favourite? Mine is the edit where Damon is in the car and-" Leo is cut off by a loud squeak and a smack to his arm.

"Yah! We don't need to share. In fact, I'm going to ban tiktok on all your phones. It's basically porn at this point." Damon's face was beet red, and Leo loved it. He looked so cute and happy, even if he was being embarrassed. The whole scene felt domestic and real.

He turned back to face you, gesturing for you to sit in the booth. You'd all been standing for long enough and he was worried people were going to stare if you stayed this way for much longer. After you slid in you looked up at him expectantly. He hesitated while Damon took the seat across from you. He wanted to sit beside you but-

"Sit with me, please?" It was all the invitation he needed. He cuddled into you, snaking his arm around your waist and pulling you close. He didn't feel any hesitance being physical with you. In the back of his mind he knew this should mean something, tell him something important. You hadn't shown any discomfort yet, even snuggling in closer to his chest. It felt as easy and natural as with his packmates. His mind rolled over the gesture, still surprised, while his beta chirped in happiness.

Speaking of which. "The guys are going to flip out when we tell them. In a good way. I bet Sungie pouts for at least an hour that he didn't get to come." Leo found the thought funny, but only because he wouldn't be the one that had to deal with his pouting aftermath. And, Sung wouldn't actually be mad, he'd be over the moon. And probably start planning for when they would move her in.

"Your pack sounds really supportive and lovely. Are any of them mated? I see you both have mating bites.."

He ran his hand along the skin at his neck, Damon doing the same and smiling absent-mindedly. Did he imagine the subtle shift in your body?

"No one else has a true mate. But we are all together, romantically. I know it's not that common anymore, especially with larger packs. Is that.. Okay?" Damon bit his lip.

You hummed, nodding your head and they both released some tension. While it wasn't out of the ordinary to have polyamorous packs, an all-male poly pack of their size wasn't common. They kept their relationship out of the public eye, not hiding it, but not coming forward with details either. The fans did enough shipping for all of them anyway.

"Of course, love is love and all that. I guess I'm just wondering how... This, us, would even work. You already have so many people to love..." Leo's heart broke at that. The way you looked down, avoiding their eyes, like you were fighting the words your brain threw at you. It was intimately familiar to him.

"You're not born with a certain quota of love available to you. Instead, your heart only grows with each new person you

68

add." He replied, lowering his tone in the way he knew people found soothing.

"Leo is right. If it were up to him, he'd love every person he met. I understand where you're coming from. I never thought I'd be able to feel so much love. But with every new relationship, every member of our pack, it's like a piece was added to my heart."

Damon reached both hands across the table now, squeezing both of theirs. His presence was so sure, so calming. Like he had every answer to every question, even if the answer was a simple 'I don't know'.

All too soon Damon's phone was ringing, pulling them out of this soft moment. He grimaced but politely excused himself. Soon he was back with a sad look. Leo frowned, his eyes going wide in a silent plea to not do what he was thinking of.

"I'm sorry... I have to go back to work now. I didn't exactly tell our manager where I was going and apparently there's only so much stalling Bin and Sung can do. Leo, did Minju leave already? Do you wanna go back together?"

It was inescapable, he thought. "Yeah, he dropped me and then left for his own studio. I'm supposed to meet him there later." He looked over at you, committing every detail to memory. The sparkle in your eyes, their colour vivid against the tone of your skin. Your shiny and soft looking hair, a halo shining from the lights overhead. Your supple lips, with the barest laugh lines, turned up in a docile smile. Every little thing was perfection. And he got to call you his mate. His.

"Don't be sad Leo. I'll give you my number and we can chat whenever you want. I need to have a meeting later anyways, and I should go over the materials they sent."

He happily took you up on it, saving your name in his phone with purple hearts around it. You all stood up, hugging briefly before heading out together. Today had been a wild ride, Leo knew he would have a lot to think about tonight as he cuddled up with whichever packmate he found in his bed.

Five

Raccoon Cafes and Lattes

You're running through an endless hall, passing closed doors on both sides. The walls are painted a dull white while the doors are dark stained oak. It's so familiar to you, but like an itch you can't quite reach, the link to why they're familiar evades you. Instead, a deep unsettled feeling spurs you on, still trying to find the end of the hall. Every few doors you try a knob, but no matter how hard you try to push and pull and turn, none open to you.

You want to scream, to bang and kick until one of them gives. You don't know why but you feel like you need to get into one of the rooms. There's something you need, but you don't know what. It's an infuriating feeling. Desperate for help, you try to take out your phone and call someone. Instinctually you try to call the person you know will help. You don't know his name, it evades you whenever you try and grasp onto it. But, much like the doorknobs slipping *under your hands, you can't seem to remember his number.*

It's an odd feeling. You just want them to come get you, to take you away from this hall of closed off possibilities. Why aren't they coming? Why can't you call them? Don't they love you? They should be here if they loved you.

You awake with a start, eyes shooting open and inhaling a lungful of air. It takes a minute for you to take in your surroundings and for your mind to catch up. Pastel teal walls, generic art, soft sheets and too many pillows. Curtains closed around floor to ceiling windows. Your hotel room, you were in your bed in your room. From the light peeking under the curtains, it looked to be already morning. Now that your heart rate had calmed down you closed your eyes again, sinking into the soft downy comforter. Your body involuntarily stretched, arms going over your head while your back arched and your legs spread out. You chuckled to yourself as you pictured your cat doing the same thing when he woke up from naps. Sometimes you really were like a cat.

Morning pandiculation completed, you turned over and grabbed your phone from the built-in charging station on the bedside table. It wasn't too early, close to 8 am, which meant you'd gotten a decent amount of sleep after you got off your video call with Mel last night. You could feel the effect a good night's sleep had on your body. For one, you didn't feel the need to mainline coffee before being able to read your notifications. What a novelty.

You started working your way through your notifications

list. There were some emails and social media mentions, some push tweets from people you followed. But what made your heart flutter and mouth twist into a delicate, almost embarrassed, smile was the two new chats that had popped up.

Leo: Morning! I hope you slept well 😊

I had to get up early this morning because I told Hyunbin I'd work out with him.

God, kill me. Please. Why did I think this was a good idea?

Oh God, he's telling me to get back at it.

It's okay, I can do this.

It's hard but worth it right?

You: I hope you're still alive.

I'd probably be sad if you died already.

Also, we have different definitions of "worth it" because I assure you, I do not find it worth it

Leo: I am alive! It was hard, but I feel great.

Did you sleep well?

You: Yeah, surprisingly actually.

Usually, I have a hard time staying and falling asleep. I pretty much survive on caffeine.

Leo: You sound like Damon

So, would you wanna get breakfast together? And maybe hang out for a while?

You: I'd love that!

Just give me like an hour to make myself socially acceptable.

73

Your heart felt so light and full at the same time. Even through text you could feel the absolute sweetness leaking from Leo. Unlike your coffee date with Damon yesterday, you were nothing but excited and happy as you got showered and dressed, the butterflies that had felt like wasps yesterday were flapping in lazy circles this morning.

You were excited about your "date" with Leo. He already felt like someone you'd known forever, despite barely spending any time together (if you didn't count the hundred texts exchanged last night). You already knew some of his past times: baking, gaming and fashion. He told you about his day working on choreography and you told him about your work trip. You hadn't told either of them your pseudonym, or what exactly you wrote. Honestly, you were a little nervous. It made you feel vulnerable to have people close to you read your work. Your writing was so personal, the characters were chunks ripped from your own soul.

Leo hadn't told you where you were going yet, which left you in fashion purgatory. Normally you would throw on a good pair of jeans, a t-shirt and maybe a nice cardigan. Simple, and comfortable. Perfect for wandering the city all day. But, Leo was an idol. Last night Mel had given you a crash course on the insanity that was Kpop. You were a celebrity in your own right. In fact, your work has a bigger audience than their music. But, you don't have piranha fans on you all the time. In fact, literature fans were generally very laid back and chill.

Kpop… Not so much. The boys were followed around constantly, their personal space often invaded. Their every move documented. Every outfit critiqued. And you were about to go out with one of them, one of the easier to spot with his bright blond hair.

No one spotted the three of you yesterday though. Maybe you're stressing over nothing. It's not like anyone would recognize you anyways. Right. Probably over exaggerating. Mel put too much fear in you of the rabid Kpop stans.

You ended up with a compromise. A cute sundress paired with your purple docs and a jean jacket if you got cold. Stylish but still comfortable. Your phone went off as you finished packing your purse, letting you know Leo was waiting in the lobby. You took in a deep breath to calm the army of butterflies trying to smash through your stomach lining; when had they gone rabid again?

Leo was, of course, handsome in a black fitted undershirt, black short sleeve unbuttoned over top and white jeans. Even with a cap and a mask he looked effortlessly stylish. Maybe you should ask him to go shopping with you. You weren't hopeless, but you could always use a wardrobe refresh.

You could tell he started smiling when he saw you because his eyes disappeared into happy little crescents, his cheeks pushing his mask up. You were a little unsure as to whether it was okay to hug him in public, but he assuaged your worries as he scooped you up in a bone crushing hug. His face buried in your neck and you felt him inhale and relax as your scent flowed through him.

75

"Hi sweetie. I'm so happy to see you. Uh… Can I scent you?"
You looked at him a little shocked, but let out a laugh as you
saw the blush creeping over cheekbones. At least he asked,
you chuckled to yourself.

"Of course, how can I say no to you?" He wasted no time and
happily buried himself back in your throat. He rubbed his
cheeks across your scent gland, making both of your scents
bloom from the stimulation. You breathed his scent in deeply
as it covered your own. Scenting was very personal, some
people needed it and others felt indifferent. It all depended
on your own needs and wants. You hadn't been averse
to scenting, your friends often scenting you, but it wasn't
something you usually sought out.

Now though, the soothing notes of vanilla that surrounded
you felt so good. Maybe it was because it was your mate who
was scenting you, claiming you for everyone to smell. Or
maybe it was Leo's natural effect on you. Either way you
happily purred and leaned into his body. When he was done
he broke away with such a content and proud look. You knew
he would be covered in your scent as well and hoped he felt
the same comfort that you did.

Leo ended up taking you all over the city. And it was probably
the best date you've ever had in your life. You started at a
cute little cafe that specialised in Japanese style croissants
and pastries. The two of you giggled your way through the
intricate offerings, poking and jiggling to your heart's content.
Leo talked about his last trip to Paris, and you told him about
the months you spent there studying.

"Tu parle Francais?" He asked with big eyes. The sunlight coming through the cafe's windows hitting his skin and making him glow.

"Certainement, je suis trilingue. J'étudie depuis la jeunesse. Quand j'étais à l'université, j'ai fait un échange à Paris. C'était une expérience que je n'oublierai jamais." (Of course, I'm trilingual. I've studied since I was young. I did an exchange when I was in university. It was an unforgettable experience.)

"Woah. Your accent is perfect. Can you teach me more French?" How could you say no to that face? So you taught him the names of the food around you and corrected his pronunciation. His love of languages made you feel even closer to him. In turn he taught you the Japanese words, his nose scrunching up cutely as he worked to perfect his tone. You could now say custard in Japanese, you were basically fluent.

After you were both well stuffed with pastry and coffee, you hopped in a cab that took you to the touristy areas of the city. Leo decided to play tour guide, pointing out things during the drive and giving you a crash course on local etiquette. It was… a lot. But your eyes still sparkled with intrigue at everything he said. He spoke so animatedly.

After a couple hours of walking around a neighbourhood that was famous for its old architecture, Leo pulled you into a building on your left for your next adventure.

"Is that a raccoon?!" You squealed out, pulling on his arm and pointing to the grey and white trash panda that was rolling around on a cat tree.

Leo smiled, watching you hop up and down excitedly. "You're so cute. Do you like it? It's a raccoon cafe, we can go and play with them."

Your mouth dropped. Leave it to Korea to have a fucking raccoon cafe. You've lost count how many times you've complained to your friends about wanting a pet raccoon. Sure they were usually wild, and you shouldn't pet them even if you really really wanted to. But they were also adorable.

"Leo Kim, you absolute gem of a human. I love it!"

The rest of your booked time slot was like a slice of heaven. Watching Leo interact with the animals with as much love as you made your heart beat furiously. Seriously, were you already falling for this man you only met yesterday? Obviously, and you don't think anyone could blame you either. He was a literal angel. He curled up in a ball against one of the cat trees, one raccoon napping on his chest while he played with another with a laser pointer. His blond hair was mussed up, yet he still looked ready to grace the covers of a magazine. But most of all, his happiness was contagious.

* * *

"Leo, I'm going to drop dead right here. How do you still have so much energy?" You were standing at a street food stall now, waiting for something Leo had ordered and promised you'd like. The afternoon was creeping by, and although it was the best day, your body was going to kick your ass tomorrow morning. How had hours gone by so quickly?

Leo snickered, handing you a stick with sausages and rice cakes. Damn, he was right, it was delicious. "I'm used to hours of gruelling dance practices followed by more gruelling workouts. Not that I'm not tired, but it's more like a content tiredness. I could go for a nap though."

You rolled your eyes. Damn idols and their perfect bodies. Not for the first time you felt a little self-conscious about your own lack of physique and endurance. You crinkled your nose and a small pout formed. You startled a bit when you felt Leo's thumb run across your lips, tilting your head to look up at him.

It was as if he could read your mind. "Don't do that. Whatever is going through your head isn't true. I promise you."

You sighed. Might as well get it out there. "It's just.. You and Damon are arguably the most beautiful and fittest people I know. I know I'm not ugly, but I definitely couldn't keep up with you. I feel like I'm lacking in comparison. And then I worry... What would people think of us together?" Your heart contracted in your chest. There it was, a worry you couldn't get out of your head.

Leo didn't break eye contact, his own gaze burning into you. There was a fierceness in there that you recognized from watching their performance videos. "They would say how lucky we are to find a true mate that is beautiful, smart, funny, witty and driven. You are more than enough for us, and seriously if you could stop being so much like Damon that would be great. Because you are both stunning and neither of you seems to believe it." His voice was fondly exasperated. And you couldn't find an ounce of deceit in his face.

That was the end of the topic according to Leo. Apparently, he wouldn't take no for an answer and told you that he'd convince you eventually. He was genuinely adorable.

"What are you doing for the rest of the day?" He asked, leaning against you with his head on your shoulder.

Your fingers were intertwined, and you had started to play with his rings absentmindedly. "Umm. I don't have any meetings until tomorrow. So nothing. Why?"

"I have dance practice soon, and then pack dinner. I was wondering… Did you want to come with me to practice?"

You were a little taken aback, not expecting the invitation. "I, uh, of course I would. But am I allowed? Wouldn't there be a lot of… Questions?" Questions about what some random foreigner was doing at a closed practice with a bunch of idols?

"No. Damon already put your name in for guest privileges. I don't know if he told our managers the whole story yet… But he will soon either way. And it'll just be Minju and me, we're practicing our solo together."

Oh. You weren't sure if that was better or worse. It was only one person, not the entire pack, which was good. But that was more attention on yourself. Surely it wouldn't be that bad right? They'd be too busy dancing to pay you any mind. And you were curious to watch Leo in action.

"Okay. I can do one more introduction, I've got the social spoons for that I suppose." You were treated to Leo's signature hug, bone crushing and all consuming. It might be your favourite thing ever.

Twenty minutes later you were pulling up in front of a sleek silver building. The light of the fading day was reflected on the chrome and glass facade. It was an imposing sight, the large blue KC visible from the road. Leo took your hand, squeezing it in support as he led you inside.

You were greeted in the lobby by a pert looking receptionist and a security guard. You bowed to them both as Leo led you to the front desk. He talked with the secretary, who was all smiles when she saw Leo. You couldn't even be jealous, you understood the joy he must bring to everyone here. After a couple minutes she handed you a badge with 'visitor' stamped across it in English and Hangul.

Leo chatted happily as he told you all about the building, what floors the recording rooms were on, where the cafeteria was and how the different divisions and departments worked. Eventually he led you down a corridor with lockers on one side and doors on the other. Leo stopped by one with his name, pulling out a set of workout clothes before running to the bathroom down the hall. You ran your hand across the lockers, finding Damon's and then over the other members you hadn't met yet. What would they be like?

Leo changed sooner than you thought humanly possible. You were lost in thought and he thought it would be funny to sneak up behind you and grab your sides. He was treated to a high-pitched scream and your wrath once you spotted him. He was doubled over in laughter as you pouted, pretending to storm away.

"No, no! Baby I'm sorry! Please, I just couldn't help myself. Aw. C'mere." You couldn't resist his stupid beautiful face and doe eyes as he pulled you into his chest. His firm, muscular, chest that definitely wasn't making you feel things. Nope. He placed a chaste kiss to your forehead and you felt like you were going to implode. You were sure your cheeks were cherry red, but if Leo noticed he didn't say anything as he pulled back and took your hand. He did hold you closer though, his hand in yours a firm anchor.

You were led over to one of the dance studios. Leo didn't knock or hesitate, he just opened the door. Music instantly poured out. The song was loud and powerful, and not familiar to you. You made a mental note to listen to more of their music.

In the middle of the well-lit room, a man was dancing passionately to the music. His focus was on his reflection on the mirrored wall and the two of you silently slid in to watch. The way he moved was mesmerizing. It was like his body was liquid, rolling and moving to an invisible current pushed forward by the beat of the thumping song. It was amazing.

As the last beats sounded out, his final movement fell into his ending position. He stood for a second before doubling over to catch his laboured breath. After a couple seconds he stood up, startling when he finally noticed the two of you in the mirror. His eyes went comically wide and his hand came up to clutch his chest. It was comical and adorable.

Leo started clapping and you hurriedly followed. "Yah, Hyung, that was amazing!"

Minju blushed at the compliment. He brought up his shirt to wipe his face of the sweat that was dripping down. You inhaled sharply as you got a full view of his toned abs and stomach. Were they all Greek Gods or something? Like damn.

"Min-Hyung, this is… My mate." Leo's smile could be heard in his voice. Hearing him call you his mate sent shivers down your spine.

"Hi! You were breathtaking just now. Truly, I'm amazed." When Minju smiled at your compliment your heart swelled. So far so good.

Minju's smile was so sweet. Leo let go of your hand to drop his stuff off on the counter and his packmate walked over to where you were standing.

"So, you're the myst-"

Whatever he said was cut off as he got within two feet of you. It was all the warning you got as his eyes went wide, pupils dilating.

"Oh God, not again." You managed to mumble out.

Yes, again. Because not a second later his own thick scent was wafting towards you. You'd think by now you'd be used to the out of body experience, to the lightning that shot through your body or the way your omega jolts awake and demands attention.

But you're not, because it's still a shock when you take in the strong smell of pine trees and Christmas. It reminded you of walks in knee deep snow, birds chirping, and branches weighed down with white powder. It was nostalgic and yet also hopeful, a smell you hoped to smell for the rest of your life, never tiring of it.

It was the smell of an Alpha. A beautiful, sweaty, lilac haired alpha who was your third mate. God oh God your third mate. Please let this be your last mate.

Six

The Singer

MINJU

Honestly, he was a little rankled that Leo had brought someone to their practice without letting him know. The fact that it was Dae and Leo's mate made it even worse. He was sweaty, his hair plastered wetly against his forehead from the hour of dancing he'd been doing before they got there. His clothes were ragged and old, sweats he'd worn for a million practices because they were worn in the best places and flowed to let the air move in tandem to his limbs. Definitely not first impression clothes. It was fine though, he told himself a bit over enthusiastically. He was still riding the high of the music, his body still buzzing.

He let himself feel the uncomfortable embarrassment, letting it fizzle out in his veins and make room for something else.

His mind wandered over to you. Leo was talking, but he let it wash over him like a wave crashing and going back out to sea. He was much more interested in you. You looked at him in awe, and he noted how cute you looked. Minju wasn't as into fashion as Leo, who always sported the newest styles and had a cult following for his OOTDs. Instead, he liked simplicity, clean cuts and solid colours. He could see the natural style you had, admiring the way you carried a simple sweater. You seemed… interesting. Someone who would have great conversations and fascinating stories. Someone who stood out in a crowd in a quiet way.

"Hi! You were breathtaking just now. Truly, I'm amazed." He blinked and flushed at the praise, a little embarrassed that he was just ogling you. A part of himself, larger than he'd admit, felt proud at your compliment. Minju wasn't one to overtly fawn, in fact he took a long time to start to accept the compliments given instead of throwing back sarcasm. His dancing was one area he prided himself however, and any praise noticing his hard work was always welcome.

There was a faint blush to your own cheeks, which he assumed came from the potentially awkward situation. It only added to the thread that drew him to you, the flush adding a beautiful undertone to your smooth skin. Your eyes sparkled up at him, they were multi toned, holding specks of different shades as well as a second colour. He gets momentarily lost in them before movement behind you catches his eye. Leo was putting his stuff away, leaving you standing there.

Minju could feel the anxiety from you without needing to

smell it. It was the small twitch of your fingers, the way your feet turned inwards to point at each other. Despite the sure look on your face. You needed to go sit down, and he should really stop staring or he's going to zone out and make it weird. He zones out too much already.

"So, you're the mys-". His foot comes down harder than it should, gravity pulling it from its half-completed step as he stopped mid-air.

Minju wasn't that clumsy, in fact he was fairly graceful. Today, however, his body betrayed him. Because as he was walking over to shake your hand, a deep inhale coated him in candied orange. The sweet citrus wrapped around his brain until it wasn't functioning anymore. He could hear it tinkling like music in his brain, notes pinging for every undertone, colours bursting as each note joined to rise in crescendo.

Instruments could never replicate the beauty he heard in his mind. But he would spend the rest of his days trying. He would immortalise the moment his alpha poked his head up and purred out in recognition of his mate. His mate, his omega to love and cherish. His omega to care for. No, their omega. His heart fluttered even harder, his rational mind at war with the emotions stirring in his chest unbidden.

One part of him wanted to run to you, envelop you in his strong arms and never let you go. The other fought back with a barrage of suspicion. Three mates... all in the same band, all celebrities, all supposedly mated to one person? That seemed highly unlikely. News article headlines raced through his mind, cases of pheromone abuse, forced mating, fraud. His alpha raged against them, inherently uncomfortable with the thought because despite all the logic, he couldn't ignore the feeling of rightness.

He itched to reach over those last couple feet, to wrap you in his arms and hold you impossibly close. He was about to do just that, give in to his instincts, when Leo's voice stirred him out of his hormonal haze.

"Hey, jagiya, are you okay? What's going on?" Leo approached you quickly, noticing the way you'd gone stock still. Both men smelled your distress at the same time. Your orange turned bitter, like an orange peel. The citrus burned his nose, but he stayed back.

Leo reached out, his hand landing on your shoulder, body moving to be directly in your line of sight. You flinched back at his touch and Leo let out a startled mewl. Minju couldn't see his face, but he could see the tenseness of his shoulders and smell the worry and hurt on him. He thinks he did something wrong.

I'm about to have two distressed mates on my hand, and I honestly don't know what to do. Do I call Dae? Would that help or hinder? Is she scared? No.. That's not quite right. What do I do?

Minju had to act quickly to figure out what was happening because both your and Leo's scents were dipping into dangerous territory. When omegas felt threatened, or scared, it could really mess with their hormones and send them to a bad place mentally and physically. Hansung's anxiety had flared up once when none of them were around. He'd been cornered by some fans wanting autographs. It pushed him into a panic, his body had gone into survival mode by shutting down. He'd been rushed to the hospital, but he was in a coma for twelve hours. It wasn't until his body was doused in scent neutralizer for long enough that it deemed itself safe to wake up. It had been the scariest twelve hours of their lives.

So he knew the risks. And this omega, you, were his mate. It was his job to support and care for you to the best of his ability. Leo, while a beta, was hypersensitive to those around him, liable to fall into a sympathy drop. His pheromones would cloud his own system and shut it down as a protective measure.

He took in a deep breath, forcing his body to relax and pump out calming hormones into the air. His hand went up to rub the back of Leo's neck. His boyfriend instantly relaxed into his touch, his shoulders lowering and muscles becoming unclenched.

"Hi, I'm Minju." He says to you, hiding his body behind Leo. You knew Leo, you'd spent all day with him. He was a comfortable known variable. "Do you see those couches against the wall?" He waited until your eyes darted around, finding the couches, before continuing. "Can Leo take you to sit down? I think we could all use a rest. Is that okay?"

His lungs stilled, holding in precious air. You silently stared at him, but didn't answer. He was starting to worry he'd pushed too far, too quick, and worked hard to keep his scent calm and under control. Your eyes broke from his and finally locked with Leo's. Minju saw the moment you recognized him, your pupils began to dilate and your body lost some of its rigidity. He sighed in relief, at least you recognized someone you felt safe with. Disaster 1 avoided. Now to get you sitting down and figure out what the actual fuck is happening. And why you were so panicked.

Leo took your hand when you finally nodded and led you over to the black leather couches. Minju took Leo's other hand, wanting some skin to skin contact after his mini heart attack. His hormones were still running high after finding his mate and he was feeling a little vulnerable. Now that the immediate crisis was averted, he couldn't help but fear what your reaction meant. You'd run from Dae, which they understood now, but Leo had said you had openly embraced him. So… What's wrong with him? Why would you be so upset at having him as a mate? Was he not as good as the others? He couldn't help but remember the previous day, in this very studio.

* * *

MINJU

Hansung was lying on his legs, being as unhelpful as always, and laughing at Hyunbin's whines and attempts to stretch around him. Sung really was their chaos gremlin, and times like these he wished he could record it and out him to Stars. Not that they didn't already know. They were stretching or were supposed to be stretching but it was mostly him groaning as his joints popped.

The door swung open and banged against the wall, making Hyunbin and Hansung jump. He was clutching his chest and looking at the door wide eyed in fear as he watched Leo run in, Dae close behind. He rolled his eyes, wanting to yell at the two for scaring him for no reason. But Leo was already halfway across the room and launching himself at them. He threw his body down, landing on top of the three with a huff.

"Leo! Yah! Are you trying to kill me?" Minju groaned. Leo was sprawled across his torso, his head burrowing into Minju's rib cage. Hyunbin growled and rolled away, kicking at Leo's legs.

Leo looked up at Minju, and the smile on his face made his heart skip. He was radiating joy, the pure joy that only Leo could give. His scent was almost sickeningly sweet with how happy it was and how it was pouring out in waves, as if the beta needed everyone within breathing vicinity to drown in his happiness. Which Minju just might at this point.

"Hyung, care to explain why your demon spawn is the equivalent of the burning sun right now?" Hyunbin asks from a couple feet away now. His face was impassive, but his tone was teasing.

Dae rolled his eyes, but his own smile was bright and pearly white.

"Leo-ah, you should tell them."

Leo turned his head so it was lying on Minju's chest but facing out towards the others, gracing them with his beautiful smile. "I found my mate! Well, our mate. My mate is Hyung's mate too!" His voice drifted dreamily, but Minju suddenly felt like he couldn't breathe.

"What? How? What?" Hyunbin voiced all their confusion as the rest of them tried to process what Leo had just said. Two mates.. They had the same mate. Was that even possible? Surely not likely.

"Honestly, I have no idea how. I'm just as surprised. Good surprised though." Dae proceeded to tell them what happened, how you and Leo had met and instantly felt the mate bond as well. And that, despite the rocky first meeting with Dae, you had taken immediately to Leo.

"No surprise there, Leo-yah is like human crack. No one can resist him, it's like resisting air." Hansung drawled from his place beside Hyunbin. Leo could wander up to any group of people and be accepted as one of them immediately. In Empire, an idol competition show they'd participated in, he often had to be corralled back to their own group because he would wander over to Steez, BYOB or even The Ladz. And no one would notice until their headcount would be one too many.

"She's so amazing. She's beautiful, and she smells like what living in an orange grove would feel like. But... There's just something incredible about her. She said we can hang out again! Hyung, can I ask her on a date?" Minju choked on his spit as Leo said the last part.

Now, Minju wasn't the jealous type. Not really. He teased Stars a lot, telling them not to look at anyone else. But that's because he's been... scared of losing their support. But with his boyfriends, he was never jealous of their time with anyone else, especially with each other. Something stirred in his gut now though. He couldn't place if it was jealousy, or something more sinister, more intrinsic. His scent soured, the normally fresh wood turning mouldy and the pine becoming burnt and acidic.

Leo shifted, looking down at him, his eyes full of worry. He sat up and scooted him so that he could cup Minju's face in his tiny fairy hands. His thumbs wiped at Minju's cheeks. "Hyungie, why are you so upset? Did I do something?"

Minju tried to shake his head and deny it, but the words came out as a croak, his throat already constricting from the emotion. He hated it.

"Oh god. I'm so sorry hyungie. I-I shouldn't have sprung this on everyone like that." He leaned down, pressing his upper body flush against Minju's own, smothering him in body and soul. He inhaled *the scent that was so Leo, letting it calm him, letting it reassure him.*

"No, jagiya. I'm sorry. This is great news and I'm ruining it for you. I'm happy for you, really I am." And he was, now that he could breathe, he realized he was happy for Leo, because if anyone deserved to find their mate, it was him.

That brought a new set of worries though, that he pushed deep down. Because now was about Leo, not himself. Taking a deep breath, feeling it fill his lungs and seep into the cracks of his heart, he let it out and with it the bad air that he'd been keeping in. He let the mask he was so comfortable in slip over his features, smoothing out the insecurity, the worry.

Leo had chattered on for another fifteen minutes, his mood like a slow poison until they were all infected. Their instructor gave up on them after two hours had passed and they kept falling into laughing fits. Luckily, they were only scheduled for another 45 minutes, but it was still a break they were all more than happy to take. That night Leo had excitedly told them he was going to try and spend his morning off with you and told whoever was nearest about whatever text you'd sent him last. He was completely besotted, and Minju couldn't begrudge the happiness you brought his mate.

It had been so easy for Leo. Yet, his brain reminded him that you'd run away from Dae at first. So maybe it wasn't entirely his fault, that or he was in good company. You had calmed down now, your scent fading off and smelling more like fresh spring breezes. Leo was seated in the middle, and Minju tried to hide his body behind him, so it didn't overwhelm you.

"I'm so sorry. I don't know…" You stopped before you finished your sentence, looking down at your intertwined hands in Leo's. It was cute, your hands were also small, even slightly smaller.

"Don't be. I should be apologising. This must be… a lot for you." You met his eyes then, and his traitorous heart stuttered with your undivided attention. Those fears he'd pushed back gained a foothold and sprang forward. Leo was the kindest, most sincere and lovable person he knew. Dae was the most driven, loyal and selfless. And you, you were their perfect equal. It made sense yesterday, they're two halves of the same whole after all. So why would you be his other half? Why would someone good enough for the two angels, be deserving of someone like him?

How could YOU be HIS mate?

* * *

Your head was pounding, the fluorescent lights beating into your ocular nerves like little stakes. The warm hands wrapped around yours felt simultaneously grounding and suffocating. And your heart, well needless to say you'd be researching whether heart transplants were possible voluntarily. Because yours was broken and needs to be replaced.

95

Three. Mother. Fucking. Mates. Not just any mates, ohhhhhh no. Three Korean Greek Gods. What even is life anymore? You must have died on the plane or something. Maybe you fell down a set of stairs looking for those confounded dumplings and this was all some weird 'hell' where any minute the men are going to turn into monsters and start laughing at you for believing for a second that you could have this, whatever it was.

Yeah, that's way more plausible.

Because, Minju, the man who was just moving like his body was made of magnets attracted to the beat of music, could not possibly be your mate. No way. Not with his beautiful wide eyes and cheekbones that could cut glass. Nor with the lean toned muscles you could see from the shirt clinging to his body, lines and grooves peeking out in the most delicious way. Even his purple hair, drenched in sweat, was slicked back in an attractive way.

A lot? This was more than a lot. This was monu-fucking-mental. Your pounding brain was trying to tell you something, but you couldn't understand it. Not over the rabid thoughts running rampant through it. Three days ago, you were living a, not exactly normal but more so, life. You came to Seoul for work, planned to visit the country a little, go to the beach and stuff your gut with food until you burst.

Today, now, you were looking into the almond shaped eyes of a beautiful man. Who was looking at you in a mix of awe, sorrow, and worry. You didn't need to place the sorrow;

you'd be sorrowful too if you were stuck with yourself as a mate. These men were at the top of their careers, only jetting forward. Sure, on paper you were an equal, but in reality it was far from it. You felt like a fucked-up version of Cinderella without the fairy Godmother.

No. You couldn't do this. One was questionable, two was surreal, and three was just a cruel joke. All day you'd laughed and bonded with Leo, admittedly falling for the ray of sunshine. You became complacent, letting the happiness cloud reality. The reality being that even if you knew next to nothing about Idol life, you knew it would be the scandal of the millennia. It wouldn't hurt you, not really, but it could destroy them.

And here they were, worried about YOU. Trying to make sure YOU were okay. Not seeing you for the ticking time bomb that you were. They were so good, so pure and full of potential, seeing Minju in his element only solidified that.

You made up your mind, you had to nip this in the bud. You pulled your hands out of Leo's, shooting him your best smile. Those years of practice had you standing up without a wobble, your perfect glass mask in place. For the best, for the best, for the best.

"It was lovely to meet you Minju. Leo, thanks for a great day. I'm going to go." It came out perfectly soft, perfectly even in tone. Perfectly practised smile.

You turned and ignored the pull in your stomach and the look of shock on their faces. Now you needed to find your bag, you'd dropped it somewhere, and get out before you broke down.

"No."

You froze, not having gone more than three feet from the boys on the couch. You willed your legs to keep moving, but they ignored you. Another thing to put on the transplant list.

"You're not planning on coming back, are you?" Minju's voice was firm, but there was an undercurrent of hurt and resignation to it. It wasn't really a question, but you felt compelled to answer.

"No." You whispered out, not daring to turn around. Not trusting your heart not to break.

"So don't go. Please. I-I know I'm not much, and I understand if y-y-you don't want me as a mate. I'll keep my distance. Just. Please don't leave them, Leo and Dae-Hyung are the best. I promise, they're worth everything."

If you could describe how you felt in that moment, you think it would feel like watching a mother bird stranded on the ground as its hatchling falls to its death, unable to help and having to watch something it loved crack into a million pieces. Watching with devastation at the unfairness of the world as it ripped part of your heart out. That's what it felt like, except it was your fault Minju was saying that about himself. You'd caused this innocent, kind, person to feel so atrociously bad.

At that point, you couldn't stop yourself from gasping out a sob, your hand flying up too late to catch it.

"Minju. No." You spun around, tears blurring your vision and body aching. He looked so sad, so defeated. "This has absolutely nothing to do with you. I would never- I couldn't. No. Just no." Words were lost to you, all that mattered was the hurting individual in front of you, tears of his own falling now.

The room was a mess of hormones floating through the air. All of your scents are sad and upset, some slightly confused beta thrown into the mix. Your omega was mewling and crying inside of you. You were so tired of her, not used to her being so active and at the forefront of your mind so much. You listened now though, because your omega was saying that you needed to comfort your mate.

Leo beat you to it, recovering from his shock and turning to Minju. He looked surprised and a little hurt. He seemed almost tentative to reach out and touch him. You sensed the elder wasn't often this emotional. "Minnie-Hyung, why would you think that?"

Minju wouldn't meet his boyfriend's eyes, staring resolutely down at the floor while his tears dripped onto his sweatpants. You approached slowly, getting onto your knees in front of him. Every movement was slow and purposeful, giving him the chance to pull away at any time. You kneeled in front of him and hesitantly reached out to grab one of his balled-up fists. Even his hands were beautiful, you noted.

"Hey. Minnie? Can I call you that? It's a cute nickname. Or do you prefer Ju?" You looked up at him, trying to catch his eyes which were now hidden behind falling hair. His hand unrolled for you, and while he didn't look right at you, he did whisper.

"Minnie's fine."

"Thank you Minnie. You can pick my nickname later, kay?" A smile, you got a small smile. It was something. It was rueful but you'd take it. "I'm sorry. I shouldn't have left like that. I seem to have a habit of running, which is ironic because I hate running. I'd probably die in a zombie apocalypse because I'd rather be eaten than run." The smile was joined by a small snort, Leo giggling beside you where he was rubbing Minju's back.

"There's some… things that I don't deal with well. I told Dae a little, so it'd only be fair that I told the both of you. I'm uncomfortable with packs. There's nothing wrong with them, I just have my own baggage. I've been alone for so long, it's both how I thrive and how I protect myself. Unfortunately, it's also become my worst habit. I push people away, good people like you. Trust me, it's something I hate about myself. But it has absolutely nothing to do with you. You, Leo, Dae, the rest of your pack from what I've heard, are all amazing people. People who deserve for their dreams to come true, and all the love and happiness that comes with it.

I don't know if I can give that to you. I don't know that I can be a good mate to one person, let alone three. And you don't deserve a subpar mate, Minnie. You deserve the world. I don't even have to know you well to know that. It's a truth I feel in my bones." Your heart thudded loudly in your chest, painfully echoing the words as they left your mouth. That was it, you'd just bared more than you cared to, to two almost strangers.

It felt worth it as Minnie looked up at you, eyes shining with wetness. His soul was visible in his eyes, entirely open and vulnerable in a way you could only dream of. He tightened his hand in your own, and with his free hand he gently wiped away the trail of tears down your cheeks. It was so gentle, so caring, that it broke your heart all over again.

"Jagiya, I don't want you to cry. Your eyes are too beautiful to hold so much sadness."

Leo smacked him on the shoulder then, slightly irritated at the other man. "Yah! And what about you, you pabo? How could you ever think you weren't enough?" Leo flew into rapid Korean, and you assumed he was chastising Minju properly for not loving himself more.

You let out a small giggle, finding the vehemence a striking contrast to his angelic and delicate face. You stopped mid-laugh as his heated stare turned on you, your stomach dropping as you realized it was your turn under the firing squad.

"And you. You're not getting out of this either. I swear to- I'm surrounded by idiots. All of you. You are more than enough.

I've spent hours with you, and you know what I found out? That you're compassionate, your laugh is like the stars made into sound, you're smart and funny and you have the most beautiful soul. Looking at you is like looking at the best parts of all of us, wrapped up in a perfect package. So, welcome to the group. You can join these idiots for the self-love class I'll be signing you all up for."

Minnie looked at you, and you him. You both held mirrored expressions, mouth agape and entirely flabbergasted. It was the small, adorable pout of Leo's lips that sent you both into a fit of laughter. You keeled over, head resting on Minnie's lap as he bent over you, using each other as headrests while your bodies devolved into laughing fits. At first Leo tried to be offended, huffing and glaring. It only made you laugh harder, clutching onto each other. It wasn't long until Leo threw his own arms around you both, his own melodic voice joining in.

Your heart had stopped thudding so loudly. Now it felt light, like it was filled with helium, and the smile plastered on your face was as genuine as it got. How had things flipped themselves so quickly? Honestly, you gave up. Clearly these boys were as stubborn as you, and you should probably have realized that sooner considering they're your mates. You weren't all that competitive, but when you wanted something, you never stopped until it was yours. You guessed it was a trait that you now shared.

* * *

"The hell do you mean there's THREE NOW?! The fuck is

in the food there? I'm actually slightly worried. I'm going to book a ticket; I have stuff I can do there anyway."

"Mel, stop. You're not flying over here unless I'm near death or incapacitated. Seriously, is someone in heat over there? Because you're more overprotective than usual."

"I resent that. I'm normally this overprotective. I just usually filter it out before it gets to you."

"That's true you know. Remember that time you went to 'find yourself' in South America? She hired someone to follow you but-" Sara's voice was cut off by Mel. "Unless you'd like to sleep six feet under tonight you better shut the fuck up."

You wished eye rolls were audible, because you're sure yours would be as loud as a car horn at the bickering couple. You couldn't see them, you were on the phone in one of the meeting rooms at the boys' company, but you knew that there would be threats of physical violence soon. You had asked for a private place to relax and call your best friend. It was the middle of the night, yet Mel was awake and so was Sara.

"Okay lovebirds. Please commit your homicide in front of someone else. I don't want to be called to testify. Mel, you get on a plane and I'm calling in a bomb threat while you're over the ocean. I love you, but I've got it handled."

"And how, exactly, do you have it handled? You can't just have a normal relationship with these guys, you know that right?" You couldn't fault her for the worry in her tone, she was dead on.

"I know. Honestly though, when have I ever had a normal relationship? Anyways, I have a plan. I need you to send me the agency's number, I have to hire an assistant while I'm here. And probably a Korean tutor. Thank God they all speak English, but I should learn.

Do you remember a couple years ago when I had that fan meet in Tokyo for the first season of the show? Well…."

Mel listens quietly as you explain the plan you'd started to form in the past half hour. You were smart, it was an unbiased fact, and you were very good at strategy. She piped in with her own comments and recommendations, but after a good twenty minutes you could hear how tired she was, so you let her go. She had her tasks from you, and the rest was on your shoulders. You quickly contacted the agency she emailed you, asking them to set up some interviews tomorrow. You were finishing up a round of your own emails when there was a light knock on the door.

"Come in." Dang, you really needed to learn some Korean.

A familiar face popped around the open door, his smile bright and dimple popping in his cheek. "Hey, the boys said you were in here. I heard what happened, can we talk for a bit?"

You smiled at Damon and waved him over to the sofa you were holed up on. He was wearing a black hoodie and dark grey active wear. His hair wasn't covered in a hat this time, and his brown waves were brushed back.

"How are you feeling?" He asked as he sat beside you, one leg crossed underneath himself to face you.

You mimicked his posture, leaning on your side against the back of the couch. Damon's eyes were so gentle, when he looked at you it was as if you were the only light in the room. Normally such unabashed eye contact would feel imposing, but with him it felt warm and inviting.

"Okay. Actually, I'm pretty tired, it's been a longer day than I'm used to." You admitted, feeling at ease enough to reply honestly. In a self-fulfilling prophecy your mouth opened in a wide yawn. You tried to cover your mouth in time, an embarrassed flush crossing your cheeks. God, you were really letting yourself go around these boys.

"I heard. Leo and Minju told me about your eventful afternoon. I'm glad you worked it out. Although, I know it's probably not fair to say this, I'm over the moon. I was, well, a little apprehensive about the whole mate thing. I worried about how the rest of my pack would take it. About how it would affect our bonds."

You let out an understanding hum. It hadn't been long that you'd known them, but even from an outsider's perspective the group was close. "Right, and working together, doing your jobs, cohesiveness is important. I get that. I guess I'm lucky that I don't have to worry about that. It's just me, and I work for myself, at my own pace. There's no one depending on me, or relationships I need to manage." It was a little bittersweet if you were being honest.

Damon seemed to sense the underlying sadness in your voice. His gaze radiated compassion and his scent became sweet and subtle. "Leo also told me what you said. It's not my place, I know that, and I don't want to overstep. But... I need you to know that we don't expect anything of you. I'm not blind to the double standards, especially the ones faced by omegas.

It's different, with Hansung. He has his own cross to bear, but I've been by his side and watched him go through it. None of us sees him as anything more than who he is as a person. Strong, independent, loving. He isn't expected to fulfil some domestic role, or 'take care' of us because of his subgender. We're a team, in our jobs and in our lives. So, don't ever think that we would expect anything from you that you weren't willing to freely give.

And.. uh, Leo told me it's hypocritical for me to be saying this, but you're more than enough. Trust me, being around you is like waking up from a dream and finding out reality is even better. I know, I know. Easier said than believed. If you'll let us, we'd like to show you."

You needed a minute to breathe, because honestly you didn't trust your mouth to not spew incomprehensible sounds right now. Maybe a whole-body transplant is doable. Traitorous body.

You made the mistake of looking him in the eyes, seeing

nothing but honesty and underneath a spark of hunger, of attraction, as his eyes flit from your eyes to your mouth. You could feel the moisture rushing into your mouth, your tongue peeking out to wet your lips. You'd blame an invisible force later on, or head trauma, but you felt yourself leaning forward. Damon met you halfway there, his own body eagerly closing the gap. His hands came up to tangle in your hair as your lips met, a deep sigh leaving your body.

His lips were as plush and soft as they looked. He moved them softly against yours, the pressure light and fleeting as he slotted your mouths together. Warmth blossomed through your body, shooting straight down to your core. The kiss was chaste, over quicker than either of you wanted, but lingering sparks in its wake. Your eyes fluttered open, when you'd closed them you weren't sure, but they were now blessed with a flushed and giddy Damon. His cheeks were dusted pink, his eyes lifted in a smile, his lips pink.

Could you let them try? What would be the harm in trying? You were adventurous, you climbed mountains, you lived in holes in the ground, you tried spicy food from sketchy places. What's the worst that could happen? They break your heart into a million pieces? Well… maybe your next book will be a tragic romance. You could cast Rachel McAdams, she's made you cry enough.

Your eyes suddenly became heavy and started fluttering closed of their own volition. Your body felt safe enough that it was prepared to fall asleep in an almost stranger's presence. Seriously, how much of a hold do hormones have over you?

Surely this would be a bad idea anywhere. Not that your body listened as it tried to drift off.

You felt the couch shift, a small breeze passing by you. You opened your eyes and saw Damon standing in front of you, his hoodie now in his arms and being held out towards you.

"Here, lay down and I'll cover you up. You can nap here if you'd like. I'll let the staff know not to bother you. We have practice right across the hall for a few hours. Did you maybe want to meet the rest of the pack and go for dinner together? You can say no, it's not a big deal."

But it was. You could sense it, he wanted you to meet his pack, his boyfriends and best friends. And you didn't begrudge him it, because you were also curious. And if you were going to try, you really needed to put in the effort. No half-assedness, only full asses here.

"Mmm. Thanks Damon, that would be nice." You laid on the pillow, cuddling into the side of the couch as he gently placed his hoodie over you. It was so saturated with everything Damon, that it was like a blanket of salty sea air. Damon chuckled as you burrowed your face in the fabric, taking in deep lungfuls of the calming scent.

"Cute. Sleep, I'll come get you later." You reached out your hand blindly, swinging it until it hit something.

"I'd like to try to." You mumbled out, half asleep already thanks to the sweater blanket. The air started to smell like hope, happiness, and joy, and you weren't sure if it was coming from you or the alpha smiling and walking to the door. Either way, you couldn't think too much about it as you drifted off into a dreamless sleep, the tingles on your lips the last thing you thought of.

Seven

One Big Family

⚯

G od your neck hurts. Eyes still closed, you tried
rotating your head but stopped when a shooting
pain shot down your neck into your shoulder.
Underneath your face you could feel the rough fabric of a
pillow, but the top of your head felt squished into something
hard. As you shook off the dregs of sleep you remembered
your less-than-ideal sleep spot. The couch crinkled as you
sat up. You started stretching as you looked around the room.
The blanket you'd been wrapped up in fell to the side, making
you shiver at the loss of heat. Suddenly you realised it wasn't a
blanket but rather a hoodie. You remembered Damon tucking
it around you and couldn't help but bring it up to your face
to inhale the soft scent.

So that's why you slept so soundly, you thought as your
mind immediately cleared from the ocean breeze. It was

110

weird having such a strong reaction to a smell, particularly an alpha's scent. Not that they ever bothered you before, for the most part people's scents were no different than their own personal brand of deodorant. Only true assholes used their scents to convey their emotions, especially intimidating ones. There have been times where you've had to run out of a room, furious that some alpha-hole had soaked the place in his pheromones. It was bad etiquette. Modern times had changed how scents were perceived, and scent blockers were common when people felt their smell may be too strong due to heats, ruts, or stressful events.

You were even more shocked to find yourself sliding the sweater over your head and onto your body, covering yourself with the calming smell. Well, too late now. You're just cold, that's all. No reason to look too deeply into it. Nope. None at all.

It was a very comfy hoodie. It was slightly too long, the sleeves covering your hands and the body hung down to mid-thigh. It felt like being wrapped in a warm hug. You made a note to start buying oversized sweaters, maybe the boys would let you replace a few of theirs... Your omega preened, chomping at the bit to cover itself in their scents. The sweetness of vanilla mixed with the salt and pine like s'mores on a warm night.

No. Get your head together. You're going to go out there smelling like a fucking carnival. Aroused, excited and probably mildly scent high. You chastised your omega, telling it to stop being a thirsty twat.

111

The door opened before you could get too far into your tirade. You flinched at the sound, head whipping over to the door. Leo was walking in, Damon right behind him. They both smiled when they saw you, and Damon's eyes widened before you got a strong whiff of pleased alpha. His eyes raked up and down your body, clearly processing the sight of you in his clothes. Shit, this is weird isn't. Crap, you've definitely made it weird.

"Uh, fuck, I'm so sorry. I shouldn't have put this on, I'll take it off." You started to lift the hem of the black fabric when both boys started towards you, voices raised and arms out.

"No! Stop, don't, keep it on."

"Not at all, keep it on!"

The two boys flushed as you stalled, confused at the outburst. Still, you lowered your hands and let the hem drop.

"Um. Okay?" Now it was their turn to feel awkward as they both looked at each other with red faces.

Leo was the one to break the silence. "Sorry, that was a little much. It's just, uh, we both really like seeing you in our clothes. Well Damon's clothes, but really all of ours because we constantly steal them."

"You don't mind that I'm... Wearing his scent?" Your words came out quiet and your own cheeks burned pink as you looked down at your feet. Wow, the floor is super interesting.

You heard a choking sound and when you looked up Damon was staring at you wide eyed and Leo was poking his side, a devious smile on his face. It took a second for the tiny tendril of arousal to reach you. "No, we definitely do not mind. In fact, I can decidedly say that we both love it."

Right, so much for innocent Leo. His eyes were hooded and his smile, which he alternated from turning on you and Damon, was nothing short of predatory. You mentally ticked off 'scent kink' on your list of facts about the lithe Aussie. You also added brat with a question mark. That was one you'd have to figure out later. And you definitely needed to change your line of thinking before you outed yourself.

Damon cleared his throat, drawing your attention back to the slowly paling man. "Right. Thanks for that Leo. But yes, you can wear or borrow my clothes any time. It looks great on you. Anyways, before I spontaneously combust or commit homicide, we came to ask if you'd be up for joining us for dinner?"

Shit, how long had you slept? Your empty stomach was telling enough. But dinner... With them?

"Us?" You asked, wanting clarification as your nerves jumped. You knew the answer, they'd all been practicing together after all. But maybe they just meant the two of them, that was possible right?

"Yeah, the whole pack. The other two would like to meet you, if that's okay?" You hated being right. No, that's a lie, you loved being right. There was too much open hope in both of their eyes for you to say no.

"Sure. Yeah, that would be nice. Ripping Band-Aids and all that. Should I go get changed or…" You fingered the cuff of one sleeve. You didn't really want to take it off, but you also didn't want to look too casual.

Leo huffed out a laugh. "No, you're good. We were just going to grab some delivery and eat in here. The rest of the guys are showering because we stink. Plus, Sungie is gonna lose his mind seeing you in Damon's sweater." You really hoped that was true as Leo cackled more, dodging a smack from Damon. It was endearing seeing them together, Damon acting the part of aggrieved older brother.

"Okay. What are we getting?" Leo settled onto the couch beside you and spent the next ten minutes going through his delivery app with you. He ordered so much food, you were a little shocked. Then again, they're five grown men who just worked out. They're probably starving. You didn't know most of the dishes, so Leo just ordered enough for you to pick at whatever you wanted.

"Usually, we eat a lot healthier. Hyunbin, Minju and I are on chicken breast diets. And Damon honestly forgets to eat when he should be eating the most." Leo sassed, pointedly glaring at the offender.

"What the heck is a chicken breast diet?" You regretted asking when Leo told you, even showing you some pictures he sent to his fans on something called bubble. You gasped in offence. "No. Please tell me you're not just eating bland pre-cooked chicken breast? Absolutely not. Do you not have nutritionists here?"

Leo at least looked somewhat sheepish as he tried to explain. "It's a little more complicated than that. It's not that we're forced to, encouraged maybe, but we have to really watch our physiques for Stars."

You turned to Damon, levelling him with a glare. He had the smarts to look down, putting his hands up in a placating manner. "Lemme guess, nothing you can do about it eh? Right. Well, not while I'm here. There's plenty of ways to make healthy, protein heavy meals that don't taste like ass. Seasoning is a thing, and has no calories. Just because you're idols doesn't mean you don't get to enjoy the simple joys in life." You picked up your own phone, making a grocery list.

"It's not that bad, really, we eat a lot, but we just don't have a ton of time." Damon cut himself off short at your pointed look. Health was something you took seriously. You didn't have a healthy relationship with food for a long time, and you worked hard to keep your mindset healthy. Food should be revered, a way to nourish your body and soul at the same time. At the barest minimum it's a way to fuel yourself, and with the amount of exercise and work they do, their tanks need refuelling often.

They were spared the budding lecture that had been at the tip of your tongue as someone knocked on the door. Damon hopped up, eager to be moving and not be the subject of your laser pointed focus, opening the door. You weren't upset though, and to make sure they knew it you let out as pleasing of pheromones as you could. You were just determined, the list you made for groceries filed away to deal with later. Because now you had two strangers to meet, that could end up being important people in your life. Your mates' pack.

Damon stepped aside, letting in a group of men all around the same age. The first through the door had his hair pushed back from his face, dressed in a simple white shirt and light grey sweats. What caught your attention though was how utterly adorable he was. His eyes were large and round, and his cheeks pushed up into cute round bubbles as he smiled at his friends. His mouth almost formed a heart as he smiled.

He was pushed out of his standstill by Minju, who came sauntering over to you, seating himself beside you on the couch, and throwing an arm around your shoulders pulling you into his side. He sniffed your hair, letting out a happy hum. "Jagi, you smell so good in Dae's sweater. I could just eat you up." You couldn't help but laugh as he buried his face in the crook of your neck, rubbing against your skin and the hoodie but not fully scenting you. You appreciated him holding himself in check. Your body had its own agenda, temperature rocketing up as you were hyper aware of every place his body met yours.

"Calm down, dinner's on its way. I doubt I would make a good appetiser." You tried for nonchalance.

You turned back to the rest of the room. The other members had filed in, dressed comfortably with partially wet hair and shiny clean faces. Christ. They were better looking in person. The new one had fluffy hair and muscles that made you lose your breath. And they were looking at you. Plain old you, dressed in a black hoodie and squished between two of their equally beautiful pack mates.

Are we completely sure this isn't a dream? A matrix simulation? Heaven?

The adorable puffy cheeked man was currently standing behind Damon, his chin propped on the older man's shoulder and looking at you with bright wide eyes.

"Hyung, she's so pretty!" Your cheeks blushed furiously at the compliment. His voice was so smooth, not quite as deep as Leo's but the tone was soft like a lullaby.

His comment garnered a smattering of chuckles and eye rolls, but mostly endeared smiles at him and, surprisingly, at you as well. You disentangled yourself from the dancer's side, getting a grumble of protest before he let you go. You stood up, Leo following your movements to stand behind you. His hand went to the small of your back, and when you looked over, he smiled at you in encouragement.

"Hi, it's nice to meet you all." You introduced yourself, remembering to bow low out of respect. These were your mates' pack mates, they deserved a proper greeting that told them you valued their positions and relationships.

117

As you stood up you saw they were also bowing at the same low angle. It made you smile, some of the tension in your body leaving as it was obvious no one was going to out you as the interloper you felt like. Taking in a deep breath for courage, you walked over to the group standing on the other side of the room.

You kept your focus on Damon, staring into his eyes that were alight with joy. It felt like you could feel his mood bolstering you. Your pulse picked up and your heart started hammering.

Then you started sweating and the room began spinning. The thumpthumpthump of your heart turned into a savage lightning storm of pain. You knew your face must have reflected the sudden agony because those eyes were now filled with worry. His lips were moving but you couldn't hear anything besides the beating of your heart.

The corners of your vision started darkening. Were you having the worst panic attack of all time? Were you dying? Was your body dying somewhere else and you were just now feeling it in your dream? All flashes of thoughts through your spinning mind.

All of them debunked as one thought shot through your body and soul. The last thing you thought before the world went dark and you felt your body start falling to the ground.

Mate. Mate. Mate. Mate. Mate.

* * *

HYUNBIN

"Damon!" Leo yelled as he caught your falling body. The room was saturated in panic and worry, and he couldn't distinguish his own from his pack mates. He could only watch as his pack alpha, leader, and lover, rushed over to Leo and their unresponsive mate.

Holy shit. Their mate. HIS mate. He has a mate? His mate is a woman? Well, that's surprising. Where is that growl coming from? Who's growling? Oh, fuck, it's me.

It was as if Hyunbin was watching this all from somewhere far away. He could see the bodies moving around him, he could feel his inner alpha thrashing around, apparently growling. But he wasn't really there. His mind was split in two, one part spinning in a dizzying circle trying to understand how he had a mate. How they all had the same mate. He'd never heard of something like that. The most he'd heard was two, and that was an oddity.

The other part was trying to force him into action to tend to his members. Dae was crouched on the ground, Leo and Minju with him as they tried to wake you up. A look to his right showed him Hansung who was just as lost and surprised as he was. He could almost feel their emotions with how thick both of their pheromones were in the room.

An undercurrent of anger wafted around him, surprising him with his own emotions. Why was he angry? He tried processing it; one minute he was smiling, reaching out to greet you, the next he watched in horror as your face twisted. His first whiff of your scent, the scent of his true mate, was full of agony and fear. He found himself pushing down his alpha, having to physically hold him back, he wanted to tear through everything to get to you. To protect you. But from who? My own pack? It didn't make sense.

Hyunbin was their glue, attuned with the pack's moods and needs. He prided himself on his perception only because it made him a better partner, a better Alpha. He struggled in his youth, during his presentation and afterwards, never truly living up to the outside perception of him. He was big and burly, a gym rat whose physique showed his hard work, and a rapper who could battle anyone off the stage. But he was also soft, playful and a king of aegyo. He loved painting and photography, capturing art in everyday moments.

Hansung mewled from his side, bringing Hyunbin back to the present.

Right. Triage first, question your entire life later.

He moved closer, his arms pulling the younger close to him, encompassing the omega who was whimpering now.

"Oh, Sungie. Sweetie. Can you look at Hyung?" Hansung moved his head from where it was now buried in Hyunbin's neck. His eyes were glossy and red, tears flowing freely out. His lips were trembling as he kept trying to open his mouth.

"Is it my fault? Di-did I do something?"

"No! No, Sung, you didn't do anything." He reached his hand up, gently wiping away the tears that tumbled down his cheeks.

"Then what's happening?"

Hyunbin frowned. He'd like to know that too. Because as much as he was trying to act cool and collected for the pack, inside he was a mess. Since finding out about Dae's mate and subsequent rejection, Hyunbin felt like he'd been constantly pushing down the ugly, inconvenient, feelings he'd been having. He was jealous, insecure, worried and suspicious. All the ugly emotions he hated feeling. Now he was being forced to confront them, as the seemingly impossible happened.

He grew up in a small pack, an older sister and brother and two loving and supportive parents. He never wanted for anything, but his parents made sure he knew the value of hard work and dedication. When he told them he wanted to be an idol, a dancer, they put him in classes, coming to all his recitals and school shows. His mother was always there with the brightest smile. "Look at my son, the dancer." She would tell everyone close enough to listen. When he later got accepted into a company as a rapper they threw a party for his closest friends, embarrassing banners and everything.

Leaving his family to move into the dorms was frightening. But he had Damon, and Minju, his reliable older packmates, and Hansung and Leo, his adorable dongsaengs. It took some acclimation but now they were his family, his pack. And they meant the world to him.

Then that was threatened. He didn't know you, or your intentions. He hoped for the best, letting the universe do its thing and being prepared to support his hyung however he could. He always chose to believe in the positive rather than the negative. When it wasn't just Dae, the worry started. Could you take them away now? Now that it wasn't just Dae? The worry became suspicion when he learned about Minju earlier that day. Were you tricking their pheromones or something? Surely that's not possible because it would affect everyone around you.

And now. Well, the jealousy was gone. You were his mate too, who would have thought? He got to have a mate, him who is said to look scary, the dark rapper who's good for only his musical skill. Once too skinny, now too bulky, never as balanced as Damon, as smooth as Minju, as handsome as Leo or as talented as Hansung. Always the middle choice, the middle child.

Him and his alpha disagreed on where the worry came from. But really it all stemmed from the same place - you.

"I don't know jagi, but we'll figure it out together, yeah? Let's focus on the good, yeah?"

Hansung perked a little at his words, only now remembering. "She's our mate Hyung! Hyung!" His smile was contagious and Hyunbin laughed at the cute puff of his cheeks.

"How is that even possible?" he mused.

Bin just shrugged his shoulders. Heck if he knew. "Dunno. But when have we ever done anything normal?" Hansung rolled his eyes, but the corner of his mouth twitched in laughter. The sharpness to his eyes was back, and Bin breathed in the calmer scents, fresh cherries mixing with his own herbaceous eucalyptus. Happier, not entirely okay, but better.

He turned his head, not letting go of his omega, as he looked over at Minju and Leo. They were hovering over Damon who was knelt beside the couch where he placed your still body. Leo's bottom lip was caught between his teeth, a bad habit he did when he was stressed, his teeth pulling at the dainty skin. Bin was most worried for him of the two. Leo was sensitive, he cared too much for everyone around him, whether he knew them or not. He was raised his whole life thinking he would present as an omega, his family and friends convinced from his delicate features and caregiving personality. When he'd presented as a beta it had hit him hard. But he was making great progress, even though he was still often mistaken as an omega, he always came to them to help him work out his feelings.

Hyunbin pushed out his own scent, hoping to breach the walls of the maknae's subconscious and give him some relief. Fresh basil and eucalyptus seeped out. He thought of every happy memory, every laugh and smile and stupid joke, and he pushed that out. He made sure it reached every person in the room, reassuring them. He heard the intakes of breath and knew shoulders would start relaxing. This was something personal he could do for them right now.

Soon enough he felt like he could breathe in more than panic from the air. They had all moved closer to the couch, almost magnetically pulled towards their new mate. The newest omega to their bunch. The newest star in their galaxy.

Minju sat on a chair at the table, turned to face the couch. Hansung was cuddled on his lap, head lolled back on his shoulder as he played with the string of Minju's hoodie. Only about three minutes had passed, but it felt like a year.

And then you woke up. Your eyes shot open, dazzling Hyunbin with their deep colour and sparkling shine. It was like a painting of the northern lights, endless tones he wanted to capture on canvas. Your eyes found his and he held his breath. Why did you have to look at him? What was he supposed to do? The fuck universe.

So he did what he always did when put on the spot or when he needed to cheer up one of his packmates. He gave you his cutest smile, popping his lip out and tilting his head, his dimples doing the rest. His members would cringe away, laughter on their lips as they ran from him and his baby face.

You didn't look away though, instead holding what might be the most intense staring contest ever.

"Fuck." Indeed, Hyunbin agreed with you wholeheartedly. Fuck.

Eight

Take Out Containers

"Fuck."

It was the first thing out of your mouth as you locked eyes with the handsome man in front of you. His light pink lips set in a pouty smile and his eyes sparkling down at you, completely at odds with the wall of muscles that was his body. You didn't know who he was, your brain was too fuzzy to remember all their names, which you still got confused when watching videos anyway. You knew he was one of your mates, but the room was too saturated with scents to pinpoint which was his.

You felt hands come up to steady you as you sat up, too quickly if the sudden onset of dizziness was anything to go by. Closing your eyes, you swallowed down the mounting nausea and tried to centre yourself. You needed a clear head to figure out what just happened.

Mentally you took stock of your body. You flexed your limbs, moving your neck back and forth. Nothing hurt, which was a good sign. Your pulse feels normal, and your chest doesn't hurt anymore. But… Something was off. It was like your heart was taking up more space. Not straining against your rib cage like before, but rather pulled gently forwards. You could feel this tugging, but you weren't really sure what it meant.

"Hey, are you okay?" Damon's worried voice floated in your ears. You looked up at him. He was crouched on the floor beside the couch, his hand on your thigh a comforting weight. You could feel other hands on you and looked to your left to see Leo sitting by your legs. He was looking at you with wary eyes.

"I'm… Okay. I think? What happened? The last thing I remember is… Oh." You felt more than saw the shift in the others as you spoke. The air in the room became warmer and the scents swirling around hit you hard.

"Right. It seems like right after you smelled the other true mate bonds you collapsed. My guess is that it was too much for your system to handle and it went into a protective state." Damon explained.

You snorted. "Sure, the most sensible thing to do in a room full of strangers is to pass out. Good protective instincts body."

126

The sarcasm couldn't be helped, this whole situation was ridiculous. The beefcake of a man snorted, agreeing with your snarky comment. You liked him, he seemed like he had a good sense of humour.

The boy sitting in his lap, the one with the biteable cheeks, sat up and watched the two of you with amusement. You were sharing a wry smile with humour guy.

"Are you sure you're okay? That was really scary." You nodded at Leo, tapping his hand with your own. You could smell and feel the worry palpitating from them all. This must have been awful for them too, after all, they'd all felt the mate bond as well.

"Well, I guess in for a penny, in for a pound?" You tried to lighten the mood with a joke, but unfortunately for you only a couple of them understood, making Damon have to translate it. You internally smacked yourself in the head, with how good their English was you'd forgotten that puns don't translate well.

"It's nice to meet you... Noona? Or are you younger?" You turned to look at the incredibly well-built man again. Did you have to repeat it in your mind every time? Probably. His fluffy bangs covered part of his eyes, but that didn't detract from his handsome features.

"Uhm, younger? I wouldn't know. I'm the same age as Damon I think, if that helps?" You'd heard about the age thing here, and heard them call you Noona before, and their other members hyung. But right now it made no sense to you, and trying to remember just gave you a headache.

Damon seemed to pick up on your confusion and explained for you. "Age is really important in Korea for proper hon-orifics. Younger males call older males Hyung and older females Noona. While younger females call older males Oppa and older females Eonnie. I know it's odd coming from your background, but you'll get used to it. If you prefer though they can speak more formally and use - ssi instead."

You shook your head. "Geeze, no, no formalities please. Damon you're the eldest right? So I guess that would make me your Noona. That's fine by me. But you can also call me by my name, we're all equals after all."

Leo had no problem smiling and calling your name, but you noticed the others just blushed. That'll be something to work on you supposed.

"What do I call you?" You asked the room at large, considering you didn't know two of them, really any of them, but also wondering if there was a word for someone younger.

Muscles answered you first, sitting up a little in his chair. "My name is Hyunbin, it's nice to meet you. I'm very happy to meet my mate." His smile was so soft, a stunning contradiction to his imposing body. Your returning smile was just as soft, your own scent blooming out in pleasure.

"Hi! I'm Hansung. Or Sung. Or whatever you want." The cute

squirrel was laughing at his own awkward start, and it was so endearing you couldn't help but chuckle.

"Well, at least now I can rest easy knowing you're not complete strangers. At least I can stop calling you squirrel and muscles in my head." Your hand flew to your mouth, unfortunately for you not fast enough to stop the embarrassing sewage that just left it.

Hansung broke into a fit of laughter. You let out a mortified squeak. You didn't think you could make that much of a fool of yourself. "Yah, Noona is just like me!" His smile was blinding when he turned it on you, his eyes twinkling in mirth.

"Didn't I tell you? She's so cute." Leo cackled in his deep voice. It set off a chain reaction, all the boys smiling or chuckling at your expense. Well, if you were laughing too at least it was with you and not at you right?

"Her laugh is so pretty. I want to put it in a song."
  "That's what I said!"
  "Bro, twinsies."

Hansung and Damon were talking rapidly in Korean. You didn't understand, it was much too fast for your beginner brain, but you admired the easy banter that seemed to light up their features even more. It worked to break some of the tension in the room.

Hansung got up from his place on Hyunbin's lap and walked the two feet to stand in front of you. Damon looked up at him, shooting him a warning in Korean, but he didn't break eye contact with you. Now that he was closer you could tell he was an omega. It made sense, a primal part of you registered, his lithe figure and beautiful features were classically omegan.

"Noona, can I scent you?"

"Yah! Hansung-ah, you can't just ask that, you ungrateful weasel." Minju yelled in tandem with Damon's warning, "Hansung…" and low growl. Hansung wasn't deterred.

Logically, your brain felt weird about this. You'd just met him, and while you'd allowed Leo to scent you, it was a different scenario. However, as you were coming to understand (not accept), your omega was a thirsty bitch who was quickly figuring out how to wrest control from you. And your omega was frothing at the mouth to be closer to its omega.

Its omega? When did we decide this? I was not part of that conversation.

"Yeah, okay." Hansung launched himself at you before you could take it back, his face full of glee. He jumped on your lap, straddling your hips and folding himself into your embrace. He was so big, but so tiny at the same time. You fell back against the couch with a laugh. How could you even be upset at this?

You managed to wave off Damon's concern before Hansung buried his face into the crook of your neck. His nose brushed against your scent gland and he began to purr into your chest, relaxing further until there was no space between your bodies. It should feel stifling, or constricting, but all you felt was bliss as his sweet cherries drifted around you and melted with your citrus. It smelled like summer sorbet eaten on the back porch of your grandparents' house as you watched the sunset, warm air kissing your skin.

"Fuck, they smell so good together. I don't know if I can handle this."

"Keep it in your pants Binnie. You're gonna scare her away."

"Yah! You little shit, I was just saying they smelled good, I'm not a pervert."

"At least he's not drooling like Dae-Hyung. Need a tissue Hyung?"

"What?! I'm not drooling. Gah. Stop. You're such a menace. Ju, stop corrupting the maknae."

"I don't know what you mean. I'm a perfect role model. Right maknae-ah?"

"Mhmm. Hyung taught me how to cook properly. If you're going to roast, roast well."

Their laughs and banter filtered through your happy daze. Your own omega was purring soundly in response to its happy mate on you. You shifted a little to get comfier, aware that you weren't getting rid of Hansung any time soon. Leo joined you on the couch, taking a seat and cuddling into you. Their scents mixed together, and you were under a cloud of vanilla beans and cherry, with a heavy overtone of your own sweet oranges. It was so comfortable, you closed your eyes and let the heat from the bodies around you lull you into a floaty headspace. It wasn't long before your whole body was vibrating from all the purring.

You heard the click of a shutter, eyes opening and clocking Damon's embarrassed grin as you caught him red handed. "Sorry, love. It was too sweet a moment not to capture. Our omegas and beta all cuddled up."

Our omegas. It sent a flutter of butterflies wild in your stomach. Sure, you'd already referred to the omega as yours, basically adopting Leo as your own as well, that had seemed as natural as breathing, if not a little startling. You wondered if this protective instinct in you was how alphas felt towards their packmates? You didn't need to know them more, you would already burn the world down to protect these two angels.

Oddly, you recognized that the same flare of protection encompassed the others. It wasn't that odd, but typically a person's omega side leaned towards care-taking urges. Not this deep-seated fire you felt to care for, and protect, the rest.

Your hazy eyes wandered over the other three figures now watch your cuddle pile on the couch. They were too far away, your inner voice growling in unhappiness. The logical part of your brain shut down, the primal part taking the lead.

"Do you need something?" Minju's voice was pitched low and quiet, trying to be as soothing as possible. He recognized the signs of someone going scent high, and knew from experience that you were teetering on a precarious ledge. One false move could send you tumbling into a negative headspace.

You simply nudged Leo to move back and patted his thigh, waiting for the youngest to move more into your side and make room on the couch. Your eyes locked on Minju's then back to the empty sliver of space on the couch and back. Thankfully he understood, despite the look of confusion and apprehension on his face. He wasn't used to watching someone's omega come out with so much force, let alone expect it to boss around an alpha. Hansung's omega usually only came out to demand cuddles, or scenting.

He settled himself down, taking slow measured steps, your eyes on him the entire time. He lifted Leo up, careful not to detach him from you, before depositing him in his lap so you could all fit together better. Once he was settled you let out a deep hum of satisfaction.

Your scent blew out in force now, and you heard the gasps from the alphas outside of your circle. You were marking them as yours, as safe and not to be touched. They weren't intimidating pheromones like an angry alpha, but they were distinctly strong. You would be thoroughly embarrassed by this later, but for now your inner wolf was happy and sated. She could still smell and hear her other mates, the two other alphas, but she didn't feel the visceral need to be close to them. You didn't know Hyunbin yet, and you trusted Damon to watch over him. You closed your eyes and waited for the food to arrive.

* * *

DAMON

Damon didn't know how to feel right now. Honestly, he probably needed a good night's rest to properly process the past few days. Today alone could send him into a coma. When he was alone, maybe in his studio, he would sift through his thoughts and feelings. Right now, he had other concerns.

One being the strong 'back off, mine' pheromones choking out the air in the room. He'd never experienced this before. He had a hunch, but he'd need to do more research before he even entertained the thought. Hansung had ever acted this possessive over any of them. It was a little odd that you had adamantly brought Minju into it as well.

He felt eyes on him and looked away from the couch to see Hyunbin staring at him. He looked like he was on edge, his body tense. But they weren't turned towards the couch, they were turned towards him.

Well, he supposed that would make sense. He would also assume his inner alpha would have a problem with this but, as he took a minute to internally check in, he was totally fine. In fact, he felt completely at ease. Huh.

"I'm good Bin, really." He looked him in the eyes and let his hold on his scent loosen a little. Once he could tell he was being honest from his calm and pleased smell they both relaxed.

"This is super weird." Hyunbin murmured. That was an understatement.

Hyunbin looked the group over curiously, his brow furrowed. "Do you think...?" Damon shook his head, sending him a look that said 'not now', which the other thankfully understood.

They sat like that for a little while, the alphas cooing at the cute noises their packmates and you would make every now and then. Soon there was a knock at the door signalling their food had arrived. Damon called out to come in, slowly getting up from the chair and stretching. An intern came in with bags of take out. Damon smiled at them and moved to help them set everything up.

It was fine until the staff moved around the table, to the side closest to the couch. There was a loud growl, low and full of the promise of violence. In a split second the happy, content, scents were overpowered by stinging citrus. It was almost enough to make his eyes water. His head whipped around, his alpha on high alert for whatever danger had made you so angry.

The staff member was frozen, staring into your glowering eyes that were poking out from behind Hansung's body. The look was all predatory, but was gone almost as fast as it had come. You blinked a couple times, your hazy eyes returning to normal.

"Oh my god. I'm so sorry. I have no idea what that was. I'm sorry." The oppressive protectiveness was gone from the air, and his whole pack's scents started mingling again. He could see your panic and shock. He wasn't the only one, as you were calmed and reassured by the others who were on the couch.

He could see the embarrassment in your eyes, the way your nose scrunched up at having soaked the room in pheromones.

The staff mumbled out an apology and said they understood, before they quickly left the room. Hyunbin met Damon's eyes with a raised eyebrow. Yeah, that was weird.

"Hey, love. It's okay, no harm no foul yeah? We're all a little on edge right now, it's been a long day. Can we move you all to the table to eat?" He approached with his hands out, visible and non-threatening.

You smiled meekly. "Yeah, of course. Gosh, I'm so embarrassed." You hid your face in Hansung's chest, who chuckled and cradled your head while he ran a hand through your hair. You did not need to notice how defined his chest was, your face rubbing into the divot between his pecs. You wanted to bite them, but pushed the intrusive thoughts down.

"Jagi, don't be embarrassed. That was super cool. I've never seen an omega go all 'roar' before." Hansung laid a kiss on your crown and you sighed. Damon found it amusing, glad that there was no lingering defensiveness. And very glad you didn't have the same problem with them approaching their members. It was normal to be protective from outsiders, in fact he hoped it meant that some part of you was already accepting them as a pack.

"Okay, come on kids. Let's get dinner before Hyunbin eats all the meat." Damon smiled fondly and went to extricate you from under a million limbs. He herded a pouting Leo and

Hansung to the table while Minju helped you up. He held your hand, and Damon didn't miss the faint blush creeping up your neck. So. Cute.

There was a quick fight about where you would sit, or rather who got to sit beside you. Damon was mesmerised as he watched the members argue while you laughed at them. When you smiled it was like your skin lit up from the inside. The arguments were useless though as Minju, still holding your hand, dragged you over to sit beside Hyunbin and plopped himself down on your other side.

"Hey! That's not fair!" Leo pouted.

"Hyung! Tell Minju he can't do that. We were gonna play rock, paper, scissors."
  "Which you would have lost."
  "Yah! Ho Minju! You traitor!"
  "That's traitor-Hyung to you. Snooze you lose."

Hansung chuckled from where he'd sat down beside Damon. How could he be so damn fond of these people? And also exhausted. Thankfully, you seemed to find it entertaining as he watched your eyes dart back and forth, trying to track the conversation that kept going in Korean.

The chatter died down as everyone started serving themselves. Leo had gotten a lot of food, and Minju was pointing out dishes for you to try. Hyunbin kept sneaking glances, blushing when Minju caught him staring at you. You didn't have a chance to get any food yourself though, as each member kept putting bites on your plate. You handled it gracefully, letting them dote on you and feed you. Seeing his packmates take such good care of you made his heart melt. He had raised them well.

Conversation was light as they ate, everyone trying to get to know you and vice versa.

"So, why are you in Korea?" Hyunbin asked around a mouthful of rice.

"Oh. Uh, I have some business meetings." You kept your answer vague.

Leo, helpfully but to your embarrassment, filled everyone in. "She's an author! She's meeting companies about the rights to the Korean translation of her newest books. It's so cool! But she won't tell us what her author name is, or what the books are." Damon giggled at the good-natured pout and glare Leo sent you.

"I'm sorry Leo! I promise I'll tell you when I'm ready."

"Is it sexy stories? Is that why you won't say?" Minju, the demon, prodded.

Your skin went up in flames and Minju cackled, proud of his chaos. "No-no!" You sputtered out.

Minju continued to hound you. "Would we know it?"

"Yeah, probably. The newest series was made into a show that I get to be part of the writing team for, and it's very popular. Like, there are ads for it in the city. I don't know that you would have read the books, as they aren't out in Korean yet."

Leo swallowed before adding, "She's like, super famous. But not the same way as us."

"Really? Jagi is famous?" Hyunbin's interest was piqued. "That's important information. For when we go out in public."

Ah, right. This was definitely a conversation they should have sooner rather than later. You looked over at him, and he could see the hesitation in your eyes. "Hyunbin has a point. Now that, well, we're all mates, we should talk about some logistics."

You sighed, putting down your chopsticks. "I agree. Leo is right, I am famous. But it's different. Since I write under a pseudonym and don't put my photos in my press, I have some semblance of anonymity. That being said, I still do signings, social media and events. People do recognize me. Not to your level though, where your fans have memorized your faces. My fans are more... Low key."

"We'll have to have a meeting with the company soon. Figure out a way to present this to the press." Damon stopped talking when he noticed your downcast eyes. A scared and guilty look filled them as you met his eyes. That wasn't a good sign.

"About that... I was talking to my friend, she owns and works for a large entertainment company. She filled me in on the, uh, craziness that is idol life. And I don't think this should become public knowledge. Not right now at least. It wouldn't hurt my career, and honestly, I'm more than well off enough to weather any storm. But, you guys haven't even hit the peak of your career. And this could really damage your image."

The room went quiet. Leo quickly translated, even though Damon knew they'd understood just fine. Once he was done the atmosphere was tense. Damon could see everyone working through their own feelings about it, understanding the logic and reality of the situation but having their own opinions on the matter.

"Do you not want to tell people about us?" Hansung's voice was quiet and broken, and it felt like an ice pick through his heart. Because it was a thought he saw echoed in all of their faces, some just better at hiding than others.

"Oh, Hansung, no. That's not it. I'm happy to tell people, and I can't wait to tell my friends. But I also know how hard you work and how important your music is to you."

"We don't like to lie to Stars." Hyunbin added. His face was sad, and Damon wanted to reach out to him and soothe him. You beat him to it, and Damon fell for you even harder as you sensed his pack's mood and began to lightly let out some calming pheromones into the room.

"I know. Your fans are important to you. And if you aren't comfortable, I'll support that decision. But, I think it's something you should discuss together first. I'm not going anywhere." Your words were like a soothing balm on a burn. He didn't miss the look that passed between you and Minju, wondering what that was about. It was what they needed to hear, even if it was a truth they'd rather not think of. Ultimately, Damon had expected to have to deal with it himself, but you had bit the bullet for him.

"She's right. It's not ideal, but this is all too sudden to dump on Stars. Honestly, it's probably what management will say anyway. It doesn't change anything. We have our public lives and our personal lives." He hoped he sounded more confident than he felt.

They all chewed over the words as eating slowly resumed. They talked about their new music coming out, asking you if you wanted to come watch them record. Minju talked about a new dance he was workshopping and the maknaes teamed up to tease Hyunbin on his newest workout he'd been trying.

"Can I join you?" You asked Hyunbin, making him choke on his food.

He pointed at himself. "Me? You want to work out with me?" Leo and Hansung laughed at his shocked expression.

"Uhm, yeah? Is that okay? I'm not an expert or anything, but with all the damn hills and stairs in this city I feel like I need to up my stamina."

Hyunbin practically glowed. He loved when someone shared

in his hobby, used to having to pester the others to willingly go to the gym with him. He chatted happily about his routine and when he goes, what he works on. You listened intently the whole time.

"Noona. How long are you staying? In Korea I mean." Leave it to Minju to bring out a whopper of a question while looking bored and uninterested.

"Oh, ah. I was supposed to be in Seoul for another couple days, then I was going to travel around the country for a week before coming back to finalise the paperwork. Then I planned to travel to Japan. I have to be at the Tokyo Comic-Con at the end of the month so I had planned some PR events to do while I had time."

Damon turned over your words. Of course you hadn't planned to stay long, it was a business trip after all. But where does that leave them? Is it their place to ask you to stay? He knew what it was like to leave his country and move here, but that was for his own dream. Would you move here for their dream?

"Can you stay? I mean, if you wanted to, could that be an option?" Leo, their beautiful maknae, asking what he himself didn't have the courage to.

Everyone turned to you. You looked at all of them, a thoughtful expression on your face. "Of course I can stay. I can travel anytime. But…"

He knew what the hesitance was. "You don't know if you're willing to uproot your entire life and move here." It was sad, it broke him to say it out loud, but nothing good came from letting things fester.

"I don't know if I can speak for the others, but personally, I want to get to know you better. I want to date you, to court you. The short time I've known you has already been amazing. I love your personality, and I want to be your person." Leo spoke from the heart. It was something Damon loved immensely, how much love and care Leo had for everyone around him and how he wasn't shy at expressing it. Hyunbin may be known for his resolve, his backbone, but Leo was steadfast in his love.

Your eyes were shiny, your emotions clear on your face. It was obvious how his words had affected you.

"Me too. I want to date you too! Leo already got a date, I call next!" Hyunbin raised his hand in the air, waving it dramatically. It set off a chain reaction.

"Yah! Age first. Dae already went, I get to go next." Minju glared.

"Hey, that's not true. We just got coffee." He indignantly replied.

Minju rolled his eyes. "That's called a coffee date, old man. Date. You could have picked something better."

"Let her choose, it's her date. Jagi, you want to come to the gym with me tomorrow morning?"

Damon got up from his chair while his pack mates argued back and forth, debating the merits of age order. He had noticed you becoming overwhelmed and staying silent as you stared at your hands. He walked over and crouched beside your chair. He turned you to face him, taking your hands in his. They were so small.

"Hey. Talk to me." He whispered.

You looked down at him. Your hair fell in your face and he reached up to tuck it behind your ear. His hand lingered on your cheek, the rough pad of his thumb caressing your soft skin. "Damon. I'm scared. This is… a lot."

He hummed. "You're right, love, it is. And none of us would begrudge you taking your time to decide. But we're all in. We want to try and figure this out. One step at a time, yeah?"

He held his breath. This was a make-or-break moment, he could feel it in his bones. There's bumps and hurdles in every relationship, and this was their first meaningful one. Whatever was decided today could change all their lives.

He held your gaze steadily.

"Okay."

"Okay?" He repeated, hope all too evident in his voice.

"I'm… well I'm going to try my hardest to be all in, Damon. To at least see where this goes." He couldn't help it, he was too happy, too full of repressed nerves. He stood up, pulling you with him into a hug. He held you close, not even wanting the air in your lungs to come between you two. As he buried his face into your soft hair he smiled. And if a couple happy tears leaked out, well your hair was absorbent.

"Did she say yes?"

Damon laughed and rolled his eyes. He'd forgotten about the four toddlers in the room. You turned your head, leaning it down on his shoulder and he held in a shudder.

"Yeah. I said yes." Cheers erupted in the room, and you laughed at the silliness of the situation. Damon couldn't imagine what was going through your mind right now, but he was glad you chose them.

"So, is Noona gonna move in?" Damon's mouth dropped open and when he felt you stiffen in his arms at Hansung's words he wanted to throttle the man. What the fuck made him think now was a good time to ask that?

He must have felt the daggers being thrown at him from everyone else because he just scoffed and held up his hands. "What? I'm asking because she said she was supposed to leave soon. She doesn't have a place to stay. So why wouldn't she live with us?"

"Choi Hansung. You pabo." Minju chastised.

145

"You don't have to move in with us, Hansung is an idiot with no filter. We can help you find a place to stay." Damon told you.

"It's okay, it's a fair question." He noticed you hadn't said no to either option. He wanted to wheedle an answer out of you, but he also knew how to bide his time. Plus, he had a secret weapon: Leo. No one could say no to Leo. It's how they'd all gotten food poisoning from trying his kitchen experiments.

Damon let you go, but was quickly replaced as Hansung slunk into your empty chair before pulling you down into his lap. He turned full clingy koala on you, wrapping his arms around your torso and snuggling in. Damon sighed as he watched you relax into the touch and ruffled his hair before turning back to the table.

His heart was so incredibly full right now. He often felt this way when he watched his pack from the outside. It happened a lot, where he would stand just outside and quietly watch them interact. It filled his cup, reminding him of why he worked so hard.

And now, there was one more person to watch light up the room. How lucky can one person be in their lifetime, to be surrounded by so many glittering stars?

Nine

Food By Bear

Where the hell are my stockings? Did I not just see them? I swear they were tucked in right beside my slacks. Ugh. I should have unpacked, I really should have unpacked properly so I wouldn't be stuck running around like a chicken with its head cut off. Can I just go without them?

You looked down at your bare legs, twisting them in the light to see if any hair was visible. You shaved a couple days ago and luckily your hair was fine and slow to grow. It was good enough you deemed, and finally gave up on your fruitless search.

It was just after 9 am and your room looked like a fashion tornado had hit it. Discarded outfit options were scattered on the bed, the chair and the floor. Today was your last meeting for your book. You'd saved this publisher for last because you had high hopes that their pitch would be the best. You'd done your research on them, and their team seemed to be very good at their jobs. There was a particular team that worked on your genre of books, and while you obviously couldn't read Korean, you'd heard good things about them. In fact, it was the agency one of your author friends had used for their last series. Needless to say, you had an emotional breakdown while trying to find the perfect outfit.

You'd settled on something simple but trendy, a black skater dress with a pleated skirt and a white lace collar. You paired it with a white lace knit cardigan in case their air con was too cold. You'd wanted to wear your black tights to finish the look, but alas your mental health couldn't handle another search right now. All that was left was to brush out your curls and apply some simple make-up. You were going for professional but approachable.

The coffee machine beeped in the livingroom and you sighed in relief. Sweet, sweet, caffeine. Whoever had the genius idea of grinding up coffee beans and boiling them to create coffee was a genius and a saint. It must have been a truly weird experiment considering the beans were inside fruit. Maybe they'd eaten the fruit and the seeds were just accidentally thrown into a pot of water or something. You were quickly lost in thought as you sipped your coffee and wondered about the origins of your preferred drink.

You were jolted out of your train of thought by your phone vibrating aggressively on the wood table. A notification popped up and you caught enough to see it was a text before it faded to black.

> Leo: Morning! What are you up to?
>   You: Morning
> Just drinking my coffee and getting ready for
>   my meeting later.
>   You?
> Leo: I don't know how you like coffee so much.
> I need so much sugar to stomach it.
> I'm taking a water break.
> Oh, looks like I'm being given the stink eye.
> Gotta go

You chuckled reading Leo's texts. It was hard not to hear his voice coming through the messages. You checked the time, you had about ten minutes before you needed to leave so you put your phone down and started packing your bag. You chose your bigger purse so you could easily fit your laptop in it. Typically, brand names weren't your thing, you opted for the best quality or best option for your use. However, you had caved and bought a Macbook Air last year after lugging around your heavier laptop started hurting your shoulder. It wasn't your first choice to write with, but it was perfect for your on-the-go meetings. You'd covered yours in cute stickers that had a rainbow effect.

Soon enough you were stepping out of the cab in front of a massive monstrosity of concrete and metal. The building was set back from the sidewalk, a small pavilion in front of it with some shrubbery and benches as well as a small fountain as its centerpiece. People were walking to and from the surrounding buildings, busy in their own worlds. You let yourself take in the sight for a moment, watching people step through revolving doors while others stepped out, most of them on their phones. The weather today was nice, and because of all the tall buildings there was a nice layer of shade from the beating sun.

You've got this. Remember, you're the talent, you're the client. You have the upper hand.

Your inner pep talk was short and to the point, just enough to calm the swirls in your stomach. You reached in your bag for your scent neutralizer and sprayed yourself quickly. You checked your neck to make sure your blocker was still on, and satisfied it was, you straightened your posture and walked into the building. You forcefully exuded bad bitch energy, wrapping it around yourself like a comfort blanket.

When you stepped off the elevator onto the publisher's floor you were greeted by a smiling woman at the reception desk across from you. She was petite but her smile was enormous and contagious.

".   ?" (Hello. Do you have an appointment?) Your brain processed enough of the words and context to understand.

". , I'm here to see Mrs. Kim Chunho."

The receptionist's eyes widened in understanding as you gave her your pseudonym. You never gave your real name, the only person who knew besides your close friends was your agent, not even your own publisher. She bowed low and said something else in rapid Korean that you definitely didn't catch. But her wave towards the seating area to your left was clue enough. You walked over, settling yourself on the comfortable blue suede couch. The area was tastefully decorated with white walls and splashes of bold colour from the couches and chairs arranged in the small area. There was a square coffee table in the middle with piles of books and magazines.

One wall was all windows that overlooked the city outside. It was the same side of the building as the entrance, looking down on the pavilion below. From up here you could see a lot of Seoul. It looked like any other big city, buildings touching the sky, cars and people filling the streets. Subtle differences, sure, but it could have been any other city you've visited or lived in. You looked at it differently now though, because there was a chance that this would become your city, your home. And you didn't know how you felt about that.

You had a few properties, as real estate was something you invested in. You have an apartment in New York City, and a condo in LA. Both used only when you needed to be there for an extended time for work, otherwise they were rented out and managed by a property management company. There was a vacation villa in a small town in Italy, that you paid pennies for as part of a tourism campaign. And then there was your true home, the cabin like home nestled deep in the forest. Architecturally, it was a modern build with dark wood

151

panelling. But it felt more like a cottage in the woods. It was your oasis of quiet. So now, thinking about living in this bustling metropolis with millions of people, it was a stark contrast to the life you'd grown accustomed to.

Luckily for your poor overthinking brain you heard your name called. You looked up to see another petite woman in a light grey pantsuit, hair swept away from her face. She looked to be in her forties or fifties, with laugh lines and a gentle face. She bowed and smiled at you, introducing herself as Kim Chunho, the editor you were meeting with. Her English was strongly accented but easy enough to understand.

She led you through a hall lined with glass walls. Open office spaces were on both sides, looking contemporary with shared coworking tables as well as nooks with comfy looking chairs. The glass partition ended, and you walked through the open space to the opposite wall, another series of glass walls interspersed with doors. These looked like small conference areas, some with blinds partially or completely obscuring the occupants. Mrs. Kim opened one of the doors and ushered you in.

You immediately bowed as you were greeted by a small team of people. You exchanged introductions before you took a seat at the end of the table facing a smart board. And so, the pitch began. You listened intently, taking notes on your computer of relevant information. Each of the team members were comfortable speaking in English and they would be the ones overseeing the project.

Your hopes weren't misplaced. Not only were they kind and honest, but they also seemed to like your work. It was a point not everyone put importance in, but it was key for you. Your work was emotionally driven and dear to your heart, you wanted someone who understood and felt a connection so that the translation was given the time and dedication needed. On top of that, their bid was generous and their schedule matched what you had outlined. All in all, you were happy to pick them for the job.

The meeting was light-hearted, but long. With questions, follow-ups, and clarifying certain aspects, as well as going off on a few tangents, an hour and a half had already passed. It was nearing lunch time, and you were eager to leave.

Unfortunately for you, business was done differently here, and you were, very vehemently, encouraged to let them take you out for lunch. By the time you were leaving the BBQ restaurant hours later you were socially exhausted, stuffed and in desperate need of a nap. You thanked everyone for their hospitality, turning down offers for dinner multiple times, and took your leave.

It was only in the safety of the quiet cab that you finally took out your phone to check your messages. Your mouth dropped open when you saw the number of notifications you'd missed.

Damon: Good luck at your meeting! Let me know how it goes!

*

Hansung: Fighting Noona!
Minju Hyung says fighting too!

*

Leo: Ack, my back is killing me. I hate physio
How's the meeting? What do you do in those things?
Text me when you're free

*

Hyunbin: Noona, you have plans today?
Ah, Dae Hyung told me you're in a meeting. After the meeting?

*

Hansung: Noona!
Helloooooo
Oh sorry, Dae Hyung said not to bother you.
Did anyone ask you out tonight yet?
Can I?
I mean, Noona, will you go out with me tonight?

*

Hyunbin: No, Noona, tell Hansungie you are going out with me tonight! Please??

*

Damon: I'm so sorry.
They're currently fighting about who gets to ask you out today and I can only imagine what they're texting you.

*

Minju: I saw this book in the store today. I bought it for you, I hope that's okay.

My friend said it was a good way to learn Korean.

*

Leo: Minju Hyung wants to know if you like cats.

He's going to send you pictures of his cats if you say yes.

Say no

Laughter was shaking your body, the taxi driver only raising their brow before brushing it off. The random barrage of messages was just the thing you needed to ease some of the tension in your soul. These boys were all so sweet. You took your time responding to each of them, updating them on your meeting and thanking them for their thoughtfulness.

You texted Damon to ask if they were still in the studio, and if Hansung and Hyunbin were still arguing. Technically Hyunbin had asked you first, even if it wasn't so much as asking you out as asking if you were busy. The thought was there, Hansung is just quicker to the point. You didn't want to cause any actual issues though.

Damon's reply came when you were walking into your suite. They were still in the studio, and they weren't fighting about it anymore, having agreed that it was your choice. Apparently, whoever didn't get to go out tonight got first dibs tomorrow. You were starting to realise that your free time was going to be few and far between for a while. You hadn't socialised this much since university.

It was still the afternoon though, and Damon reassured you that they still had a few hours of work left. Which meant you could easily nap and recharge before your date. With whoever you choose.

After a minute of internal debate, you decided to text Hyunbin, telling him you'd love to do something. You quickly followed it with a text to Hansung, telling him you were his any time tomorrow, or later this week. A part of you had wanted to choose Hansung because it felt easier. You already felt comfortable with him. Maybe because of all the cuddling you'd gotten yesterday or maybe it was an omega thing. Hyunbin was... More daunting.

You'd gotten to know him a little yesterday, and he seemed like a great guy. He was funny, outgoing, and doted on his mates. But he was still an unknown alpha. And that made you uneasy. It shouldn't though, and you berated yourself for falling for the stereotypes that these men clearly didn't fall under. You couldn't help it, it was this bone deep awareness that alphas had the potential for danger, even if every other part of you screamed that Hyunbin was safe, that you would be safe with him.

Ultimately it was this niggling fear that pushed you to make your call. You had to be around them, three of them. It was better to get it out of the way now then have it cause issues later on.

Hyunbin was quick to respond, with an entire row of happy emojis. It was adorable. You made plans to meet him in the lobby at 8 pm. He said to dress nice, and that he was taking you out to dinner. A classic date. It made you happy to have an idea of what you were doing, and even happier to know you had a few hours to nap before you needed to start getting ready.

You wasted no time stripping your clothes off and cocooning yourself in the fluffy duvet, passing out in moments.

* * *

HYUNBIN

He could hear Dae's pacing in the hall outside of the bathroom. Hyunbin just rolled his eyes and finished running the cream through his damp hair. He knew Dae was worried, but this was too much. It was just a date; one he was more than capable of going on. He grabbed the diffuser, flipping his hair and drying it the way the stylists had taught him.

Once he was done, he opened the bathroom door and almost walked right into Dae. He caught himself on the other's shoulders and steadied them both. Dae looked at him with a sheepish smile. How could he be mad when he looked that cute? It was unfair.

"If you keep going, you're going to wear a hole through the floor. You need to relax, Hyung." He let go of Dae and made his way down the hall to his bedroom. He left the door open because he could hear Dae following him.

"I know, I know. I'm sorry. I don't mean to hover, I'm just nervous."

Hyunbin didn't look up or stop what he was doing. He'd learned by now that it was best to just let Dae work through things on his own.

"This is the first date, well the first 'date' date any of us are going on with her. I don't want anything to go wrong. Not that I think you would do anything! Ugh. I'm just gonna shut up."

Hyunbin laughed as Dae threw himself face down on his bed. He really was over dramatic sometimes. But he got it, there was a certain amount of pressure. It was one of the things that had motivated him to ask her out first. She'd likely have a harder time with one of them, the alphas, then she would with their other pack mates. Better it be him than one of them if it went sideways.

Plus, he could be damn charming when he wanted to be. He said as much to Dae who groaned and rolled over, watching him get dressed from his spot on the bed.

"You think I don't know that? I was putty in your hands on day one and you know it." There was the dimpled smile he loved.

"Relax, it's fine. I'm not planning anything crazy. I know she's not comfortable with alphas, so I booked us in at that little pop-up restaurant Sungie loves. It's quiet and there aren't many people. Plus, it'll be free of prying eyes. Then there's a night market we can go to if she feels like it." He'd put a lot of thought into the perfect, easy, night.

He turned back to the mirror, looking over his outfit. The restaurant was on the higher end scale, not suit and tie, but not casual either. He'd opted for a pair of fitted black pants, and a navy dress shirt that he knew hugged his chest in a flattering way. He put on his everyday jewellery, a ring and bracelet, and added one of Hansung's chain necklaces. His hair was pushed out of his face and slightly curly. He looked good.

Dae got up from the bed, coming up behind him and circling his arms around his waist from behind. He laid his head on his shoulder, leaning into his back as he watched him in the mirror.

"You look amazing Bin." He whispered, leaving a sweet kiss on the side of his neck that had Hyunbin blushing. "Now, go before I either panic more or rip these clothes off you." Hyunbin chuckled but acquiesced.

* * *

HYUNBIN

He'd borrowed a car for the evening, wanting the privacy of driving them around himself. He pulled up in front of the hotel, handing the valet the keys and telling him to hold it as he'd be right back.

Stepping into the lobby he was greeted by a blast of cool air. The place was well appointed, luxurious looking sofas and dim chandeliers the main points of focus. The floors were black marble, which was accented by the white walls and white furniture. It was a little too two toned for his taste, but still nice looking.

Checking the time, he saw he was a couple minutes early. Not wanting to draw any attention he took a seat on one of the sofas and texted you that he was there. He hadn't been nervous all day, but now that he was sitting there, mere metres from you, his palms started to sweat, and he couldn't stop his knee from jumping up and down.

Fortunately, he wasn't left alone for long. He heard the sound of heels clicking towards him and looked up to see you walking over. He stood up quickly, his breath catching in his throat.

You were stunning. Your hair was brushed over one shoulder, cascading down your chest. Your eyes were bright, and your lips popped in a luscious red lipstick that made them look utterly delicious. His gaze travelled the length of your body, admiring the way the fitted black dress you wore hugged your curves. He blanched a little as he saw the slit that worked its way open as you walked. You were wearing red strappy heels that matched your purse and your lips; a vision in red and black.

"Hi." You smiled as you stopped in front of him.

Hyunbin took a step forward, kissing your cheek and lightly holding you by the waist. He stamped out the flare of disappointment when he couldn't smell you. You were wearing blockers, which was fair, and he should have expected it, you were going out in public after all.

"Hi. You look beautiful. Ready to go?" You nodded and he kept his hand at the small of your back as he led you out to the car. He opened the door and waited until you were safely inside before grabbing the keys from the attendant and getting in the driver's side.

"Where are we going? You look great too by the way." There was a slight flush on your cheeks, and it made his stomach flip. Hearing the compliment from you was different than when Dae had said it earlier that evening.

"Thank you jagi. We are going to a special restaurant. In a secret location." He winked at you as he drove through the streets, and you giggled.

"That sounds fun. I love trying new foods. Whenever I visit somewhere I look up the trending places, or the secret hidden gems."

"Really? That's good. This restaurant changes location every night, only open some days. You need an invitation. It's why I chose it, so we can relax and not stress. It's funny too, the food is cooked by a person in a bear costume."

You looked over at him in shock before laughing. The sound was loud and genuine, and absolutely enthralling. "Seriously? A chef in a bear costume? That's so random!"

The drive didn't take too long, and you told him about the craziest places you'd eaten in your travels. He doesn't think he'd want to eat off of hot rocks in the forest, but it did sound cool when you talked about it. He pulled into the underground parking of an office building, finding a space easily since it was nighttime.

The two of you walked through the empty space, footsteps echoing on the concrete. He noticed how close you stepped into him as you got in the elevator. His smile was a permanent fixture on his face now, happy that your body language said you were at ease around him. Taking a risk, he took your hand in his, holding his breath until he felt you intertwine your fingers in his own. He looked over at you to find you softly smiling at him. His heart did another flip.

The ding of the doors opening popped the little bubble you were both in and you giggled. He leaned down to press a chaste kiss to your temple before leading you both out of the elevator and into what looked like a regular office space.

A person seated by a door to his left stood up, tablet in hand. Hyunbin gave his name, the man checking it off on the tablet before leading them through the door. The door swung inward to reveal a wide-open room. There were a few tables spaced far apart, the candles on them and around the room the only illumination. At the far end was a projector setup playing an old film. The sound was playing over speakers and only slightly louder than the clatter of utensils and hushed conversations. They were led to a table close to the front and tucked into a wall.

Hyunbin pulled out your chair for you, earning him a playful grin. His hand brushed your shoulder as he helped you push yourself in. There was a barely perceptible shiver down your arms at the touch. He took the seat adjacent to you, trying to hide his smile at having such a reaction on you, so you could both watch the movie, or each other. He didn't think he'd be paying much attention to the movie.

"Are there any allergies?" The staff asked.

Hyunbin turned to you, translating the question. You shook your head.

"No, thank you." The man bowed and took his leave. Hyunbin looked around the room before looking back at you.

"He didn't leave a menu?" You seemed confused, your brow furrowing in a cute way. He wanted to run his thumb along the crease like he did for his members, but he held himself back.

"No menu. Chef decides, they bring whatever he makes. If

you don't like it, you don't have to eat it. It's usually very good, with seasonal ingredients." It was one of the things that drew him to this experience. He loved that every menu was different and made with whatever was in season. It made for the freshest foods. He had a moment of doubt though, he hadn't asked if you had foods you disliked. He knew foreigners sometimes didn't like all types of Korean food, especially the spicier dishes. Shit, he should have asked.

"Oh, cool! That sounds super fun!" His tension deflated at your excitement. You were so easy going. He couldn't bring Minju here, he was so picky about his food. He really only brings Hansung or Dae. Leo is easy about his food but is so often on and off some stupid diet that it's hard to find the time. He shouldn't be one to talk, typically his meals are bland and protein heavy because of how often he works out, but he truly does love food.

The first course came out rather quickly. The waiter placing the plates in the middle of the table for sharing. There was a dish of seared scallops with fried rice cakes cut into thin strips and a take on tteokbokki sauce. Another was a fresh salad with lamb and a cranberry vinaigrette. Lastly, a kimchi pancake tower made of mini pancakes. It looked like the chef was playing with fusion dishes tonight.

He watched as your eyes lit up as you took in the dishes. He pointed them out one by one and explained what they were. Without thinking he took a piece of the lamb and salad, as well as the best scallop, and gingerly placed them on your plate.

He hadn't thought that it would be weird for you until you sputtered and looked at him with a mix of confusion and amusement.

"Do you do this for everyone?" Your tone was playful, if not a little teasing.

He flushed and pulled his chopsticks back, putting them on his own plate. "Sorry jagi. I'm used to eating with the members. I'm not trying to control what you eat." Fuck. Now his brain was running a million miles a minute. Did she think he was being an alpha-hole and trying to assert himself or something? It's instinctual for him now to give the first bites to his boyfriends, almost programmed into him.

You looked at him for a second, and your gaze turned sympathetic. When you put your hand on his forearm he almost melted into the touch. "It's okay, I'm not mad. It's a cultural thing, right? I've seen it on Kdramas, the mom putting extra meat on their kids plate. It's sweet that you're so nurturing. You're the least scary alpha, Cho Hyunbin."

"No, Dae Hyung is the least scary. He's a big baby." Your laugh bubbled out, catching you off guard. He smiled at the flash of emotions on your face, wanting to make you laugh more.

The rest of dinner went smoothly. He continued to sneak you food, but only when you were distracted. It couldn't be helped; he wanted to coddle and care for you. The noises you made whenever you tasted something you liked were so cute. He laughed the first time and cooed, which he was rewarded for with a smack to his bicep. The two of you grew warmer and warmer, your conversation flowing easily.

By the end of dinner your chairs had scooted so close you were almost in each other's lap. He could feel his skin tingling across his arm where you leaned into him. He was cursing himself for not wearing a sleeveless shirt so he could feel your skin against his own. His mind kept wandering, wondering how your skin would feel under his hands, how the rest of your body would feel pressed against him, the pesky layers of clothing out of the way. It was driving him crazy, he needed to distract himself before he grew visibly hard. He was currently showing you some pictures of their vacation in Jeju, his phone propped on the table in between the two of you.

"Hyunbin-ah! Is that you?" The voice startled him, his arm immediately wrapping around you and pulling you into his side protectively. The tension left the minute he looked up to see two men standing in front of their table.

"Wooyoungie, you idiot. You startled me. Hi, Tae-yah. Did you two just get here?"

His best friend grinned and plopped himself down in the chair in front of him, inviting himself to their table. Hyunbin rolled his eyes; his friend was never able to read the room. At least Tae had the decency to look apologetic, slapping his packmate on the back in reprimand. Wooyoung only smiled wider, thriving on the chaos.

"No, we just finished. We were heading out when I noticed

a dark storm cloud over here and knew it could only be our baby dark rapper." His eyes were going to roll out of his head at this rate.

"Yah, stop being mean. It's nice to see you Bin-ah. Sorry for intruding." Tae smoothed over Wooyoung's over enthusiasm.

"So... I would have expected you to be out on a date. But then I see this vision and I'm wondering where you kidnapped her from? Hello Miss. Oh. Does she speak Korean? Are you holding a foreigner hostage? Chyah. I thought we'd talked about this."

He was never so glad for language barriers before. He looked over at you, and sure enough you were smiling politely but looked thoroughly confused.

"This is Wooyoung, my best friend. And this is Tae, my other friend and his packmate." He explained in English.

"Oh! Nice to meet you." You bowed your head to each of them introducing yourself, and Wooyoung reached over the table to shake your hand.

"Nice to meet you as well. Do you work with Hyunbin or...?" He always forgets that Tae is the one with the most English in their group.

But his tapered off question needed an answer as both men looked between you quizzically. Shit, what was he going to say? He didn't want to lie to his friends, but you had been clear yesterday that you didn't want people knowing. He met your gaze, trying to come up with a discreet way to ask. Luckily you seemed to read his inner turmoil and patted his hand comfortingly.

"It's okay, if they're your friends and you trust them you can tell them." You didn't sound put out by it, and he was grateful for your easy-going demeanour.

He turned to face the two others, who were now very obviously on the edge of their seats. "Wooyoung, you need to stay quiet and not yell. Okay?" Wooyoung nodded his head. "She's my true mate."

He still expected Wooyoung to make a commotion, he was an expressive person by nature. Yet, both of them froze in place. He watched the emotions flit across their faces, disbelief, shock, uncertainty and finally joy. They looked at each other before breaking into huge smiles.

"Congrats man! That's amazing! Why didn't you tell me? How long have you known? I have so many questions." Wooyoung's voice was surprisingly quiet, and he was staring at you in a way that made Hyunbin tighten his hold on you ever so slightly. It wasn't sexual, or predatory, but there was too much curiosity in his eyes. It was like how he'd looked at Leo when they'd first met, and Hyunbin knew how quickly he'd 'claimed' their friendly beta as his. He wasn't sure you'd be as open to Wooyoung's brand of intensity.

"Doesn't Dae-Hyung have a mate too? Did he find her?"

Tae asked in English, clearly trying to include you in their conversation.

Hyunbin hesitated. Another bomb to drop. "Yeah, he did actually."

Tae's face softened, obviously happy for their shared hyung. "Oh, that's great. That story made me so sad. Yoon cried for hours. Joo was worried for Hyung." Hyunbin felt your body stiffen. He wished he could smell you to know what was going on in your head, no matter how personal that may be. He worried that bringing up the fresh trauma wouldn't be good for you. As bad as it had been for his hyung, he knew you had gone through a lot too. Were still going through a lot.

Wooyoung, perceptive as always, sensed something amiss. "Bin-ah. What aren't you telling us? Did something happen with Dae-Hyung?"

Hyunbin didn't have time to answer because you took the opportunity to speak up yourself. "Uhm, I'm also Damon's, or uh Dae's, mate. In fact, the whole group is fated with me." In another situation he would have found their gobsmacked faces hilarious. However now he was just worried about you.

"Okay. There's a store downstairs, we'll get ice cream and meet you by the cars." Tae got up, shooting Hyunbin a pointed look and a much softer one to you before grabbing a still floundering Wooyoung and dragging him to the door. That could have gone worse, he thought.

"You okay jagi?" He turned his attention back to you. You shook your head a little, but still gave him a smile. He could tell it was strained, but he didn't think now was the time to push it.

He stood up and held out his hand to you, helping you up. He held it tightly as he led you out of the room, thanking the staff with quiet bows. Thankfully he didn't need to waste time paying, it was all paid upfront. He pressed the button to call the elevator, taking the wait time to really look you over. You seemed calm on the outside, but he caught the way your free hand was fidgeting with the skirt of your dress. A nervous tick he'd noticed the other day- you fidgeted with your hands a lot.

The elevator dinged, and in the blink of an eye he was steps away from the car. The parking lot was still fairly empty, only a handful of cars on this level. You sighed and moved to lean against the side of the hood. Hyunbin joined you, now playing with your hand in both of his. It was so small, so dainty.

"Jagi, I'm going to ask something, and you tell me no if you want, okay?" You hummed, looking up from where you were watching your hand in his. "Can I take off your blockers? I want to smell you. It's just us, and Wooyoungie and Tae are family." He could see a little bit of hesitance in the way your lip twitches, but you nodded anyway. He was gentle as he peeled off the patches, glad you hadn't opted for the thick gel that he'd have to wipe off.

He was immediately enveloped in the warm hug of your citrus.

170

His own scent spiked in response, leaking to wrap around its counterpart and make a beautiful mix of greens and oranges, like a fresh summer salad. There was a tinge of anxiety and unease in both of your scents, but it was so soft and small that Hyunbin felt relieved. He knew it wasn't the most boundary appropriate thing, to use someone's scent to read their emotions. It left no barriers and could be inappropriate. But he'd always felt better when he could tell what his partners were feeling, where their headspaces were so he knew how to help.

He found his body pulled towards you; two magnets pulled together by force. He stopped when your chests were almost touching, waiting to sense any reluctance or warning from you. When your scent only softened slightly, he let himself close the distance. He was still slow, keeping his hands on your upper back and giving you the time to step back if you wanted. He wrapped you in his arms and laid his head on your shoulder. His nose brushed against your neck, but he stopped short of actually scenting you, despite the strong urge.

Your body fell compliant into his own, but you kept your face turned away from his own neck, which he understood. His scent, while calm and light for an alpha, probably still screamed alpha at you.

"Awwwww, cute! Look at you love birds all cuddly!" Hyunbin cursed as you startled in his arms, body going stiff and rigid. Why was it so loud in here? He grabbed your wrist in one hand while the other rubbed your back. Even as he pushed out calming pheromones, he could still feel your pulse beat quickly and unevenly through his fingers. Was it the loud noise? Or was it something to do with his scent? He tried to tamp down the self-consciousness that threatened to leak out.

"Can you be more loud? Or are you trying to get someone's attention on us?" He growled. His voice came out rougher than he'd intended, but his mate was a step away from trembling in his arms and he hated it.

Wooyoung had the decency to look apologetic, and once he noticed the deer in headlights look on your face he slowed his steps, his posture shrank so as to seem smaller and therefore less threatening. "I'm sorry. Sorry Noona."

Wooyoung came over, ice creams in hand. He reached out, offering you the first choice from the options. You graced him with that addictive smile of yours. While you looked at the offerings, you absentmindedly stuck the tip of your tongue out of the side of your mouth. Hyunbin could see Wooyoung's eyes sparkle at you, recognizing his own amazement in them. He had no doubt you would charm your way through the rest of the Kpop-groups if given the chance. Which he would definitely not let happen.

He took one of the treats at random, eating pieces but mostly watching your expressions. Through the whole night he'd been completely smitten with the way you wore every emotion so honestly and unredacted. It was like watching your thoughts flit across your face.

"Thank you for the treat. It was delicious. I guess you have a lot of questions. I'll answer what I can, but Hyunbin might be better." Tae translated what you said into Wooyoung's ear, both of them silently nodding.

Before they could ask anything, especially anything inappropriate, Hyunbin launched into an abridged version of what happened. Sometime through it the duo had moved to stand beside them. He could smell their soft mix of scents now, Wooyoung's sweet almond and Tae's rich leather. He kept his eye on you, but it seemed like you were comfortable with them both. You even let Wooyoung give you a side hug, and put up with his tactile personality.

"Noona. Poor you! You okay? You tell if Binnie bad. We fix." Hyunbin rolled his eyes at the theatrics, but you laughed and leaned into him. It warmed his heart how you were getting along with his friends.

"Yeah, Noona. Five mates, the crazy Galaxy too. That's a lot. We're here if you need anything. You're family now too." Tae added, refining Wooyoung's choppy English. He felt so lucky to have friends like this.

"Thank you, I'm so happy Hyunbin has such caring friends. I haven't seen the crazy yet, but I'm sure I'll be able to handle it. And if not, I'll send them to you to knock some sense into them." They all laughed at that, happy that the mood wasn't so serious anymore.

They talked for a short while longer, but he could tell you were getting tired, your eyes drooping, so he wished his friends goodbye and promised that they would get together soon, both packs. The ride back to your hotel was quiet as you stared out the window, but it was comfortable.

Pulling up to the front of your hotel he all but sprinted around the car, opening your door with a flush on his cheeks. He escorted you up to your room, your arms barely brushing each other as you rode side by side in the elevator. A current buzzed just under his skin, making him itch to close the gap, to pull your body so close not even air could come between you.

All too soon you were pulling out your keycard, the beeping of the lock echoing in his mind like some kind of death toll. He didn't want the night to end, didn't want to step away from you and watch you close the door. You turned the handle, propping open the door and stepping half-way in before you turned to him. He tried to decipher the looks that crossed your face, but they were gone too quick. It couldn't have been desire he saw, right? The night had gone well, yes, and you had warmed up to him, little touches coming freely and more often.

You stepped back into the room, facing him as you held the door open, beckoning him forward. He wasn't going to question it, simply stepping across the threshold and into the room. As soon as his body was fully in the room you leaned forward, your one free hand grabbing the collar of his shirt and tugging him into you. He swallowed down the nerves riding their way up his throat.

174

His surprise was quickly overridden by joy as your lips crashed together. He groaned softly at the feel of your warm lips moving over his own, eagerly chasing them. His arms wrapped around you, bringing your chests flush. Arousal spiked through him as he felt you, feeling the curves of you so close. His hands travelled up the arc of your back, one tangling in your hair while the other held you steadily at the nape of your neck. A shiver passed under his fingers and your mouth parted in a sigh. He took the opportunity to press his tongue into the opening, licking and prodding at your bottom lip.

The kiss was heat incarnate, the loud smacking of wet lips and tongues dancing together and mapping each other's mouths. Hyunbin bit back a groan as you started to roll your hips into him, his own body moving of its own accord to meet yours. His mind was beginning to fog over, all he could taste was oranges and flowers, and if the two of you kept going he wasn't going to be able to stop from chasing the source of that taste until his mouth was firmly on your other set of lips.

With a determined, but reluctant, deep breath he slowly detached himself from you. His hands lingered, playing in your hair as he stared into your eyes. He wanted to laser engrave this moment on his brain; the way your lips puffed up, lipstick slightly smeared at the edges, eyes sparkling and blown wide with lust, and finally your blushing pink cheeks.

"As much as I want to continue this Doll, we should slow down." Your brow furrowed, but before you could get lost in your mind, his thumb came down to smooth out the wrinkle, tracing gently down your cheekbone and grazing your lip. "I promise you, the next time I have you to myself like this you won't be walking away." Your scent leaked out, making his ego flare at the arousal his words and lingering kiss caused. He leaned forward, leaving a delicate kiss to the corner of your mouth, saying his goodbye and watching as you closed your door.

The night had gone so much better than he'd hoped, despite the sudden interlopers. He hadn't really thought about what it would be like telling his friends or family. Or introducing you. He'd dreamed about it, but it was such new, and uncharted, territory. Maybe he'd avoided it purposefully because there was the chance it didn't work out.

As he left the hotel, riding down in the elevator with the taste of your tongue on his, he started to think about it. How happy his mother would be to have another daughter. How you would get along with his sister, even if that didn't bode well for him. Or how his dad would probably be so proud and happy for him. His family meant a lot, as much as his pack. So he couldn't wait to introduce you.

On the way home, car silent and his head running with hopeful dreams, he called his mom.

"Hi, mom. I have some news, is dad around?"

Ten

Girl Boss

K eys, wallet, phone, mask. A mantra you repeated to yourself often enough that it came with its own rhythm. It was the last thing you would think before leaving anywhere, as they were the four essentials you needed whenever you left the house. Today keys encompassed hotel keys more so than house keys, but it was still the same idea.

Satisfied you had everything you left your room. You checked emails as you walked, which was probably a bad idea with your penchant for clumsiness, but some God of luck was watching over you today as you didn't trip on your face. Today were the interviews for your assistant. The agency had reached out yesterday, sending you a handful of resumes to choose who you wanted to interview in person.

You were impressed. Most of the candidates were highly

educated, more so than your average assistant in the states. You'd heard the job market was harsh and competitive here, but you really didn't expect anyone with a post grad applying for a temporary job as a glorified translator. You were grateful though; it made your job easier as you had a wide pool to choose from.

You narrowed it down to four candidates. The applications hadn't had their gender or subgender, which you'd been adamant about. Instead, you wanted to focus on the people who you thought you'd get along the best with. And someone who could be trustworthy. Now with your new… relationship status? Whoever it was, you needed someone around that you could trust knowing about you and the boys.

The placement agency was in a nice three-story building. The front was made of grey brick, and it shared the space with a dentist and an education centre. The lobby was bright, the overhead lights almost overbearing like they were trying to make up for the lack of natural light. You were greeted by a secretary who brought you back to a meeting room. There were plush leather armchairs across from a nice couch. On one side was a table surrounded by four chairs and a whiteboard, while on the other was a refreshment station stoked with water bottles, juices, and snacks.

A middle-aged woman with silver-streaked black hair was already sitting when you arrived. She stood to greet you, introducing herself as the hiring manager you had been in contact with, Im Joongae. She informed you the candidates were already there, in another room and filling out an aptitude test. You nodded, you're sure she knows what she's doing.

You had a few minutes to yourself as Joongae excused herself to check on the applicants. Your knee bounced anxiously, the heel of your boot clacking on the tiled floor. You checked your phone again, deciding you needed a bit of a pep talk. Things were just so different here, you felt out of your depth.

Damon picked up on the second ring. "Hey, I thought you had interviews today?"

You signed. "I do, that's why I'm calling actually. It suddenly dawned on me that I have no idea what to ask or say. These people are all probably smarter than me. Not to mention, I have to ask them to sign an NDA, two actually, and I don't know how to bring that up naturally. What am I even going to need them to help me with while I'm here? Besides translating?"

"Hmm, you're right, that sounds overwhelming. I think you should break it down into easier to swallow parts. What's your main problem you want them to solve?"

"The language barrier. I think I need a translator the most. Although, a tutor or someone willing to teach me would also be a bonus."

"Great, so someone fluent in English and comfortable with the nuances of both languages. What next?"

"I guess business would be the next important thing. I have a lot of events coming up, not to mention deadlines and new releases this year. So, someone to keep on top of that with me."

"That's great. So someone to translate who's organised and able to handle your schedule. That's not asking too much, I'm sure you'll find someone."

You exhaled; you were already feeling calmer. His voice had that effect on you, which was slightly weird, but you didn't dwell on it. "Right. Anything else I should know?"

Damon hummed on the other side of the line. "Well, there will probably be a certain amount of distance between you. Respect for position and seniority is really big here, so they may be more formal with you. It can come across cold, or indifferent, but it's the expected reaction here. Oh! Work culture here is different, longer hours are normal and bosses are often overly critical. It's a big problem. All that to say, be prepared to fight them to back off a little."

You inwardly cringed. Boundary setting, fantastic. You'd grown better at setting boundaries, but it was always at a distance. It was harder to do with people you grew close to, or saw everyday. You supposed this would be easier though, since it would be for their benefit and not yours. "Okay, thanks Damon. I really appreciate it."

"No problem! So, uh, I know it's not really my place to ask but…"

"Like a Band-Aid Damon, just rip it off." You prompted him when he didn't continue his train of thought.

"Are you interviewing omegas only or, uhm, alphas as well?"

The only thing that stopped you from going into a rant on how it's none of his business and that their subgender has no bearing on their ability was the crack in his voice. He was probably beating himself up enough about it. "I don't know, I asked them to omit it from the applications. Are you okay with that? If I hired an alpha?"

It irked your inner feminist to even ask that, as if anyone else deserved to have an opinion on the matter. Yet, at the same time you recognized that he might be uncomfortable, and it was only fair to ask. Whether you took it into consideration or not was up to you.

"Oh! No! Not at all! I don't care who you hire, as long as you think they're the best choice. They're your assistant, not mine. I was more thinking about your comfort, I don't want you to be put in an uncomfortable position or feel threatened if there's an overbearing alpha."

Again, you underestimated the man. You felt a knot of guilt and were immensely grateful no one was around to see the flush in your cheeks from the embarrassment. It was maybe time you took a step back to readjust your own prejudices. Just because you'd had bad interactions with men, with alphas and pack alphas specifically, it wasn't fair to put that baggage on Damon's shoulders. He wasn't holding you to any toxic omegan standards, he deserved the same consideration in return. Plus, he hadn't even shown any trait or red flag that you'd become accustomed to. Seriously, you were setting yourself up for failure if you kept expecting the worst while being shown nothing but the best.

"I'm sorry, I shouldn't have assumed. That's my bad, Damon."

"Don't apologise, you have nothing to be sorry for. I totally get it, I knew the question could come across as insensitive. Sorry!" You could picture him rubbing the back of his neck, probably sitting in front of his computer with his own look of embarrassment.

"You know, I'm going to start thinking you're Canadian if you keep apologising so much. At the very least I'm going to apply for honorary citizenship on your behalf." The joke lightened the tension, and you heard his chuckle over the phone. It warmed your heart, the heat seeping into your blood and making its way through the rest of your body. You felt lighter now, more ready to tackle the day.

You said your goodbyes, letting Damon get back to whatever it is he was doing while promising to text him as soon as you were done. Shortly after Joongae returned to the room, one of the applicants in tow. You stood up to bow and shake their hand, and so the interviews began.

The whole process felt like a whirlwind. Joongae took point in asking the hard questions, and you were happy you weren't on the other side of them. At some points it felt more like a nosy aunt critiquing your life choices than an interview. The applicants weren't phased though, and they all did quite well. It wasn't until the last one that you really felt that connection.

Lili was a recent graduate, having finished her master's in business. Her hair was dyed this luscious cocoa brown with streaks of burgundy. You wanted to know who her stylist was here, because it still looked so healthy and rich. It wasn't her looks that grabbed your attention though.

"I'm actually a huge fan. I've been reading your work since your first book. It helped me learn English. I followed your career, and my dream is to follow in your footsteps. I know they say not to meet your idols, but you're my role model and whether I get to work for you or not, just to know you would even consider me is an honour."

You hadn't realised the company had advertised the position with your name. It made sense, but part of you was surprised you'd have someone who considered you a mentor here, who would even know to follow your career.

"When I read about your interest in investment, I started learning about it myself. It's why I decided to major in business. In an interview I read you said, 'every woman needs to be the master of her own finances' and that really resonated with me. I never want to be reliant on someone else for something so critical. There's not a lot of women, especially omega women, in the business world. But you took your seat at the table and were unapologetic about it."

It may have been ass-kissing, but you didn't get that vibe from her. And if you could help someone on their own journey, you'd always try. You spoke some more, laughed over your shared love of reading cheesy romance novels and cosy mysteries, and once you decided your gut was giving you the thumbs up you had her sign the NDAs to start working for you. One for yourself, and anything she would have to do on your behalf or that involved anyone in your life, and one sent over from KCE for the boys, who she was bound to run into and get to know. Lili took it all in stride, not baulking at the many pages of legalese in front of her. She didn't even ask any questions as to why she had to sign something from one of the biggest k-entertainment companies.

"Great! So, when can you start?" You smiled at your new assistant.

"I'd say right now, but that might make me look overly eager."

You laughed at her honesty, happy that she felt comfortable around you already. "How about tomorrow then? Joongae-ssi, is there another room where I can speak privately with Lili-ssi? I'd like to explain some things that fall under the NDA."

Joongae nodded in understanding. She assured you this room was fine, and to take your time as she processed the paperwork for the employment contract. Once the door was closed behind her you turned back to Lili. "So, do you have any questions for me? Ask me anything that's on your mind."

Lili hesitated for a moment, seemingly organising her thoughts. "Not really a question so much as curiosity. Are you working on a secret project or something? While I'm super happy you're here, I don't really understand why you're working from Korea."

"Understandable. I came to find a publishing company for the Korean translation of my latest series. I was actually supposed to leave yesterday. The reason for all the secrecy, and why I'm staying in Korea longer, is because I met my true mate. Well, mates, is more accurate."

Lili's eyes went wide, but her shock turned into joy as her mouth widened with them. She was smiling so brightly and genuinely. "Wait, did you say mates? As in plural?" You simply nodded, watching as the information settled over her. This was the first test, you supposed.

Understanding replaced the surprise fairly quickly. "Ah. They must be idols then, or someone who works with idols. That's what the other NDA was for wasn't it?"

"Exactly. It's important to protect myself, but the damage that could be done to their careers would be much worse. Do you listen to Kpop?" Lili nodded. "Oh great, because I could use some lessons on the Kpop world. Honestly, I'd never heard of Galaxy before, or any other Kpop artist besides Blackpink and BTS."

"Wait, did you just say Galaxy? Holy shit! Which ones are your mates? Oh my God. Is it Hyunbin? He's soooo dreamy.

No, wait, let me guess. One of them has to be Baek Dae, you give off the same boss energy."

Lili was ticking things off her fingers as she went through the list of members, weighing their personality traits and gushing over their looks. Clearly, she was a fan, but it was also endearing to watch how animated and excited she got talking about them. She would be the perfect person to teach you all about them and their music.

You decided to put her out of her misery. "You're not wrong, Damon, or er, Baek Dae is one of them. The truth is, all of them are my mates." It still sounded weird to say.

Clearly it was as weird to hear as Lili went slack jawed. You thought you'd broken her as she just stared at you silently, mouth agape. She didn't so much as speak, as squeal, breaking her silence.

"That's so cool! I'm sorry, I know I'm fangirling, and I promise I won't do it in front of them. But that's amazing. I've never heard of someone having so many true mates. I get why it all needs to be kept secret. Honestly though, I'm so happy for them. They truly deserve this happiness, and to have you as a mate. Well, they're incredibly lucky. Do they know who you are, how popular your books are?"

You shook your head. "They know I'm an author, and that I'm successful at it. But I haven't told them my pseudonym or what I write yet. I know they've all seen the show, and Leo has read my books. I think maybe Minju as well. I don't want them to know just yet, so that's something else you'll have to keep on the down low."

Your phone vibrated in your pocket. You took it out to see a text from Hyunbin asking how your day was going. Little butterflies took flight in your stomach. You hadn't gotten to see him after your date, but he, and that kiss, was constantly on your mind. It had been one of the best dates of your life, and he had been so sweet. He sent you coffee and breakfast the morning after, and the two of you had started regularly texting.

"Which one of them has you looking so fond?" The slight teasing tone told you that you weren't being very subtle about your little crush.

"Hyunbin. He just texted to ask how I'm doing. God. Have they always been this sweet?"

Lili smiled, an edge of playfulness to it. "Oh, you have no idea. I can come over tomorrow and show you all their worst kept secrets?"

"That sounds perfect. I should probably get some ammo under my belt because they are sweeping me off my feet all too quickly."

You exchanged information, making plans for Lili to meet you at 9 am tomorrow morning so you could start getting things rolling. You needed to find an office space, rebook your plans for the con, and figure out the visa process to stay here longer. And there was the issue of finding an apartment.

* * *

That was what you thought about on your trip to the boys' company. You couldn't stay in a hotel the entire time, more accurately you didn't want to. You were quickly tiring of take out, and wanted the comfort of your own space. Your own kitchen. The confession from the other night played in the back of your head. They had, sort of, offered you to live with them. But they hadn't brought it up again, which made you wonder if it was a genuine offer or something that was said in the heat of the moment. Maybe they rethought it. It's understandable, having a new person in their space would be a big deal. It sure was for you, and you weren't sure you were comfortable moving into a pack's house after only knowing them a week.

It was a decision you could waffle on by yourself for ages. At the end of the day, it needed to be talked about and made together, as a team. You didn't love it, but you'd have to bring it up with Damon at some point. That some point didn't have to be today though, you were more than happy to procrastinate.

Your cab pulled up to the company building and you thanked the driver as you got out. This time you didn't bother looking at the building, instead walking in as if you'd been there hundreds of times, instead of two. You knew the drill though, and you signed yourself in. Damon had given you a visitors pass, so you only had to flash it to the security guards, and they would call the elevator for you.

Music was pumping out of the practice room as you drew near. You recognized the title song from their last album. They had said they were practising a new version of the choreo for their upcoming tour. You didn't want to interrupt their flow, so you watched through the window until they were finished the run through. It looked so cool. You knew barely anything about dancing. You liked it, sure, but that was dancing with your friends like a bunch of idiots. This... this was an entirely different beast. You watched as their feet moved in synchronised movements, every turn, flip and toe point carefully executed. It must take them so much control to move in sync with each other, hitting the beat at the same time at the right angle. It was a maths nightmare for you.

The music finished, the instructor clapping to let them know they had done well before giving out instructions you couldn't hear but that looked like small adjustments. The boys politely bowed before collapsing on the ground. You chuckled to yourself. They looked so tough and cool thirty seconds ago, now they looked like they wanted nothing more than to become one with the floor. It was a good time for you to enter.

At the sound of the door opening all eyes turned to you. That wasn't unnerving or anything. Besides the boys there were a couple managers, who you haven't met yet, their instructor and what looked to be interns or maybe assistants, as they were hovering behind the other staff members. You remembered your manners, bowing to the staff and introducing yourself.

189

Minju was the first one to come bounding over, covered in as much sweat as the first time you'd met. It was a funny kind of Deja Vu. He went to open his arms to hug you but stopped himself at your slightly disgruntled face. You liked him and all, but he was a little rank right now. And you were already a little lightheaded by the barrage of scents. It was like a pheromone sauna in here. You definitely didn't need some embarrassing repeat of your traitorous body's reaction to all their scents in front of their staff. The fact that his clothes were sticking to his body, rigid six pack outlined clear as day, had nothing to do with it. It also had nothing to do with the heat pooling in your gut or the wetness in your panties.

Why? Why do they still look like walking sex after dancing for hours? God has favourites.

"Ah, hyungs, noonas, this is our mate we told you about." He took your reaction in stride and spoke to his staff instead. You were stuck on the last part though, how he just casually brought up something you had decided to keep secret so openly. You looked at him with panic in your eyes. Minju put his hands up, realising quickly why you were upset. "Oh, Noona, it's okay. These are our personal staff. They know everything."

That did not quell the panic. In fact, despite his noble intentions, Minju had basically thrown a lit match into a dry pile of brush. Poof, forest fire started. Thankfully Damon was already on his way over and saw the entire interaction.

He put a hand gently on your elbow, not an overwhelming

touch, but enough for a point of contact to ground you. "What he means is that our staff have all signed the strictest NDAs, not that they would ever leak anything anyway. They've been with us since debut, and we trust them implicitly. These three are our managers, and the other two are their assistants. Our instructor is also under the same restrictions."

It was like one of those forest fire planes, flying overhead and dumping an entire lake over the flames. The fire was out, but you were left soaked and a little sore from the impact. You wanted to trust them, you knew the boys did, but trust for you was earned, not given. Still, you should try, make an effort.

"It's nice to meet you." You said in your best Korean. Which was at least understood, and if your omega preened a little at the proud look Damon shot you, well that was no one's business.

One of the staff members, singular other woman in the room, smiled and bowed, repeating the greeting, as well as the two assistants who looked a bit confused. The woman turned and whispered something which had their expressions turning into not-at-all-disguised-surprise. In fact, they looked a little shell shocked. The two elder men didn't look as impressed. One was an older man, likely in his forties, while the younger seemed to be only a little older than you. The younger one seemed… not disinterested, but more like it was of little importance to him who you were. Not in a bad way either, you didn't feel like he disliked you, just that he was indifferent. You could work with that.

However, the older man was giving you a look like you'd just suggested putting ketchup on his ice cream. It was a mix of contempt and distaste, and it made you immediately defensive. You've seen this look more times than you could count. It was the 'what is someone like YOU doing here' like you were some street urchin who found their way into the lord's house. You see it all the time from men who think your place isn't in the boardroom but the bedroom. And you thoroughly enjoyed knocking them down a peg.

You didn't want to have to, not to people who meant something to the guys. But clearly this man wasn't going to leave it alone. You weren't surprised when he ignored you and instead turned to Damon and began speaking rapid Korean. Of course you couldn't understand anything, but the air was becoming uncomfortable. Minju was shifting on his feet, looking back at you like he was worried about your reaction. And Damon's scent was spiking in annoyance, his jaw flexing in a way that clearly said he was trying to keep his cool.

"Excuse me. I may not know Korean, but I know my name and I know how to read a room. Would you like to take this to another room? You're making everyone uncomfortable." You laced your tone with sickly sweet venom. Too sweet to be outwardly rude, but cutting enough to tell him you weren't joking around.

Damon and the man held the world's shortest staring contest, and that was all you needed to know that the man was an alpha. Because only alphas, male or female, could be so pig-headed and smell like they're about to set fire to something at the same time. You put a hand out, waving in between their faces. The man shot you a glare but said something to Damon before walking out the door.

Damon's eye twitched but he turned back to you. "You didn't have to do that, I had it handled."

"I'm not something to be 'handled' Damon. Anything that has to do with me, or our mate bond, is my business and I'll handle it as I see fit. And I sure as fuck am not going to sit here and be talked over by some alphas." Your tone was icy and your words hit like a hammer. You could see the anger fade into hurt and guilt. You felt slightly guilty yourself, you knew he didn't mean harm but the action itself was problematic. Better they figured out now that you didn't like to be belittled.

"I wasn't talking over you. It's just, this is a delicate situation."

You waited until he looked at you so you could level him with a pointed look. "Damon, I'm aware you're the leader, the pack alpha. So I will grant you some leniency because I know it's coming from a good place. But do not leave me out again, please. The idol world may be your world, but the business one is mine. Don't forget that I also hold my own power, and I've gone head-to-head with much more powerful people.

Now. Let's go follow your manager. He clearly has something to say. Sung, could you come here please?"

Hansung looked up from where his head was bent with Leo. You weren't naive, you could feel the stares on your back and knew they were all listening and watching. And anxious from the smell of things. He got up and hesitantly approached. You gave a soft smile to the anxious omega. It broke your heart a little that he looked so wary, like he was in trouble or something.

"Sweetie, can you take my card and grab lunch for everyone, your staff too? That would be so helpful." You grabbed your wallet from your purse and handed it to Hansung. "And maybe grab some drinks too. Whatever you all want, it's on me today." You winked at him before turning to smile at the others.

There was a chorus of thanks, and a single voice of protest from Damon that you shut up with a glare. They would have to learn that you were more than capable of treating them. He had the sense to back down looking contrite. His anger seemed to be retreating, and now that he wasn't actively sweating his features just looked tired. His eyes were dark and hollow, and his skin was paler than the other day. You made a note to check in on him after.

The manager was waiting in the room across the hall, the same one you'd had dinner in the other night with the pack. He was sitting at one end, leaned back in his chair, and tapping his hand impatiently on the table. You took a deep breath before sending a quick text off on your phone. You'd prepared for this situation, you were ready for however this turned out. He really picked the wrong person to insult.

* * *

DAMON

Damon was fidgeting with his hands. He wanted to grab your hand and hold it tightly, but he could read your body posture and tell you wanted to be left alone. Something had changed in you, and he was both confused and intrigued. He knew he'd have to have a proper conversation about what had been said in the practice room, he really hadn't meant anything but clearly, he'd said something wrong. He knew he was overbearing when it came to his members, and he thinks that maybe he'd let it bleed over to you as well. Which wasn't fair or necessary. He didn't want you to think he thought you were incompetent or unable to deal with things yourself. He was just an overprotective alpha sometimes.

But you, you surprised him. He'd been angry at what Hunjung had said about you, especially with you right there. He'd dismissed you exactly as you'd called him out for. But, while he had thought you'd be upset or hurt, you seemed annoyed. As if you were annoyed at the inconvenience of having to deal with someone like him. And it was evident now. He watched you sit at the nearest end of the table; your movements were sure and smooth as you slid into the chair. You folded your hands in front of you on the table and stared Hunjung right in the eyes. He caught a glance at your gaze when he sat beside you, and he shivered from the ice in it.

"Do you understand English enough to have this conversation or should I call my assistant to translate?" You broke the silence, voice taking on a steel edge, devoid of emotion.

Hunjung scoffed before answering. "English is fine. Let's get to it then. What do you want?"

Damon stared at him. He'd never heard his hyung speak so coldly to someone. Let alone look so suspicious and accusing. He opened his mouth to reprimand him but your subtle hand wave at him stopped him.

"Are you implying there's something to be gained here?"

"You know there is. So, what is it? Money? Fame? Whatever you want, the company will give you to leave."

What the fuck was going on. Damon felt like he'd been thrown into a movie halfway, completely at a loss as to what was happening. When he'd talked to the company, they'd told him everything was fine, that they'd figure some things out and get back to him. He knew it wouldn't be easy, but this was completely out of left field. His veins were turning to lava, running hot with the anger that was quickly reignited in him.

"Interesting. So you think I'm a gold digger, or what, an attention seeker?" Your tone was so calm. Too calm for the words coming out. Hunjung only snorted before you continued. "Look, before you embarrass yourself further. I will give you a pass today, only because I can see you're acting in what you think is the best interest of the guys. You're being an asshole, but I get it.

In about a minute you'll be getting an email. After which I expect a heartfelt and profuse apology to myself and Damon.

First though, let me be clear that this tactic is disgusting, and you should be ashamed of yourself. You think I'm easy to intimidate because I'm a woman and an omega. You think you can just insult me, make me feel inferior and I'll cry about it and accept whatever you want. Well, bad news for you."

Just as you'd predicted Hunjung's phone went off. He looked at it suspiciously before opening it. Damon watched as he read whatever it was, and was befuddled as the man's face paled. He looked back up at you with pure fear on his face. What the fuck did he just read? Damon looked over to you, but your face hadn't changed. It was like a carving made of ice, completely bereft of emotion despite the heavy words you just said.

"Uh, I'm confused. What's going on?" He asked the room at large. The fire was becoming itchy and suffocating with all this uncertainty. He felt like he was falling with no control over his descent.

"Your manager just read an email from the CEO. He really should have been more cautious and done his homework before assuming I was some harlot. He just realised who I am, which is someone with more power and money than anyone he's ever worked with. He's also just been told that there's a new major stockholder. Which is me."

"What the fuck?" He was caught, his emotions and thoughts pulling him every which way. For one he felt a little betrayed. You'd clearly done this behind his back, and he didn't like it. Yes, you were his mate now and he cared about you, but this was his career, his company he'd poured blood, sweat and tears into. Which led to an anxious feeling. There was a hell of an important conversation to be had, but not now, not in front of someone else.

Then there were the bigger feelings. The awe, that you rendered his manager speechless. That you even thought of this plan, predicting something like this would happen. And that you bought fucking stocks in the company. Exactly how rich were you? And to top it off, the desire. Watching you affect someone, an older alpha who was held with a lot of fear and respect in the company, and have them crumble at a few words. All without a hair out of place. It made him want to push you, to grab you and bend you over until he tamed the ice queen out of you and you were screaming his name. Damon shook his head, willing the growing hardness in his pants. That was so fucking hot.

He hadn't even realised he'd said the last part out loud until his eyes were met with your own. The ice melted for him, showing him that spark of mischief he was so personally acquainted with from his own members.

"I'm sorry for not telling you. Honestly, I wasn't expecting it to go like this, or this quickly. I was hoping I could have a meeting with you and KC so we could talk things through and make a plan." There was guilt in your eyes, but also something you were holding back.

"But how? How do you know the CEO?"

"I do actually. I know some of the board members too. I own shares in one of their brands, and the other is in a book club with a friend of mine; I met her last year. Actually, I already knew your CEO. His daughters are fans of the books and show, so I met them all at my last fanmeet in LA a couple years ago. I still have video calls with them on their birthdays and send them all my books. They're super sweet. He's in full support of whatever we decide to do. I may have also bribed him with tickets for his family to meet the actors when they come for their press tour." You winked at him.

Wow, he was gobsmacked. Not only were you connected, but it was also really sweet that you kept in touch with the girls even before you knew any of them existed. He had a soft spot for kids that you seemed to share.

"Right, we can talk about all that later. And Hyung, don't think I won't be speaking with you. I'm pissed about what you said. You have no right to make a unilateral decision or mistreat people like that." His leader voice came out strong and brooked no argument.

Hunjung looked between them for a minute. He stood up abruptly and walked over before lowering into a deep bow. "I'm very very sorry. Please accept my apology. I would not have said anything if I knew." Damon was irked by the apology, but that was probably coloured by the fact that you had predicted this very scenario.

"You knew this would happen." He voiced the statement.

You took a last glance at the bowing man before turning to him, a sad look on your face. "Like I said, the idol world may be your world, but at the end of the day it's just a business. And that's a world I've had more than my fair share of incidents like this. Someone always wants to throw their dick around."

That sadness was something he couldn't exactly understand, but he thinks he kind of knows. He'd fought the stereotypes and the critics who thought Galaxy wouldn't ever be successful. They blazed their own path and that came with its own people swinging their dicks around. He'd seen it all the time as a trainee. He supposes he should have known you would have had the same battles in your own world.

It makes sense because he's already seen how strong you are. And today he's seeing exactly why they get to have you as their mate. You're strong enough for it. Probably stronger than all of them. Now he really, really wants to know more about your work. Who were you that you held so much sway, so much power? It was intoxicating.

"You may go. Hansung is bringing dinner and I'd like you to join us. Despite your actions to me I'd like to start over. Consider today in the past, but not forgotten. I will be watching, and expecting only the best for them from now on." Seamless as that the ice queen was back.

Hunjung bowed again, apologising and thanking the both of you at the same time. He was grateful you were as generous and understanding as you were fierce. Tension among his team was a distraction he didn't want or need.

When he'd closed the door Damon turned to face you fully, taking one of your hands in his own. "I'm... I don't even know what I am right now. Proud? Amazed. But also, a little upset. You should have talked to me. Buying stocks in the company? That's scary. It scares me that you can just do something like that."

"It wasn't a hasty decision. After I realised that Minju was also my mate I knew that there would be complications. I didn't want any of you to be forced into any decisions by money hungry accountants. If you didn't want to pursue our relationship for your career, then that would be your choice and I would respect that. But I worried that they would threaten and force you into something you didn't want. So, I put this all into play. And I know... it's a lot. But the stocks are actually in your name as well as my own."

"What?" He didn't think his heart could take anymore. Was this what a stroke felt like?

"Damon, I would never do something to jeopardise your career. And I wouldn't want you to feel like I was holding something over you, or have the media spin it like that. So, I bought equal stocks. You own a large chunk of the company now. And you have a meeting next week. I hope you know what this means."

Understanding dawned on him like being struck by lightning. He looked at you, looked into your gentle smile and comforting eyes.

"I… I can have full control."

You nodded, squeezing his hand. "You can have whatever you want, do whatever you want. You answer only to the highest management now, and even then, you have the board behind you."

He didn't know if you even grasped the gift you'd given him. Even he himself couldn't believe it. It was the greatest gift he's ever received.

He couldn't hold back anymore. You were everything he'd ever dreamed of and more. He stood up, pulling you up with him. His hands grasped your waist and lifted you up, sitting you on the table in front of him. He moved between your legs, one hand tilting your chin up towards him. His heart raced as your lips met. So softly at first, a romantic meeting between two lovers. It was too addicting, you were too addicting to stop. His lips pressed harder, gasps and moans curling in the air around the two of you.

You were as desperate as he was, your hands moving down his torso and under his shirt. Your eyes flew wide, and you bit back a moan as your hands came across the hard planes of toned ab muscles. Damon laughed into your lips; his smile wide as he blushed.

"Yeah, I'm gonna need this off. Now." You growled out, pulling at the offending clothing article.

Damon was happy to oblige, stripping it off and tossing it

to the side. He watched your face, drinking in the way your pupils dilated and how you started biting your bottom lip. The air was drenched in arousal. His cock strained against his sweatpants; that did little to hide it.

"May I?" He asked, his hand playing with the bottom of your own shirt. You nodded, giggling when he pulled it off in one quick movement. Fuck, he thought, looking down at your breasts in a lacy white bra. The tops were flushed beautifully, and he was seized by the desire to taste them, to have them in his mouth.

As if reading his mind your hand snuck to the back, popping the clasp of the bra before leaning forward and letting it fall from your arms. Holy shit that was sexy. Damon's nostrils flared and he dove in. He took one pert nipple in his mouth, tongue rolling along it, while he ran his fingers around the other. He bit and pinched, sucking marks into the soft delicate flesh. You leaned back on your hands, giving him more access as he switched between them. Low moans leaving your mouth, broken only by the sharp inhalations when he would bite down.

"Fuck, Damon." He could listen to you moan his name all day. Saliva ran down your lips, your face heated and mouth raw from trying to silence yourself.

Damon let them go, working his way towards your neck. This time he stopped on your glands, not skipping a beat before sinking down on it. You moaned obscenely, feeling the jolt of his erection pressed into you. You were putty in his hands as he sucked and bit, leaving darkening red marks all across your neck.

His face was flushed, his lips as bitten as your own. He looked down at you with awe and hunger, equal parts marvelling at his luck and wanting to rip you to pieces. The responsible leader was gone, and in its place was a man starved. He loved his pack, his mates. But fuck has it been too long since he's seen a pair of tits. Hyunbin's man-tits excluded.

He held back, breathing deeply to gain some semblance of control. As much as he wanted to fuck you right here on the conference room table where anyone can walk in, that wasn't how he wanted your first time to go. He wanted the time to devour you. To worship every inch of your body and mark it for the world to see.

"Is this okay? We can stop." He asked you tentatively.

"No, I don't want to stop. Just… Let's take it slow. I don't know if I'm ready to fuck ten feet away from a bunch of people just yet. Maybe next week." Damon laughed, smiling down at you and pressing his lips to yours, one hand caressing down the side of your face, lovingly tucking back some stray hairs.

"Of course. Whatever you're comfortable with. I could just sit here and smell you and be happy."

You laughed at that. You couldn't help taunting him, rolling your hips up into his, brushing along the tightness in his pants. "You sure about that? Because I can feel something different."

Your voice dipped in honey and lavender, coated in sweetness and rolling down his neck teasingly.

Damon bit his lip, his eyes closing. His hips bucked forward, chasing the pressure and grinding into you. Your panties were already soaked, and he could almost hear the slight squelch as his thigh pressed into you. Your body shivered and responded in kind, riding his hip as the pressure of the firm muscle was just the right kind of taunt.

"If you keep moaning so loud, the others are going to want to join. And I don't think you're ready for that." His remark jolted you out of your haze. He chuckled, his gaze roving down your body again.

"Fuck." He breathed out. "Your tits are so… one day I'm going to fuck them." His dirty words sent your mind spinning. His hand caressed down your stomach, light barely there touches tingling. His fingers edged along the fabric of your pants before moving down. He palmed your pussy, feeling the wetness that was leaking out and the way you stiffened underneath him. "But right now, I want to taste you. I bet you taste like sin."

You were nodding, "Yes, please" coming out broken and needy. He sat up, hooking his fingers into the sides of your waist band before yanking it and your underwear down and shimmying it off your body. The cool air was both refreshing and torturous. Instinctually you closed your legs, but he leaned back over you, prying your legs apart with a frown. "No, no hiding. Let me see." His eyes floated down, taking in the soaking mess in between your legs. He licked his lips, that devilish smile back. You didn't have time to breathe before he was bent forward, tongue licking a thick stripe up your slit. His voice deepened with a moan.

"You taste so fucking good."

Your hands tangled in his hair, pushing him deeper into you. He chuckled, understanding the silent command and didn't keep you waiting. His tongue entered you, lapping at your juices, and you clenched around the muscle. His cock twitched, achingly hard as he imagined himself sheathed in you, your walls clenching around his member. He ate you out like you were a Michelin starred meal.

Hands clenching harder in his hair made him moan into you, your legs trembling in response. He could feel your orgasm coming. When he closed his mouth over your clit, taking it between his teeth and sucking, the pressure finally exploded. The air was knocked from you, a long moan leaving your lips, your legs snapping closed around his shoulder and shaking from the intensity. He massaged your legs, gently lapping at your pussy while you came down.

Eventually you managed to open your eyes, breath still coming in heavily. Damon was staring down at you with heavily lidded eyes and a satisfied smile. He brought his mouth down and felt you shiver as you tasted yourself on him. Your hand came up, holding his chin in place as you broke away, coming back to lick at his chin. He gaped, you were licking him clean of your own juices.

You purred up at the beauty on top of you. "Sit down. Now."
Damon's eyes widened but he did as he was told, anticipation
seeping out of him. You wasted no time, switching places
with him as your hands deftly unbuckled his pants, quickly
pulling them down and open enough for his cock to twitch
out. Your hand grazed along its covered length, a wicked
smile appearing at the little moan that left his lips.

You freed it from his boxers, pushing them down to join the
offending pants in dick-purgatory. You looked offended that
they kept it from you. His cock was veiny and large, his pack
often told him he should get it cast so they can make toys out
of it. Its tip was shiny with precum, red and throbbing in your
hand. Damon threw his head back, his hands balling into fists
as you placed soft butterfly kisses all over the length.

Your tongue poked out, licking a long stripe up the underside.
He watched in muted fascination as you nibbled your way up
the length, holding himself back with every ounce of strength
not to grab your face. Finally, your mouth sunk over him,
taking in his head and sucking it into your mouth like a
vacuum. You gave it a few extra hard sucks, clearly enjoying
the spasming you created, before falling further onto him.

Now, he wasn't the biggest dick in the group, he knew this,
but he was still big enough that he hit the back of your mouth
before you could take him all in. His eyes closed and mouth
laid open slack jawed. You bobbed up and down, your hand
working at his base and cupping at his balls. Working yourself
up to it, coating him in your saliva and precum, you pushed
forward, taking him to the hilt. Your nose pushed into his

groin, and he looked down at you. You were looking up at him, your eyes filled with tears. Damon's hands clenched at his sides, his whole body held still as he tried desperately not to fuck into your mouth. You stayed like that for a second, your throat closing around him and sending shocks through his cock. A few delirious seconds and you moved up, quickening your pace as you tried to take in as much of him as you could.

Damon tried to watch, he really did. He wanted to remember the way you looked, eyes glazed over and teary as your mouth closed over him. The image of his cock in you would haunt him, and he loved it. But the way you moved your tongue, and the suction of that pretty pretty mouth, was too much for him. He felt himself tense, his cock thickening, and he knew he was getting close.

"Ah-fuck. Cl-Close." He tried to reach you, to pull you off in time, not wanting to cum in your mouth since he hadn't asked how you felt about that. He panicked as he felt his orgasm barreling further, but you only sank down further, taking him in all the way and clenching his balls. It tipped him over the edge and he came down your throat. You swallowed around him, taking everything he had to offer. His eyes rolled back, his head tilting backwards as he moaned out your name over and over again, like a prayer.

Instead of popping off him you continued to suck, pulling hard at his tip. Damon groaned and whined in over stim-ulation. His body convulsed and he was a pleading mess underneath you. You chuckled and showed him mercy, letting go with one last kitten lick to his tip. You gently tucked him back into his pants, standing up and leaning over to return the kiss from earlier. Now it was his turn to taste himself.

He wanted to collapse on the table. Maybe he could convince you that it was, in fact, an ideal place to nap and you would crawl up there with him. But you were moving away, already putting your clothes back on with trained efficiency. He wanted to know how you did that, how you just sucked his soul out through his dick and then put yourself together like it never happened. He wasn't ruling out superpowers at this point.

"C'mon let's go see what kind of weird ass lunch Sungie got. I bet it's those intestines he loves."

Damon laughed. Yeah, lunch with his pack, with you, sounded like the best way to help him digest this afternoon. The two of you may be going in smelling like a brothel, but it would be worth it. He held your hand the whole way, not letting you out of his reach through the entire meal. He's not sure he ever wants to let you go.

Eleven

Sleep With Me

~~∘⚬♋⚬∘~~

Y ou were typing away on your laptop when you leaned forward and immediately regretted it. You had set up shop in the meeting room across from the boys' practice room for the afternoon. They weren't all there anymore, they'd split up after lunch for their own individual schedules and lessons, but the majority were still somewhere in the building. Damon had offered for you to come work in his studio, but it felt too early to invade his privacy like that. And you're certain neither of you would get the work done that you need to. So instead, this wooden table and uncomfortable chair became your home base, which led to the reason for the pain shooting through your back.

It had been a long time since you'd worked anywhere this uncomfortable, probably not since your uni days where you'd study just about anywhere. Back of the bus, a cafeteria table, under a tree in the quad. Success was really changing you; you'd gotten too used to plush executive chairs and padded reading nooks. You snickered as you heard Mel's voice in your head calling you a princess for complaining that the new office chair you'd bought was an inch too high. You'd tried to explain that the one inch threw off your entire posture but gave up when she bent over cackling at you.

The clock on the bottom of your screen told you it was nearing the early evening, the afternoon having drifted away. You didn't feel like you'd accomplished much, it had mainly been housekeeping stuff. You updated Mel, giving her your new assistant's contact information. You hadn't spoken on the phone in a few days, not since finding out about your complete set. You felt like a Pokémon trainer, Gotta catch 'em all. She'd sent you an essay of an email, and the two of you had promised to have a lengthier talk later. Honestly, you were both glad and suspicious she'd been MIA. She was either busy or plotting something. She still sent you pictures of your demon spawn cat, so that made you happy. He was living his best life, terrorising all living beings.

You supposed now was as good a time as any to pack it in. You shut off your laptop before sliding it in its cover and placing it in your bag. You grabbed your empty Americano cup and walked out of the room, tossing it in the recycling on your way out. You were headed to the elevators, debating on the risk versus benefit of getting another coffee so late in the evening, while massaging your lower back. You stopped halfway down the hall to lean over and stretch, trying to rid yourself of the stiffness.

A hand landed on the small of your back while you were bent over, making you scream and straighten out. You whipped around, ready to throw fists at whoever dared to touch you, when you came face to face with a flustered looking Minju.

He held his hands up, stammering as he tried to explain himself. "I'm so sorry! Did not mean to scare you. Sorry!" His eyes were panicked and shooting around, as if he were checking for witnesses to his absent-mindedness. He was dressed in a new pair of sweats, hair fluffy and slightly damp from a shower.

Laughter had you looking behind him, finding Hansung doubled over against the wall. He was gasping for breath he was laughing so hard. He looked up to point between the two of you before falling back in a fit of giggles.

"Choi Hansung you pabo. *Do you want to die? I'll happily stuff you with tissues.*" Minju growled, his embarrassment fading to exasperation. The whole altercation helped to calm your racing heart.

Minju turned to you, his smile reflecting how sorry he was for scaring you. "Noona, you okay? You're hurt." He pointed his finger towards your side, where you'd grabbed once you had decided you weren't in danger of kicking someone's ass. You were definitely in worse condition than five minutes ago.

Still, the ingrained reflex of never wanting to be a bother took the wheel and you were shaking your head. "Oh, I'm fine, it's okay!" You tried waving your hand, which resulted in suppressing a jolt of pain down your shoulder and into your back. You needed to get home, and maybe rob a pharmacy.

"Yah, you're as bad as those idiots. Hansung go get my bag from my locker. And tell Hyung that our mate needs to see our physio doctor asap. What are you standing there for, go!" Hansung scurried off after Minju's quick, but somehow still chastising words. How did you feel chastised without understanding anything?

He turned back to you and gestured for you to come closer. You obeyed, head hung low after being caught in your lie. His touch was gentle as he spun you around. He tapped your shoulder before pointing to the hem of your shirt. You blushed but nodded and he lifted the back of your shirt up. Little butterflies fluttered; you weren't shy about the showing skin, but the ink staining it wasn't as well received in some countries as it was back home.

He took in a sharp breath before lifting the shirt higher. His fingers grazed along your side and back, tracing what you knew was the outline of the tattoo you sported. It took him a second but soon he was refocused on his task, poking gently at you in different spots.

"Jagi, your tattoo is beautiful." You let out the breath you'd been holding. "This hurt?" Your pained mewl gave him the answer he needed but you still nodded. Your muscles spasmed and you bit back a cry. "You're straining. I'm going to put on cream and tape, then you need medicine and to go see a doctor."

It wasn't so much a question as a fact, and one you didn't have the nerve to disobey when you saw the sternness in his eyes. Hansung saved you from a lecture you could see brewing, jogging up with a gym bag in hand.

"Here Hyung! You okay Noona? What happened?" He hit you with those big doe eyes and you were done for.

"It's nothing really. I was working in the meeting room this afternoon and I guess the chair wasn't great for my back."

Hansung pouted, his lower lip sticking out in a way that made him look both adorable and hilarious. "Even Dae-Hyung doesn't do that. You should have come to one of the studios. I was just upstairs, we could have worked together."

Your heart fluttered at how much these boys cared about you already. They were so warm and welcoming, attaching themselves to you at every opportunity. Sometimes you wondered if they understood boundaries and personal space, but mostly you found it endearing. A cold sensation jolted you back to the man at your side, who clearly didn't have boundaries as he rubbed ointment on your lower back and side without warning. The cream was cold, but his hands were soft and warm. You found yourself leaning into him, losing yourself a little at the ministrations.

Hansung leaned against the wall in front of you, reaching out to hold your waist on the opposite side. His thumb ran in circles as Minju eased some of the aching with a gentle massage before applying the physio tape across your back.

214

You wanted to close your eyes, fall into the fire that was slowly igniting in your stomach. That was when Hansung noticed the flash of colour. He stepped up to your front, holding you against his chest as he looked down at your back, taking in your tattoo.

"Woah! Noona, that's so cool! Can I see the rest? What is it? When did you get it? Did it hurt?" He tried to reach out and touch it during his barrage of questions, but Minju smacked his hand away before lowering your shirt.

"Pabo. I just fixed it, don't touch it." Minju shook his head and caressed his hand down your back. Your whole body broke out in goosebumps. Thankfully you were completely covered, now, so no one could see it. The devious glint in his eyes told you another story. The fire flickered and intensified. Clearly your libido didn't care about injuries.

"Hyunnnng! I just want to see it. I want a tattoo, but I think it hurts too much." Hansung didn't pull away from you even though your shirt was down, instead he hooked his chin over your shoulder and grabbed your waist with both hands. You felt your stomach flip and the hairs on the back of your neck stand up. This close you could make out the faint cherry blossoms that clung to his neck and clothes. His blockers must be almost washed off, but you weren't upset in the least. In fact, you gravitated towards his neck, taking in a subtle breath of the omega's sweetness. It calmed your fluttering heart, but did nothing for the arousal.

Minju closed in on your back, his arms twining around your

215

waist over Hansung's. He rested his head over your other shoulder, turning his face to not so subtly take in a deep breath of your own scent. "Mmm, you smell so good. Happy omega." Your face was probably crimson at this rate. Having an alpha compliment your scent made your knees weak in a way that your inner woman hated. Did that stop your omega from purring? Nope. You just desperately tried to reel in your dirty thoughts so they wouldn't know how big of a -.

Hansung shifted closer, ending your train of thought, not an inch of space between any of your bodies anymore as your purring vibrated through your bodies. Part of your brain registered that you were still in an empty hall, in a not so empty building. Not that that had made a difference the other day…

You felt the edge of his nose whispering over your skin, the barely there sensation making your head tilt back. He took it as permission, pressing his face further into the crook of your neck. His fingers tightened on your waist in an almost painful way as his lips brushed over your scent gland. It was quickly followed by the warmth and wetness of his tongue as he licked a stripe over it. The air felt ten times colder on the wet skin as he pulled back. You had to bite back a moan.

"Mmm. Jagi. You taste like heaven. I want to roll around in your scent." Hansung's voice came out low and husky. It sent shocks of arousal to your core. You were mere seconds from slicking up in this hallway.

A door opening and closing down the hallway shocked your

system. You cleared your throat, hands going to Hansung's shoulders to pull him from you slowly. He whined and tried to cling to you harder. Unfortunately for you that meant digging into your side that was still sore. You flinched which caused a chain reaction of Hansung apologising followed by Minju smacking him on the arm and letting out a lot of fast Korean you thought sounded suspiciously like swear words.

The three of you moved apart. You already missed the warmth and comfort of Hansung's body. "Noona, where are you going now?" Hansung asked as you walked over to the elevator, pressing the down button.

"I was going to go back to my hotel, maybe rest and take some ibuprofen. Why?"

Hansung stood beside you, his hands in the pocket of his jeans. "Can I... uh, can we hang out? Just us? I want to know more about you." His voice was so soft, his entire self seemingly shy and unsure of himself. In the days you'd gotten to know him, you'd never seen Choi Hansung as unsure of himself. It made him look younger, more vulnerable and you wanted to wrap him in a hug.

"Yeah of course Sung. What do you wanna do? I don't know if I'm in the right state to do much moving around..." You felt awful now, like your body was decrepit and holding you back.

Hansung was quick to perk up. "That's okay! Let's watch a movie." It was a simple suggestion, but it made him so happy.

He didn't look disappointed or put out in the least. You never knew what to expect with them, you would have thought that as idols, young ones at that, they'd want to do extravagant things. Not stay in and watch a movie.

The universe liked to prove you wrong it seemed. Because Hansung was practically vibrating with joy as he raided the suite for every pillow and blanket he could get his hands on. He was building a veritable nest in the living room. The TV was hooked up to your laptop, where he had a Studio Ghibli movie loaded up. It wasn't one you've seen, Kiki's Delivery Service and My Neighbour Totoro being your go-tos. He was chattering about the plot and his favourite character while you put the snacks you picked up on the way in some bowls.

Once Hansung was satisfied with the mountain of fluff he flopped down on his stomach. He looked up at you, his head propped up on his hands. "Noona, come! The nest is ready." You happily walked over with your loot. Immediately you noticed the space smelled so strongly of him. You couldn't help yourself as you lowered yourself down and wrapped a blanket around you. Hansung rolled over, nudging at your arm with his head hanging upside as he looked up at you from the ground.

"What do you want Sungie?"

"Can we cuddle?"

You smiled as you opened up your cocoon. "Of course love, you can cuddle with me anytime." Hansung let out a happy sigh as he settled into your side, and you wrapped the other side of the blanket around him. His body melted into yours, you wrapped your arms around his waist. You laid your head on top of his while he rested on your chest.

The movie played, with Hansung mouthing along to some of the lines. His eyes were alight with rapt attention. You caught yourself watching him half the time instead of the movie. It was hard to reconcile all these versions of him you knew. In the videos you'd seen of their performances he exuded confidence and pure fuck-boy energy. It was… very attractive. Then there was his high spirits and constant jokes. He was fun and genuine, breathing life into everyone around him.

And here was yet another new side of him, you were learning. Soft, quiet, cuddling into the warmth of your body and making your heart want to stay like this forever. The movie ended and Hansung looked up at you expectantly.

"It was great, Sung, you were right. But, I think Calcifer was my favourite. Why do you like this movie so much by the way?"

Hansung pondered for a moment, running his tongue over his lips while he thought. "I think… it's because they both deserve more than what they got. Like, look at Howl. He's a powerful wizard, but he's so lonely. People only want him to give, but not give back. But he still fights for them. And Sophie, all she does is work. Her friend has no time for her, her mother lies to her. But they see each other. Really see, you know?"

Huh, you hadn't thought about it that much. But clearly Hansung had, and it seemed to be something that struck him in the heart. You understood, you had your movies or books that stuck with you the same way. The characters you would see yourself in, which made them so much more special to you.

He cuddled into you once more, flicking through Netflix to find something else to watch. He continued talking after a quiet minute. "When I was young, we moved abroad. It was hard, I was home-schooled, so I did not have many friends. Then I came back here and became an idol. My only other friends are idols. I'm lucky, I have my pack, but sometimes I want to be seen as more."

You ran your hand through his hair, feeling the soft strands slip through your fingers. Your heart broke at his quiet confession. It must have been so lonely, for all of them, to grow up in such a suffocating industry. You had your own baggage, but the suffocation was different, less eyes on you and more limitations. You couldn't exactly empathise, so you took your time before speaking again.

"I'm sorry Sungie. I can't imagine what it was like to mature and go through your life under a magnifying glass. I have some friends who were child actors, and teen movie stars. It really fucked them up. One of them... One of them didn't make it past his 18th birthday.

I was lucky, I could hide behind my pen name and live a regular life. I still went to college, still had regular friends. But even then, when people learned who I was, it was like something would shift. I let myself open up once and it ended poorly. It made me paranoid, and eventually I just pulled away entirely. It was safer to just stay away from people, than risk the heartache of finding out you were being used. It's why I still use a pen name, despite my face being known now. I'm scared."

It was Hansung's turn to reassure you, his hand rubbing calming circles on your thigh. It wasn't sexual, it didn't ignite a fire in your stomach. Instead, it felt soothing, like he was anchoring your frayed nerves to his movements.

"I'm sorry baby. Is that why you don't want to make this public?" Your stomach clenched at his words. Was that why?

"Maybe. A part at least. The biggest part is my worry about the backlash you would all face. But I guess a part of me is still afraid. How many people would try to use me to get to you? Or use you to get to me? It would break my heart if any of you got hurt because of me." You felt the truth of the statement as if it were tattooed on your soul. Flashes of memories long past tried to force their way to the forefront of your thoughts. You pushed back, you didn't want to relive that. They weren't them, they weren't him.

His hand kept up its soothing rhythm, moving on to drawing random patterns instead of just circles. "Don't worry about us, we're strong. It's worth it to have you with us. Really

Noona."

You smiled down at him. He really was too sweet, it had your heart melting and for a nanosecond you thought about what it would be like to be in a public relationship with them. Going on dates, laughing openly without worry. Those happy scenes were quickly replaced by rabid fans, plummeting stock prices, and sad mates. The flash of a condescending smile, newspaper headlines tearing you to pieces. No, it wasn't something you would, or could, entertain.

So, you did what you did best. You deflected, switching the topic to what you two were going to watch next. There was a brief debate on the merits of horror movies, to which you vehemently told him there were none and he was insane, before you realised you shared a mutual love of Harry Potter. Your evening became a movie marathon as you started with the first one and worked your way through.

By the second movie you were both falling asleep. You were so tired and achy; you knew sleeping on the floor would fuck you up the next day, yet you didn't have the energy to care. You fell asleep in a haze of cherries and honeyed oranges, your arms wrapped around his waist as his body laid half on top of yours and your legs tangled together. It felt like a puzzle piece sliding into place, the great satisfaction of completion.

* * *

You woke up with a groan. You might actually need to rob a pharmacy now. You cursed your past self for being too lazy to move to the bed. Off to the side a phone was ringing. You blinked open your eyes, trying to pinpoint whether the shrill ringing device was within reach. Hansung was curled into your side, one of your arms trapped underneath him. His breathing was shallow. You cooed at the sight of his mouth slightly ajar, hair tousled in his eyes. He looked so peaceful.

You finally found both your phones, thankfully within reach. You very carefully grabbed them so that you didn't wake up your sleeping omega. Your phone was checked first. It was almost 7 am, and there were ten missed calls and too many missed texts to count. Hansung's phone began ringing, Damon's name popping up on the caller ID. You cursed silently before deciding to answer it for him.

"Hey Damon, it's me." You whispered.

Damon exhaled sharply. "Thank fuck. What the hell -? Where are you both? Why didn't you call or text?" His tone was clipped and stressed, and you immediately felt terrible. You'd both texted the group chat yesterday that you were going to watch movies at your place, but you totally forgot to tell Damon that Hansung was staying the night. Clearly, he'd forgotten to text as well.

"I'm so sorry! We fell asleep watching something and forgot to tell you. Hansung is here, he's sleeping right now. Want me to wake him up?" The guilt was eating a hole through your stomach lining. You never had to tell anyone where you were, or what you were doing so it completely slipped your mind that it's not the case for Hansung. Maybe not even for yourself?

"No, let him sleep a bit more. I'll be over to get him. Next time let me know, okay? I was worried."

"Of course, I'll remind him to tell you and I'll try to be more on the ball about it if one of them is with me."

"Not just them, you too. I don't expect you to fill me in on your every movement, but I would like to know that you're safe. I didn't just worry about Hansung last night."

You were confused and conflicted on how to feel. On the one hand, it was said with such sincerity and it made you feel valued and cared for. But, on the other hand, you couldn't help but feel a flare of discomfort. It always started small, maybe even out of goodwill, but you've seen how it quickly becomes obsessive and oppressive. Your old pack was enough of a lesson that you wouldn't let yourself be controlled again.

You stayed silent for long enough to make Damon worry as he hurried to explain himself. "Not, not that I'm trying to police you or something. I know I'm not your alpha, or your partner or anything. Gosh, I don't even know what we are. But that's not going to stop me worrying about you."

"Damon."

"Yeah?"

"You're rambling."

"Ah. Yeah, my bad."

You chuckled. "It's okay. And I know you're not trying to restrict me. It's just... Well, I've been there. I've had the overbearing alpha who policed my every move, and it was suffocating. But I also recognize that you're not him, and you don't deserve my suspicion. I'll try and keep you in the loop, I promise." It was the best you could offer right now.

It seemed enough for Damon though, as you could hear him relaxing over the line, the smile back in his voice. "I'm sorry too, I should have been more cognizant of how I was acting. I promise to try and be less protective."

"Thanks Damon. And, for what it's worth, I also don't know what we are. So I guess this is uncharted territory for all of us." You blushed a little at the confession. You hadn't put much thought into it, too consumed with the whole 'mate' thing to think about labels.

"You're our girlfriend, obviously." You nearly jumped out of your skin at the sleepy words that came from your side. Hansung was blinking up at you, a huge lazy smile spread across his face. You would be mad about the eavesdropping if you weren't having a conversation basically on top of him.

"Yah! Choi Hansung, how long have you been listening? You little menace!" Damon yelled over the phone, his voice cracking at the beginning. Clearly you weren't the only one flustered at the younger's bold statement.

"That's something you can't decide for your whole pack, Sungie. I appreciate the thought, but I don't think everyone else feels the same." You smoothed his hair down.

"I do. I mean, uh, I would also like you to be my, our, girlfriend. And I'm pretty confident everyone else feels the same." Damon coughed out. You snickered at the awkward cadence of his voice.

"Nooooo. I want Noona to be pack. But girlfriend is okay. For now."

"I swear to g-. Ho Minju you little shit, stop listening to my conversations. Binnie! Come get the little weasel before I can't hold myself back. I'm so sorry, no one is pressuring you about that, we're still getting to know each other and-" Damon was cut off as his voice became muffled. There were some scrambled noises on the other end of the phone and laughter followed by running footsteps and a door closing.

You looked at Hansung with your brow raised, thoroughly confused by what was going on. He shrugged before moving to lie on top of your torso, cuddling into your neck and scenting you. The living room became even more covered in citrus and cherry pie, making your head go happily hazy. You could feel Hansung start to purr as he peacefully lazed on you.

"Noona? Let's go on a date today." Minju's voice was clearer now, echoing in the room he was in. There was pounding on the door, but Minju only giggled. The antics made you smile, and you wished you could be there to see the chaos in person.

"Sure Min, I have some things to do this morning, but I'll be free in the evening. What do you want to do?"

"It's a secret. I'll text you. Okay, bye girlfriend Noona!" You didn't have time to respond as Minju's voice faded out and you heard a commotion on the other end before Damon got his phone back.

"I'm putting you all up for adoption. Try me." A loud laugh bubbled out of you at Damon's words. You'd heard something about him being dubbed the dad of the group, but this was your first time really experiencing that side of him. You had to admit, you'd be exhausted too having to deal with the chaos that was your mates. Well, you supposed you'd be in that position soon enough.

"So… Does that make you my boyfriend?" You teased.

Damon audibly gulped before answering. "Uh, yeah. I guess so yeah." His smile was so bright in his voice you could almost see it. "I have to go now, but I'll see you both soon. Sung! Get your ass up and in the shower, I'll bring a change of clothes." You both said goodbye before you hung up, putting the phone on the floor with your own.

"So… how much trouble are you in?" You asked Hansung while you rubbed his back.

"I think you mean 'we', you're my accomplice, you heard Dae-hyungie. He'll give me lecture and then we'll fuck until he's not mad anymore." Hansung cackled as you choked on your own spit. That was more graphic than you'd anticipated, and it was way too early for you to be picturing that or getting so hot thinking about it.

"Damon is right, you are a menace. And I know just how to deal with the likes of you." You stared down at him with an intimidating smile before you pounced. You tickled his sides, making him squirm and laugh until he was breathless. You continued your attack as you both rolled around, Hansung sometimes getting the upper hand and attacking your sides back. Eventually you both collapsed, tired and panting but still laughing at each other. You shooed him away to shower, leaving a robe by the door for him.

You decided to take the quiet time to check your to-do list for the day and make yourself a coffee. Lili would be here in about an hour. You had planned for her to take you shopping, you needed a new phone and Korean Sim card as well as some other necessities. You also wanted her to pick out a laptop and phone for herself for work purposes, but you hadn't told her that yet. You figured it would be harder for her to say no when you were at the store. Then you had an appointment with a realtor to look at some apartments. Mel was dealing with closing up your house and hiring a groundskeeper, but you wanted to put Lili on that asap so you wouldn't need to put anymore extra work on your friend's plate.

Wobbling around in pain all day wasn't your idea of a good time. However, you noticed that since you'd woken up the pain had been a ghost of itself. In fact, it wasn't more than a lingering ache. You should be feeling a lot worse, considering you completely ignored Minju's advice and then slept on the floor. And while your back had been stiff this morning, you also hadn't noticed any pain during your impromptu tickle-fight. Strange.

You were completely engrossed in your thoughts when you heard a knock on your door. You opened it to see Damon standing there, hands filled with bags. He was wearing a leather jacket over a black shirt and ripped black skinny jeans, while a black cap sat on his head. You chuckled at him fondly.

"Are you auditioning to be a grim reaper? I hear the salary is too low to afford those brands. Come to think of it, I don't think I've seen you in any actual colours, only monotone shades." You teased him before stepping aside and letting him in.

He rolled his eyes but took your jabs with a light-hearted laugh. "Not you too. I like black okay! There's nothing wrong with that."

You smirked. "I know, most of my own wardrobe is black. I just like to see you get all riled up, it's cute." Damon blushed at the compliment, turning away to distract himself by taking things out of the many bags he was carrying.

"Did you call Hyung cute before me?? Noona!!" Hansung wailed as he dramatically entered the living room, towel wrapped around his waist. Your eyes were drawn to his bare chest, following the lines of his abs up to his pecs. His hair was still wet and dripping, so you watched as one brave water drop made its way down his collarbone and down the carved edge of his right pec. You marvelled at how defined he was, and how absolutely snatched his waist was. He was built like an upside-down triangle, his shoulders wider than his waist and hips.

Damon's laugh shook you out of your staring contest with Hansung's perfect marble skin. Your gaze shot up and you turned to glare at him. He held up his hands in surrender but there was an infuriating smirk that was only fuelled by the pink in your cheeks. He couldn't possibly know the sordid things you wanted to do to his packmate's chest. You turned back to Hansung, seeing the same self-satisfied look in his eyes. He'd done this on purpose, you were sure of it.

"Choi Hansung, why aren't you wearing the robe I put out for you?" Your voice was too high to be natural. It wasn't fair, why were they so handsome?

Hansung just shrugged before moving to rustle around the bags on the table. "Hyung, did you bring coffee?" You rolled your eyes, but the shock of his bare chest was starting to fade. The view of his back, and his defined muscles moving as he reached however…

"Of course baby. You're a monster without caffeine." Damon slid a container with two iced americanos over.

You snatched one, having completely forgotten about your

now cold and abandoned cup in the coffee maker. "Me too. Thanks Damon." The boys chuckled and joined you to sit at the table. It turns out the bags, besides one for Hansung's clothes, were full of breakfast. It was a suspiciously large amount.

"I may have gotten extra for you to keep here, in case you get hungry at night." The answer came as you eyeballed the array in front of you. "And, uh, Minju may have also threatened my life if I didn't make sure you had a big breakfast." You choked on your coffee at that, Hansung rubbing your back while he snickered. The possibilities of the evening flashed behind your closed eyes, ideas running rampant about why you'd need so much energy.

"He'll feed you to death if you're not careful." Damon admitted, thankfully mistaking your flush, with Hansung agreeing before grabbing a container and stuffing his cheeks. You were happy he had such a good appetite, especially with how small he was. But, after seeing so much of him, you were reassured that it was a healthy small, and not a dangerous small.

You picked at the nearest dishes to you, but didn't eat too much. It was still too early for you and your stomach would rather be filled with caffeine and water. The boys talked about their upcoming day, each having different things to do and places to be. You tuned them out as you went back to your computer. Your phone pinged, letting you know that Lili was leaving and would be there in half an hour. Earlier than you'd told her to, but you appreciated that.

"Noona, what are you doing today?" Hansung asked around a mouthful of food.

"It's my assistant's first day so we're going to do some shopping, finally get a new phone for Korea, and grab her some things for work. Then we're going to go look at apartments and probably come back here later to set her up with all of my emails and contacts. Oh, and apparently a date with Minju tonight."

The room was eerily silent, something you had yet to experience when you were with them. It was odd enough that you looked away from the email you were typing. Damon and Hansung were having some kind of conversation with their eyes, Hansung tossing his head in your direction aggressively and Damon narrowing his eyes and pursing his lips at the other. They both looked… upset? On edge?

"Did I say something?" You tried to break the tension that was now making the hairs on your neck stand up.

Damon turned to you, startled out of his silent battle with Hansung. He turned to you, his face now looking apologetic and sad. "No! You didn't do anything at all. Sorry, we shouldn't have ignored you like that."

Hansung interrupted, "Dae-Hyung has something to tell you." Damon snapped his head back towards the younger man. If looks could kill, Hansung would be at least severely crippled. Maybe have lost a hand.

"Right, do you two need a minute? Because this is starting to sound like some kind of big reveal in a drama and it's too early and two coffees too soon in my day for that."

Damon looked back over at you. "It's nothing serious, Hansung is just a shit disturber. You said you were going to look at apartments?"

Your stomach twisted, so that's what made them uncomfortable. "Yeah… is that a problem?"

"No, not at all. You can live wherever you'd like. All I ask is that one of us checks out the place with you to make sure it's in a good neighbourhood. But, we were hoping that you would, uhm, stay with us?" His voice went up on the last part, making it seem like more of a question than a statement. Was he asking you to stay?

"Oh, so you were serious the other day." You'd thought about it, but you weren't entirely convinced.

"Of course, none of us would have said something like that on a whim. We had a pack discussion about it, and it was unanimous."

Part of you prickled at that. They'd discussed it but never asked you how you would feel about it, or even that it was an option they were discussing. Obviously, it was a choice they all had to make, but you felt like you should have been clued into it existing. So much of your life the past week happened to you, not with you. You were someone who thrived on controlling your own life, a trauma response you held onto strongly.

You forgot you weren't wearing blockers, and your mood was easily picked up on through your scent by the other two. A strong burnt orange smell wafted around the room making Hansung whine and Damon move closer to you. He reached out a hand, laying it on top of yours. Hansung got up, dragging his chair over until it was butted up to your own. He sat down, circling your waist with his arms and pulling you into his chest. His very bare chest.

"I'm so sorry. Just forget we even mentioned it, you don't have to do anything you don't want. I know, living with five men you barely know is insane and would probably be weird for anyone. We didn't think about it. We'll make sure you find a nice apartment, maybe close by so we can visit, if you want, and we'll go shopping to make sure you have everything you need. There's a store that sells -"

"Damon. Rambling. Again." You cut him off before he gave you a headache. "I'm not mad, or upset. Not really. And it's not about living with you guys." You paused, not sure how to elaborate on why you felt pushed away, talked over and left out.

You took a deep breath before continuing, grateful that they were letting you take your time. You needed to get your thoughts together. They'd had a pack meeting, but was it really such a shock? It wasn't completely new information, and they had brought it up, you just weren't sure it wasn't a joke.

"You had a whole conversation about this, made a decision on it, without involving me. I understand the pack needs to make its own choice, but you should have told me it was something you were considering seriously. I know it was thrown out there, but it didn't seem real, you know? It would have given me a chance to think about whether it was what I wanted to do, or even think about as an actual possibility.

I'm not mad or anything. I guess, it's going to be hard to adjust to this. We each have our own ways of doing things, and now we're going to have to adjust to accommodate each other."

"Sorry Noona. We didn't think. Does that mean you don't want to live with us?" Hansung's voice was soft next to your ear.

"Hansung." Damon chastised. "You don't have to answer that. I'm sorry too, I should have considered that. But you're right, we do have some changes to make. Thank you for communicating that though. It must have been really hard. This is why I'm so confident in us though, as long as we're open and we communicate we can make it work. And really, we'll support whatever you want to do. But the offer is there, we truly would love for you to stay with us."

You hummed. You also appreciated the openness you'd felt with all of them so far. They seemed to have very healthy relationships, which only comes from years of being together. It was a goal you'd strived for in all your past romances, only achieving it with Mel. Which was why you ended up staying such good friends. And why you avoided relationships… until now.

"I think you should move in with us. Leo is already decorating your room. He wants to know your favourite colour. Plus, if you live with us, we can have morning cuddles every day." You laughed at Hansung's sincere plea. He had a point, you loved cuddling with him. And it wasn't just because he was currently shirtless and smelled like cherries on a summer day.

"I'll think about it, okay?" You hoped it would placate them. Now that you'd been officially asked, or told, you needed to think more seriously on it. Maybe you could bounce the idea off Lili. The biggest worry you had was that living together was a high stress endeavour. It can make or break relationships, and yours was so new, you didn't want to set it up for failure.

Hansung pressed a kiss against your cheek. It was soft and warm, full of love and care. And left you putty in his arms. Damon gave him a warning look. But Hansung only stuck his tongue out.

"What? I can kiss my girlfriend if I want. Right baby?"

"Yah, that's our girlfriend." Damon winked at you.

You were dead. You were sure of it now. It was the only logical explanation as to how you were currently being called pet names by two of the most handsome men you'd ever seen.

Laying in the half-clothed arms of one of them.

Yep. RIP.

Twelve

Patty Cake

༺✦༻

"No Eonnie, absolutely not."

"Lili, please. I'm your boss, you should listen to me."

"Still no. I can't, I'm perfectly fine as is."

"You said you want to be like me, right? That makes you my hoobae, and me your Eonnie. I think by Korean law you need to do as I say."

"Ugh. You're pulling cultural rules on me? That's a cheap shot."

You look up at the salesman who's looking very confused trying to follow your conversation in English. You shoot him a smile and point at the phones, tablet, and laptop, showing him your card to get the point across that you wanted to buy them. He understood the unspoken command, smiling as he happily wrung everything up and worked to start setting up the phones with your new Sim cards.

"Eonnieeeee." Lili's whine was adorable and only worked to make you laugh.

You patted her on the shoulder, trying to give her a sympathetic smile. She never stood a chance, when you wanted something, you got it. And you wanted to get her the best electronics so she could do her job easily.

"Sorry not sorry. I promise you weren't leaving without them. If it makes you feel better, you can just pretend they belong to me for business purposes." You shot her a wink and she rolled her eyes. She talked to the employee while he packed things up, giving him your details and email for the receipt after you paid.

The Samwei store was the last on your list for the morning. You'd wanted the new flip for a while now, and it totally wasn't because it came in lilac. Definitely not. That would be fiscally irresponsible. You would tell your accountant it was a necessary business expense.

There was a magic to a new phone, all shiny and ready to explore. You lost yourself in setting up your accounts, blindly following Lili through the mall. When you looked over, she was putting something into the case and clipping it shut. You'd gotten her the regular version of the newest model.

"What are you doing?" You asked curiously.

A pink flush crept across Lili's cheeks, and she didn't want to meet your eyes. She was hesitant but eventually showed you the back of her phone. There was a picture of Minju, rather a photocard as you'd recently learned. So this is what those are used for.

"Why are you so embarrassed? He looks cute on your phone."

"Because he's your mate and you actually know him." Lili sounded like she wished the floor would swallow her whole right about now.

"Lili... Is Minju your bias?" Another new term you'd learned but didn't really understand. You couldn't even pick a favourite latte flavour, your favourites were forever changing.

You hit the nail on the head though as Lili hid herself behind the bags she was carrying. "Oh God. Please never tell him. I'll die." You shrugged, promising her no such thing.

"Wait!" A sudden thought hit you and you held up your phone next to hers. "Mine won't fit a photo card!" You wailed a little dramatically.

Lili looked at you like you had three heads. "Not to be rude, but why would you put one in the first place? Wouldn't that cause problems?"

You grinned deviously. "Not problems, but I should keep them on their toes. And who knows, maybe I want to put in a random other idol just to rile them up."

Lili clutched her chest in mock shock. "Devious. I like it, I'm taking notes."

You were getting along swimmingly with your new assistant. She was funny, quick witted and extremely competent. You learned that her parents had sent her to study abroad because they thought she'd be better marriage material with an Ivy League and English background. You both snorted at that. Lili was an omega after your own heart, laser focused and quick to dismiss societal expectations. Taking her under your wing was going to be a treat.

The two of you listened to music and Lili introduced you to some girl Kpop groups while you had lunch at a cute sushi restaurant near the real estate office. She played some songs from the junior artists at the boys' label, which was good for you to know about. You really liked Ordinaries, they reminded you of your emo rock stage in high school. You never really grew out of your alt rock phase, and their sound immediately pulled you in. What you were surprised with though, was the girl groups. They were young groups, but the vocals were amazing. You wanted to meet them, especially after learning that one was another Aussie implant and like Damon's little sister.

All too soon you were sitting down with the realtor and going over some listings that checked your boxes. Lili was great at vetoing ones in bad areas or had bad management, which left you with three that were good enough to go visit in person. The realtor chatted mostly to Lili, which left you to stand back and observe.

The price to size ratio was similar to New York, which is to say everything was fucking expensive. You already missed your large cottage and garden. You'd given them a large budget, but the places you were visiting were mostly one or two bedroom units. They were nice, but there was just something missing. You couldn't pinpoint it, but they were all better than the hotel.

One in particular was better than the rest. It was close to the boys' work and overlooked Olympic Park. The view was breathtaking with one wall made entirely of glass. It was a corner unit, so the balcony wrapped around. The kitchen was open concept and marble, and the living room had a hidden TV stand that descended from the roof. It was all very high tech and modern. The real selling point was the bedroom. It was like a warm cave, the walls lined in velvet panelling, and the bathroom separated by a waterfall wall. It was the first time you'd seen something like this, but you could imagine letting the waterfall lull you to sleep.

"The last one was the one, wasn't it?" Lili asked once you were outside. You'd told the agent that you'd think about it and get back to her tomorrow. You needed to talk to Damon anyway, he'd asked to come see whichever one you chose.

"Hmm." You hummed noncommittally. It should be the one,

and you should be as excited as Lili is. It's in a great area, there's amenities in the building, and the price is within your limit.

Lili eyed you suspiciously, as if she was trying to peel back your layers and get to the truth. "Right. Well, if you didn't like any, we can go to another agency. Or we can book you into a long stay hotel. They've got suites that are better equipped."

You shook your head. "No, I don't think we'll find anything different. And this place was great. I'm just in my head because it didn't feel complete. But it's a great place and I shouldn't be so picky."

"You know you can talk to me about anything right? I signed an NDA, two actually, but on top of that I would never betray your trust. I'd like to help." She sounded so sincere.

You took in a deep breath, debating it but speaking before you could talk yourself out of it. "They invited me to live with them. The pack."

Lili's eyes grew wide, her mouth forming an O as she digested the sudden confession. "Oh. That's great though! Or is it not? How do you feel about it?"

"Honestly... I don't know. On the one hand I'm flattered. My omega wants to pack up our shit and move in like yesterday. But... We've known each other for like a minute. It feels rushed, and what if that's the reason it all falls apart? Because we rushed into things? And then there's the fact that I would be living with a whole ass pack. A very touchy-feely pack. With three alphas. It's a bit daunting."

"Those are all valid points. Honestly, millions would kill to be in your shoes. Living with all those good-looking guys. Oof. But I do get your point. I don't know that I would be comfortable living with alphas while I'm unmated. It's old fashioned but I can't help it. You basically are though. Mated."

The thought was said so casually, as if it wasn't a life altering fact. You were kind of mated, in the most general sense. No one walked away from their fated mates, if they did it would be for a serious reason. Could you accept that? That if you stayed you would eventually be mated and in a pack for life. Nope, this was too much for you right now. That was a later-you problem.

Your mind was so busy ignoring your problems that you hadn't noticed you were already back at the hotel. You shook yourself together enough to get some work done with Lili. You signed her up for her own emails and got her in contact with everyone she would need. There was even time for a quick video call with Mel, but only because she was in Europe on business, so it was morning for her. Mel and Lili got along great and had a blast making fun of you. Fantastic, you'd hired a clone of your nosy best friend. No wonder Minju was her bias.

Lili even helped you get ready for your date. She only almost freaked out twice, she'd gotten better at getting her fangirling under control. You were still definitely filming it when she finally met the boys. Her fashion sense was better than yours though, so you let her rummage through your "closet", or rather your overstuffed luggage pushed against the wall, while you primped and preened.

By the time Minju texted that he was there you were throwing your purse together. Lili left you with strict instructions on your make-up and styling and you'd followed them to the tee. You were wearing a strappy navy-blue dress that hugged your curves lightly. It fell to your knees and had a modest square neckline. You'd paired it with some white flats and a white distressed jean jacket. Your hair was styled up and out of your face and your make-up was light and neutral. Except for your lips, those were a deep bright red, somewhat of a signature look. The outfit was genius really, because if you lost the jacket, it could easily be dressed up enough for dinner.

You met Minju in the lobby, and not for the first time that day you were struck by how beautiful one of your mates was. His hair was styled down framing his face in straight strands of vibrant purple. He was wearing a dark blue dress shirt tucked into white jeans, and you couldn't help but laugh that the two of you had managed to match so completely. He laughed as well and pointed between the two of you.

Hearing his laugh healed over every bump and scrape from the day. You could go sit in a car all night and it would still be worth it just to hear it. You reached out your hand. Minju was quick to grab it and lead you on your mystery date.

* * *

MINJU

He had to constantly remind himself to stop staring. It had been a struggle since he saw you walk over, all smiles and laughter. He couldn't believe that you were matching, it was like fate was trying to convince him even more of how perfect you are for each other. He didn't need the reminder; he was already sold. He did take a sneaky picture to send to the pack chat. They were going to be so jealous.

"So where are we going?" Your voice floated over to him. The sweetness of it warming his insides.

"It's a secret! If I tell you, it's not a secret." He wiggled his eyebrows playfully, earning him an exasperated giggle.

The ride to the event was short, but you both had enough time to talk about your days. He watched as you lit up when you talked about your new assistant. You already seemed like a proud sister; it was cute. He knew you'd be a great mentor; you had the same leadership quality he saw in Dae.

The car stopped and he jumped out, running to the other side before you could open the door yourself. He wanted to go full gentleman today, you deserved nothing less. You stuck out your tongue, mumbling something about being an independent woman, but he didn't miss the smirk or the slight blush on your cheeks as he helped you out of the car. You stepped out on the sidewalk and looked around confused.

"Minju, where are we? It looks like everything's closed here."

You weren't wrong, but he smiled sweetly. "Trust me. Come on, you'll see."

He took your hand, trying to not get goosebumps from the closeness, and led you to a rather plain looking door. The windows were all shuttered and to the outside eye it looked like an empty bakery, maybe a cafe. He produced a key from his pocket, unlocking the front door and leading you in.

He felt a trill of joy at your confusion and the slight hesitance in your posture as you moved through the dark room. He could have flicked on the lights, but instead opted to lead you with his phone flashlight. Call it his love of chaos, but mostly he loved surprising his dates. There was something intoxicating about watching their faces turn from questioning and apprehensive, to shocked and joyous. It kept them on their feet around him, never knowing what he had up his sleeve. Would they get caring, doting Minju, or menace to society Minju. Even he didn't know half the time.

He steered you to the back of the room where a heavy door

swung open. He flicked on the lights and watched your reaction.

"Uh. I still don't get it… we're in an industrial kitchen?" He smirked at you, holding himself back from pinching your cheeks. You looked so cute when you were confused.

He walked around to the opposite side of the stainless steel worktable in the middle of the room. There was an array of ingredients and dishes, everything set up with mis en place in mind. There were two neatly folded white aprons off to the side. He took one of them, shaking it out with a flourish that made you smile. He slung it over his head and tied it before answering you.

"Right Jagi, we're going to be making dinner. And if you're really good I'll give you a treat for dessert." He winked.

You chuckled, your smile wide and excited as you joined him. "Why do I have a feeling we're not thinking about the same kind of treat?"

Minju shrugged, working hard to keep the smirk from his chiselled nonchalance. He took the other apron, using the opportunity to wrap his arms around you, brushing his hands across your stomach and sides. "I guess we'll have to see how good of a girl you are."

His heart thumped at your little snort of amusement. "Okay Master Minju. What's on the menu tonight? Souffle with a side of Boeuf Bourguignon?" He stared at your lips, arousal budding at the way your tongue moved through the exotic words.

"Not exactly. Although if you keep up with that attitude, you'll be on the menu next." He teased, reaching for the bowl farthest from him, and coincidentally making him lean right over you, bodies rubbing against each other.

Your breath hitched. "Who says that's not exactly what I want?" You threw right back, but it lacked the bite from earlier, the flush in your face belying your attempt at being smooth.

His eyes crinkled as he laughed. It felt good to be wanted back, to have the same effect on you that you held over him. But his growling stomach kept him in check; mostly. He couldn't help one last jab, tilting his head close to your ear as he whispered. "Like I said, we've still got dessert."

With you adequately flustered, and his own arousal flaming far too high, he set to work, explaining the plan for dinner.

He'd rented the kitchen for the evening, having it stocked and prepped with all the ingredients needed to make homemade pizza. When he chose the bakery, he noticed the wood fired oven they used for some breads and knew he needed to try this. The way your eyes popped and your smile grew told him he'd chosen correctly.

"So, what toppings do we have?" You asked, eyes searching the counter.

"I got everything." He waved over the bowls and containers arranged nicely on the table. He had requested a variety of meats, vegetables, herbs and cheeses. He'd even gotten pesto and red sauce to choose from. There were bottles of olive oil and balsamic. Pride filled his chest as he looked over the veritable spread; he provided for his mate with his love language of food.

"Wait." Your voice ground his preening to a halt. What was wrong? Did he get something you were allergic to? Shit, he didn't even think to ask.

"What is it Jagiya?"

"There's no pineapple." If he could bottle your pout, he would keep it on his shelf and look at it every time he had a hard day. There was no way you were pouting that cutely over not having pineapples.

"On pizza? Ew, you're like Dae and Leo. What is with foreigners?"

You gasped, clutching at your chest dramatically. "Excuse me. Pineapple is the superior pizza topping and I will not be taking questions. Especially from someone who has smoked salmon. Who puts salmon on a pizza?"

"Italians." He smiled. You rolled your eyes and scoffed. "There will be no pineapples on my pizza. But I can get some for you, if you insist on ruining yours."

You squinted your eyes at him, and he thought this must be how the others feel under his cold scrutinising gaze. A small shiver ran down his body. It was eerie. Just as suddenly your face softened, and you chuckled quietly. "No, I think I can manage with the literal heaps of choices we have. Seriously, we might as well make spares for the pack with all this."

The two of you moved in sync, the atmosphere clearing of the near disaster. It was so easy to be around you, he felt himself relax in a way he normally couldn't around outsiders or non-family. He was constantly watched; someone always waiting and prodding to see if the "cold hearted Minju" was real. It was and it wasn't, most of all it wasn't anyone's business. But with you he could laugh, and joke. The air felt light in his lungs and his face hurt from smiling so much.

He flipped the starter on the stove, lighting one of the burners before lowering the gas to his desired amount. He put a heavy steel pan down, pouring in a generous amount of oil.

"Jagi, can you watch this for me? I have to go start the oven. Be careful, please, the fire is high on here."

You rolled your eyes at him and playfully pushed him away. "I can manage just fine. I probably cook more than you. It can't be that different from an electric stove." Your cockiness made him groan. But he figured he would only be a few feet away, and it was just browning some onions, what's the worst that can happen?

He really should have expected it, he did jinx it after all. He was finishing stoking the coals when you screamed. Actually, it was less a scream than a loud string of expletives.

He whipped around, running over to you with his heart thumping painfully. He could smell the rancid smoke of something burning and his mind panicked. You were flailing around, fire arcing around you. When he got close enough, he yanked you to him, probably harder than necessary. The fire was coming from the hand towel you were still stupidly holding. The fire was licking up the cotton fabric and he watched in horror as it swung back and caught on your dress, a light smoke coming from it.

His instincts had never kicked in so fast. He picked you up in his arms, throwing the fiery rag on the ground and stomping the flames out before carrying you over to the sink. One hand was turning the tap on while the other patted down the singed area, sitting you up against the counter. He could see that it hadn't broken through the fabric, but he still splashed water on it.

His heart continued its erratic beating while he worked your dress up, exposing the pinking area on your hip. Your face was flushed, likely a mix of what just happened and the fact that you were now half naked on a countertop. Seeing that there was no longer immediate danger his pulse slowed, and the adrenaline began to fade. It made his veins feel like they were stretched too thin.

"What the hell?!" He growled. *"What were you thinking? That was so fucking dangerous. I left you alone for one minute and you almost set yourself on fire! What would have happened if I wasn't there? Are you aware of what could have happened to you? Do you have a death wish? Are you trying to give me a heart attack?"* His face was red as the anger exploded out of him. As the panic subsided, the simmering anger bloomed in the empty space, blowing out of proportion. His skin vibrated with it, which was unusual for him. He didn't get angry, not like this.

He also realised, seeing your shocked, confused and slightly teary expression that he had yelled all of that in Korean and you likely hadn't understood a thing. He took in a shaky breath, willing the anger to go away, to little avail.

He tried again, grinding his teeth and speaking slowly. "What happened?"

"I'm sorry." Your lip wobbled.

Fuck. He wanted to be angry with you. He was angry, but not at you. It's not like you did it on purpose. He exhaled, counting in his head. You were already scared of alphas, he needed to redirect all this instinct driven energy. "I'm not angry at you. I'm sorry Jagi, I don't want to scare you. I just… You need to be more careful. You're precious, you're ours. You need to take better care of yourself."

He risked a look in your eyes, finding you staring at him intently. There was so much depth there, like your eyes were playing out a story for only him to watch. Your eyebrows drew together, and he could see the cogs working in your brain. It seemed like the fear was subsiding, if that's what it was, and in its place was a war for dominance. His inner voice giggled as it pictured that movie, the one with the animated emotions. He bet your joy was adorable too.

His own inner emotions were fighting on where this memory would end up. Anger was fighting hard, out of breath and puffed up on hormones. But, surprisingly enough, to him at least, his alpha wasn't siding with him. No, his alpha was backing his insatiable lust, the horny little demon in his head pushing him to claim you. His alpha was wholly focused on possessing you, every inch: mind, body and soul. He needed to claim you to keep you safe. Or at least that was the backwards logic that was starting to filter into his conscious mind.

Possess you. Take you. Teach you that you belonged to him, and you needed to keep his belongings cared for.

A low humming started in his body. He leaned forward, stopping inches away from your face. His eyes never left yours, gauging your reaction. The worry was still there, but you made no move to stop him. Neither he, nor his alpha, could wait any longer. He closed the distance, his lips falling onto yours with force. He pressed his body closer, arms wrapping around your waist and pressing against the small of your back, tilting your body into him.

You didn't respond right away, lips frozen, but you also didn't pull away. Minju kept going, pressing insistent kisses until you warmed, your lips slowly moving to match his pace. But as soon as you did it was as if a fire lit in the both of you. The kiss gained speed, friction, and mess. He devoured your lips like they were tonight's appetiser, flavoured in spit and the wax of lipstick. Your scent enveloped him in a cocoon, radiating arousal and elation. His own head felt filled with cotton as his alpha instincts took the front seat.

He let his hands wander, starting at your knees, feeling the smooth skin heat on contact. He moved up, fingers gliding softly, teasingly, on the inside of your thighs. He could feel the trail of goosebumps in his wake. He pushed up under the rest of your dress, grasping onto your hips and playing with the band of your underwear.

Your pace stuttered, lips stilling on his. He smiled into the next kiss, drawing teasing circles just under the waistband, moving closer to your core before slipping away. He could feel you tense under his little dance, and it wasn't long before your breathing became uneven, the smell of slick hitting his nose and making his cock twitch to attention. He was fully hard now, his own arousal swirling in the air.

As much as he loved to play with you, and he would, tonight he needed to follow his gut. And it wanted him to be burying himself in yours. His left hand grabbed a handful of your hair, tugging and arching your head back. Your mouth popped open, a sensual gasp leaving you. He dove in, his tongue dominating yours as he explored your mouth. Both of your breathing came in pants now, your rushed and smacking lips the only other sound in the room.

He moved his wet lips down your jaw, licking a stripe before following it with kisses. When he got to your neck he took in a deep inhale before latching his mouth on your glands. His eyes rolled back into his head. He would be scent drunk if he kept this up much longer, your pheromones so strong and delicious he began rutting into you. His constraining pants rubbing his cock painfully.

Suddenly he felt hands reaching down, running over his chest, and down to his buckle. You hooked two fingers in the band and pulled, the button popping open with the force of it. He chuckled into your neck, resuming his path of biting and kissing down to your collarbone as you unzipped his pants.

He gasped into you as your hand curled around him, holding his smarting cock tightly. You freed it from its prison, stroking it and sending shivers down his back. Your hand looked so small wrapped around him. And then you set his insides on fire. You guided his cock forward, pressing it over your panties. He moaned as he felt the wetness on his tip.

"Is that what you want, Alpha?" Your husky voice whispered. His head snapped up, eyes blown wide at the title. He had half a mind to question it until he saw your own lust dilated pupils. His own need and heat reflected back on him. You wanted to play as bad as him.

"You're a little brat, aren't you?" He all but growled, his voice low and heavy.

You smirked, a twinkle of mischief and darkness in those eyes that he wanted to devour. It awoke a primal part of him. "Maybe." You shrugged. That was as good as a yes. His insides exploded in anticipation. The things he could do to you, the games the two of you could play… He shook his head, laughing lowly.

"We'll see about that another time my love." He smiled, thrusting his hips forward, his cock pressing into your folds over your panties. He revelled in the loud moan ripped from your lips. Your pretty, wet, lipstick smudged lips. He released your hair, tugging off your dress. His own shirt quickly followed, as did your bra. He marvelled at you, at the pink dusting your soft silky skin, the hardness of your nipples, the patch of goosebumps that followed his thumb as he caressed around your areolas.

His mouth latched onto your pert breast, sucking your nipple in and rolling it between his teeth. He watched as your eyes closed and you let out little noises full of lust. He loved the weight of them in his hands, massaging them as he traded off. You were squirming in his hold, back arching as you pushed your hips into him.

"Please. Ju." You moaned after a particularly hard bite.

"Tell me what you want princess."

You huffed out, your annoyance only spurring him on to tease and draw it out further. "You. I want you. In me. Now."

Minju laughed into your chest, sliding off your nipple to bite and suck across the spongy tops of your breasts. He could feel your impatience, and as much as he wanted to be in you, he also wanted to see how far he could push you. Maybe it was his own variety of punishment for earlier.

You didn't like his plan so much, taking matters into your own hands. Your palm closed around his member once again, guiding it to your entrance. In a smooth move you thumbed your panties to the side and jutted forward. Surprising him, you were able to get him a few inches inside you. He nearly took over to bottom out right then, you felt so good, so warm and tight. He could feel your heart rate pulsing through your walls.

A growl tore out of his throat, his alpha evidently not happy with the change in dynamic. He pulled away, a dark look on his face. You returned it with equal petulance, no regret in your actions. He would have to teach you then.

He reached for you, dragging you off the counter and flipping you over it. He pressed his palm down on your back until your chest was flat on the cold steel of the counter. He smirked at shock on your face when the cold registered.

"That's not playing nice darling." He crooned, keeping one hand pressing you down while the other pushed his pants down the rest of the way. Your ass was pushed out, presenting for him as your juices glistened in the overhead lights. You were so slick it was starting to pool and run onto your thighs. He stroked a finger through your wetness. You looked so good like this, he wanted to snap a picture.

As you squirmed uncomfortably on that counter, he leaned over and grabbed his phone, getting the perfect shot of your soaked through panties. Then he hit record, using his other hand to rip them right off you. You yelped in surprise, head snapping back at him. He was grinning from ear to ear.

"Did you just take a picture before ripping off my, perfectly good and expensive, panties?" You sounded shocked, but your scent pumped the room with the smell of arousal.

"Want me to delete it? Or should I send it to the group chat?" His brow quirked at you, wondering what you'd choose. He let out a pleased hum when your cheeks blushed, and you shrugged your shoulders.

"It stays between us, never use my name with it." He didn't need to be told twice, tapping away at his phone before he put it down on the counter.

Your mouth opened but he interrupted you, he could sense the attitude returning so, in a last-minute decision decided to shove the drenched panties in your mouth. Your eyes went wide, and your body stilled. His stomach twisted as he felt time slow. Did he cross a boundary? He hadn't thought before doing it… shit.

His worries were assuaged when your eyes rolled back and a gush of slick ran down your pussy, a low whimpering moan heard around your gag.

He almost came right then, untouched.

"Little brat likes being put in her place. Now you can't say anything stupid. I'm going to fuck that pussy now, and you're going to be good and take it." He breathed, lining himself up with your now bared entrance. He didn't bother prepping you, after all you'd already had him halfway in, and the amount of slick alone would help the glide. He pushed himself in, bottoming out in one smooth motion.

He had to still himself, hands holding onto your hips, as he fended off the intense need to rut and come. He wouldn't be a one pump chump, he would never hear the end of it. No, he wanted to fuck you until you couldn't take it anymore. So he did. He set a languorous pace, thrusting deep and hard, changing angles once he found your spongy sweet spot. Your moans were intoxicating, a steady stream of nonsensical gurgles as he pounded relentlessly into your g-spot.

He longed to be buried in you for hours, the glide along your walls sinful, so wet and somehow so incredibly tight. You kept sucking him in at every stroke, your walls puffy and inflamed with arousal. His hips bucked, his pace stuttering as he felt himself near his climax. He slipped his hand around your leg, dipping one finger over your clit. It only took a few circles before you were clenching around him, your body twitching as you were about to reach your own climax.

He leaned over you, whispering in your ear. "Come for me." His finger flicking your clit hard, triggering the domino effect. Your orgasm hit you like a truck, your legs spasming and body shaking while your walls clenched around him impossibly tighter. It triggered his own climax, and he continued fucking you throughout it, moaning loudly as you milked him dry, his cum filling your cervix.

His alpha instincts roared, and he found himself biting down on your shoulder. Not hard enough to break the skin, not a true mark, but a bruising reminder. A claim that would be seen for days. It read "Minju's" to his alpha caveman brain.

He stayed like that for a moment longer, laying over top of you, buried deep, as he kissed and licked over his claim. Your groan of pain had him standing up, gently bringing you with him. His hands soothed over your stomach and chest where it had been pressed down.

So busy in his blissed out state, he missed how rigid you'd gone in his arms, or how your scent no longer filled the room with fresh blossoms but rather tart soured oranges. It was only once the scent invaded his olfactory nerve that he suddenly became aware. He stiffened, spinning you around in his arms with a concerned face, looking you over for signs of injury, something to explain the intense shift.

"Are you okay? Did I hurt you?" His eyes roamed your face. It looked like you were shell shocked, mouth closed in a tight line. Your eyes were watering but there wasn't sadness in them. It looked more like anger, and by the way you flinched back when his hand came to reach for your face, he'd guess fear as well.

"I-" He was at a loss. "What did I do?" He whispered out, voice reflecting his sadness at having hurt you somehow and not knowing.

The anger flared in your eyes, and you blinked back at him. "Seriously Minju? You fucking marked me." Your own voice broke at the end, tears finally falling down your cheeks. Your pretty cheeks that used to be flushed pink but now looked paler, devoid of colour.

"I- well yeah, but it's not permanent. I thought you liked biting?" He was more confused now.

"Biting! Minju, that wasn't biting. You marked me to claim me. I don't care if it's not permanent. You did that without asking. You can't just claim me like some piece of fucking furniture. I didn't consent to that." Your voice rose as you kept talking, anger rolling off you in waves now.

He felt the laser heat of your gaze on him, and he gulped. He'd really fucked up. In the moment he hadn't given it a second thought, letting his alpha get his possessive needs met. They marked each other all the time, sometimes even just playfully. He didn't think it was a big deal. He repeated that out loud, wincing as your eyes narrowed and you stepped back, backing into the counter as you fixed him with a glare.

"Of course you would think that, that's such an alpha-hole thing to assume. What, every omega must be just gagging to be marked and claimed right? We need an alpha to piss on us to make us worthy, to protect us from the big bad wolf out there." Your words were venomous whips. He shook his head, trying to bat the words away, but they sunk into his skin anyway, like searing sparks.

"No-no, Jagi I would never think that." He held his hands up in front of him, trying to calm or trying to defend himself he didn't know.

"You didn't think, Minju, that's the problem." Your hurt bled into your words now. Oh, you weren't just angry, you were hurt, he realised. And suddenly it hit him like a speeding semi-truck.

He'd really fucked up and he didn't know how to fix it.

* * *

Your head was foggy with thoughts and emotions. There was anger; anger at not being listened to, to being used and treated with such little care. That was an emotion you were ready for; you knew why and where it came from. You felt vindicated in your anger. The other emotions were more complicated.

The ghosts of teeth whispered along your skin like a cold winter wind swirling through the crack in a window. You'd been frozen in fear in the moment, your body tensing and dreading whatever would come next. You didn't even feel him finish, thrust into scene after scene of nightmares from your past. Scenes of another alpha, alphas, using that exact action to make you submit, to threaten you into obedience.

"It would be so easy to mark you, make you ours forever. You'd like that wouldn't you? A nothing omega like you, not even good enough to breed. You'd be lucky to end up with us." His voice mocked, rocking into you and turning your stomach over and over again.

> *Your whimpering was met with dark laughter. "Pl-please don't. I pro-promi-se. I won't... won't do it again." You choked on your tears and phlegm as a hand circled your neck.*

> *"Better not. Or I'll make sure no one ever wants you again. You think your family would let you walk away from us if you were marked?" He laughed again, the feeling of ants creeping over your skin making your entire body shake.*

It was a part of your past you left buried, not unearthing it even for therapy. You were afraid if you let it air out it would burst into dust, creeping into every crevice of your mind and leaving you incapable of escape. Yet now you have to fight to return it to the depths of hell, unable to care for the rest of your surroundings or your current emotional state.

Breathing was becoming harder, your lungs heaving in shallow and quick breaths. Shit, you thought, recognizing the beginning of a panic attack. The adult, responsible, thing would be to get help, to tell Minju and have him calm you down. However, right now Minju was resembling them in your fractured psyche, and the mere thought of him touching you at the moment sent you further into a panic.

So, of course, you did what you do best. You ran. Ran out of the kitchen, barely sparing a thought to the scorched dress you threw over your head, or the missing underwear. The plan was straight forward, your hindbrain in complete control: get out. To where? Well, that was a great question because you neither had your phone nor your purse with you. You got points for at least remembering clothes.

The door to outside burst open, the cool late summer air soothing the heat and sweat on your face. You ran in no particular direction, you picked on and went. Thankfully you stayed in a relatively straight line. The neighbourhood you were in was modern, wider side streets and sidewalks, which meant less twists and turns to get lost in. After an unknown amount of time, probably no more than five minutes, you found yourself walking to a small park. It was actually just a couple benches and some calisthenic equipment, but it was well lit and didn't give off "serial killer training ground" vibes. You collapsed on one of the metal benches, the cold seeping into the thin fabric of your dress. It was grounding, helping the fuzziness and adrenaline clear from your system.

Shit.

Shit. Shit. Shit.

You swore internally a few more times as the quiet night let your brain slow enough to process everything. How had that happened? What had you, he, done? Now that your emotions were burnt out and mellowing, the panic left you numb enough to look at the situation in a different light.

Minju had bit you, a bite yes, but not that kind of bite. It wasn't a mark. You repeated that over and over again. It wasn't, not really. Yet you still felt this indignant rage settled in your stomach. You wanted to scream at him. How dare he? Who did he think he was? Just because he was a super hot celebrity didn't give him the right.

But what if he didn't know? The little angel on your shoulder spouted. Maybe it was a devil in disguise. Problem for another day.

He had to have known, to an extent. Right? Surely Damon would have said something, given them a heads up or retold the explanation you gave for that first day.

You didn't tell them this though. How are they supposed to know your triggers if you don't tell them the whole truth? Yep, definitely a devil.

The demon wasn't wrong, but logically you could infer...

Inferring isn't knowing. Oh my God shut up already you griped at the invisible being in your head.

So what if he didn't figure that out? You still don't go around marking people without their consent. Period. The voice was suspiciously quiet at that. Although marks weren't as popular as they used to be, it was still a permanent mark on someone's body that meant something. It was a symbol, and potentially a painful memory. Albeit not legally binding, as you had been brought up to believe. Therefore, marking someone was not done on a whim, and definitely not without a conversation.

Thinking it through helped ease some of the tension in your chest. You were still angry, but it was a low ember instead of blazing fire. The fear had subsided as well. You understood where it came from, but now you could remember the look of horror on Minju's face when he realized something was wrong. He knew he'd fucked up, whether he knew why or not. That fact alone cut all ties with those horrid memories. They would never have felt regret.

Now you were stuck somewhere in the cold, burnt up dress, likely reeking of sex and panic, with nothing on you to help you get back home. You had really done it now, you self-chastised. A headache was beginning to form and as a lovely cherry on top your stomach grumbled to remind you of your missed dinner. This might be up there as one of the worst dates you'd had.

You were thinking over your two choices, stay here and wait to be found (hopefully sooner rather than later) or try and retrace your steps back to the cafe. Your pride told you the bench would make a fine bed and that you'd slept worse places. It was a tempting argument, that you luckily didn't need to indulge in as your name was called, startling you. You turned and saw Minju running over to you.

His face was radiating panic while his brow was drenched in sweat. He was running at full speed, and it looked like he'd been running for a while. Did he run around blindly looking for you?

He stopped just short of your bench, leaning over and bracing himself on his legs as he panted. "You-." He stopped to catch more of his breath.

"Min. Just come sit down first. I'm not being held responsible if you burst a lung." You told him, your voice soft but scratchy with leftover emotion. You slid over, and he respected the distance, seating himself gingerly at the other end.

You gave him a moment to collect himself. He looked... distraught. "Noona. I am so sorry. Please forgive me." He bowed at his waist, his hands out and rubbing together in a praying motion. That confused you; you'd ask about it another time but assumed it was a cultural thing.

"Why?"

His head popped up and he straightened slowly as his brow furrowed. "Why what?" He asked, confusion clear in his eyes.

You exhaled, reigning in your inner fighter. Words. Adult words. "Why are you sorry?"

"For hurting you." He answered like it was the simplest thing. You had never wanted to roll your eyes so bad in your life. But you were bigger than that, you were trying.

"Minju. I'm trying really hard not to lose my shit right now. Do you know why what you did was so wrong?" Calm. Cool. Collected. Mel would be proud.

To his credit he noticed the shift in you, straightening his posture and taking a minute to seriously consider before answering. "Honestly... No? I know marking you was not okay. But I didn't think it would hurt you so badly. We, the pack, mark each other all the time. Not always during sex, sometimes when we need reassurance, or we feel very possessive that day. I didn't think, and I know that I should have. I'm sorry." There was so much raw truth and vulnerability in his gaze.

Some of the tightness left you again. You wouldn't admit to the little shit eating voice that it may have been partially right. Over your dead body. Yet, even with the heartfelt apology, you couldn't let it go. The ghost of it was still there, the memories knocking at the back of your skull. You didn't want to fear them, didn't want to mistrust them.

They had shown you nothing but the best, surely one negative could be ironed out. You could work with them on it and try to move forward. Taking in a deep breath you decided.

"Minju. What you did wasn't okay for so many reasons. Yes, you didn't think and you didn't ask. Those are things you should do with anyone." You paused. "I do understand a bit though. You have all been together for a long time, and from what Leo has told me it's been the only relationship some of you have had. I will give you grace for that.

But, and this is a strong but, we all need to sit down and have a conversation before any sex happens again. I have boundaries, and you crossed them. I didn't feel safe, and I didn't feel cared for. I don't know what Damon has told you, so I'll tell you now. Trusting alphas intimately, physical or emotional, is not easy for me. There are things from my past, triggers and traumas, that will never go away. And I need to feel like they're being respected."

You inhaled, your mouth dry from your Shakespearean ser-
mon. Warily, you watched the information being processed
by Minju. His face was scrunched in concentration. After a
minute he nodded to himself before turning to you.

"I am sorry, again. More sorry now that I know why. You're
right, of course you are. And I, as well at the pack, will do
anything you need. Please don't hold it against them, they
are so much better than me. This was my dumb mistake. I
should have known, I did know how you felt about alphas,
it was obvious. I just didn't make the connection. And I will
continue to apologize for as long as it takes. Longer. I-." He
stopped mid rant. His eyes were beginning to water as he
looked at you, that vulnerability coming back.

"I was so scared I fucked it all up and lost you. I couldn't
handle that. I don't... I don't ever want to be why you leave,
to ever take you away from the others. I'd rather you leave
me and stay with them." His voice wobbled, caught in a wave
of sadness.

You felt a pang of empathy. Minju constantly put himself last,
it was always pack first. In fact, it was that way with all of
them. You'd seen it in all their little gestures and interactions.

Minju's voice continued. Your eyes meeting his tear-filled
ones. He reached a hand out and you let him take yours. "I

wouldn't want to ever take them from you either. They would, could, make you so happy. As happy as you make them. I see you with us, I see all of us being good for each other. Despite my clear flaws."

Your breath caught in your throat. Damn, this Casanova for striking your soft spots. Those embers sizzled, going out almost entirely. You didn't think they would ever leave, there was going to be a sore burn mark for a long time to remind you and keep you from fully getting comfortable.

But Minju was here, he was learning and willing to do the work. That had to count for something right? Like you always say, you can forgive, though you never forget.

"Jagi? Your hand is so cold. Should I take you home?" Minju asked, enveloping your hand in both of his.

You thought about it for a second, until your stomach remembered pizza was promised. And as drained and tired as you were, pizza always won out. Besides, who didn't like cheesy carbs after an emotional rollercoaster where you relived some of your worst memories? Coffee and carbs, your two true best friends.

"No, I think I'd like to get back to our date. I was promised pizza, even subpar pineapple-less pizza." You winked. Your humor was honed by trauma, it shone brightest when you were using it to bury your human self. And she needed a break, you could be non-human for the night and process later. Eventually.

The two of you continued your pizza adventure, walking back holding hands and making an absolute mess of the kitchen. You were very happy you weren't cleaning up. Minju took lots of cute pictures to send to the group chat with the members. You looked exceptionally cute with flour smudged on your brow and you asked for a copy to put on your next book jacket.

Soon the night was wrapping up and you were sitting in his passenger seat. You were exhausted as you slumped in the luxurious leather seats. Normally you would have asked him to sleep over, but after the events of tonight you decided time to yourself was best. Instead, he walked you to your door, giving you a chaste kiss goodnight.

The standard hotel bed had never been comfier, a cloud of softness for your knotted muscles. Running wasn't your friend, why was it your instinctual reaction? Can you change it to napping? Maybe you would have been better off being part possum.

Despite wanting to go right to sleep, you forced yourself to crawl to the headboard. Snuggled into the pillows you called your human best friend, the one not made of coffee or carbs. Mel picked up on the second ring, too bright and chipper for your late timezone. Nonetheless you soldiered through and told her about your night. The two of you talked for hours, something you were both used to and grateful for. Mel was always there, to offer advice or just listen and cry with you. You did a bit of both together, Mel having her own feelings on your past.

It was into the early morning when you finally hung up. You felt cleansed, but so thoroughly drained. It was worth it though, Mel had given you great advice and helped solidify your decision. Everything was moving a little too quickly, it was time to take a step back and reassess. You definitely needed to have a conversation with the boys.

Which scared you most of all. Because, despite everything, you found yourself falling for them. It was sudden, and you were sure to be partly driven by hormones. Nonetheless, they were your soulmates, the ones fate herself had decided would be your perfect equals. Skipping steps seems a lot more natural when you already know you're meant to be together.

Doesn't make it any less terrifying. You were just glad the big bump was out of the way. You didn't need to hold your breath and wait for the other shoe to drop. You could take your time, work through this as a team, and come out stronger.

You had all the time in the world right?

* * *

Somewhere deep on twitter a picture pops up:

IS THIS MINJU???
   - Who's that girl with them?
   - OMG ARE THEY DATING?!
   - no way.... but why is he hanging on to her like that ummmm is that a mating mark?!!!

view 158 more comments...

Thirteen

KPopducation

Leo: Noona
  How could you??
  I thought I would be your first kiss
  And then I find out I wasn't even your first dick

                                    You: Leo
                                    Baby
          You know I wasn't a Nun before, right?
  Leo: That's not what I mean, first from one of us!

      You: I'm sorry baby, you should have said
                                      something
                What can I do to make it better?
  Leo: It's okay, I'm not actually mad

But I would like a hug and a kiss
If you want!! Oh God, I mean forget it

You: Leo
Calm down

*

Damon: Why is Leo smacking his head against
a wall and muttering something about you?

You:
[screenshot attached]

Damon: Right
I'm so sorry, he crossed a line, I'll talk to him

You: Not you too

Damon it's fine, I'm not mad at him at all. It
was kinda cute

Damon: How are you feeling?
Min told us what happened last night
I know he said it already, but I'll say it again.
I'm so sorry. That should never have happened.
I've had a talk with everyone, we're all on the
same page, and we're all more than happy to sit
down and talk about anything you need

You: Thanks, I appreciate that.
I had a good talk with Mel last night and I think
we worked through some things. A talk is
definitely on the calendar, but I'm okay.
Thanks for trying to take care of me sweetpea.

*

Hansung: Noona, I think you broke Leo and Dae-Hyung

*

New Group Chat created - Boyfriends

Noona: Ok, you pabos. Listen up because I'm
only going to say this once.
You can joke around however you want with
me, if I get upset, I'll tell you
And if you want to ask for a kiss, or something
more, you can
I might say no, but you can still ask
Minju got first dibs because he took the chance
Fortune favours the bold my dears

Sung: So pin you to the wall and fuck you next
time I see you, got it
  Damon: Hansung I swear to god
  I didn't think I'd ever have to say that
  Hyunbin: I want a kiss too please
  Sung: Come here, I'll give you a kiss Hyung
  Damon: Yah, no kissing in the dressing room
  Minju: Stop acting like you don't like it
  You kiss us all the time
  Leo: Noona I'm so sorry
    You: I'll give you something to be sorry for
                if you keep apologising Leo
  Sung: Uh oh. Noona sounds like Minju-Hyung

> **Minju:** Good
> **Hyunbin:** Oh no, they're teaming up already
> **Everyone run**
> **You:** Minju, dear, please give them all a good
> smack for me
> **Minju:** Anything for you Noona

For the first time since you'd met them, you had a whole day to yourself. The boys were filming all day and would only be back late at night. You were secretly happy for the break. Their company was always fun and welcome, but you were a quiet creature that thrived on isolation and space. You needed this day to recharge your emotional and social batteries. You checked your to-do list, seeing all the places you wanted to visit but hadn't had the time to. There was quite a bit. You figured you could cross a few off your list and sightsee today.

Your plans were foiled by your assistant, quickly and thoroughly. When you'd told her you'd be out for the day because the boys were busy, she immediately decided it was the perfect time for your "Star-vention" as she called it. She gave you an hour to wash up before she showed up at your suite, dressed in comfy clothes and carrying a bag of snacks.

Your education into Galaxy began. Lili came prepared, you had to give her credit for that. She had a playlist ready, dozens of videos and tiktoks ready to show you. It was a little overwhelming. You'd done your own searching at the beginning of all this, and you'd found such a mountain of content, but it was mainly fan edits, or compilations. Which were funny, and cute, but at the time you'd tried to concentrate on them as an entity, their music and performances. Or maybe it was just because you found their stage presence enthralling.

Lili had a plan though, not just your YouTube or tiktok rabbit hole method. "You need to see them from the beginning, which is their reality show."

"Were they on a competition show against other teams?" Your knowledge of reality shows was American Idol and Masked Singer. Which honestly, you barely watched. The only one you'd watched to the end was Total Drama Island, and that was animated satire.

"It's a different system here. If you want to be an idol you either get scouted or audition for one of the big companies, like KC. If you're accepted you become a trainee, which may be one of the hardest experiences in someone's life. You're then trained and work towards being put in a group to debut. But that only happens if you're good enough AND fit whatever style or look they want.

Dae had it rough. He was a trainee for many years. Most trainees come in their teens, or late teens. Damon came over at 13, he lived his entire adolescence in that system. He eventually found his group, and they filmed a show called 'Star Searching'. If I'm being honest, I don't want to rewatch this. It's traumatising. But it's also a rite of passage."

Lili hadn't been joking. You sat huddled under a blanket, watching hours of the show. You watched much younger versions of your mates laugh, joke around, and find their way. Their relationships were already so strong, despite some of them only knowing each other a couple months. They worked tirelessly, and you saw the raw talent as well as the fire and passion that drove them.

"Who's that? There's like two people I don't recognize."

"Oh, Jeon Yeonku and Chen Shi."

"Did they not make the cut or something?"

"No. It's, uh, more complicated than that. Actually, it was a touchy subject and no one really knows what happened. The story is that they left for personal reasons, but it was all hush hush."

"Huh. Okay."

But it also brought tears as you saw them struggle. You watched Damon falling asleep on his laptop, watched the way his face became graver, and his excitement faded into anxiety and sadness. It was like he was running for the goal, but the path he was on was tearing chunks of him away. Then the anger really started.

You watched as these boys, because they truly were boys, all of them minors at this point, get torn to shreds. Forced to do ridiculous tasks, running up and down subway stairs, making fools out of themselves on the street for strangers, pushing their bodies past normal limits. They had them training day and night, filming content of every aspect of their lives. And then, when the boys poured their hearts out they were critiqued left and right.

"Leo-ssi needs to lose the freckles. His skin is already so dark, his image won't sell well. He's too foreign." The words were so carelessly thrown around, not minding that the subject was sitting right there. The camera panned in and you could see the sadness in his eyes, the way he shut down. It continued on, poking at their weight, their height, their skin colour, their rapping or dancing. Jab after jab as you watched the lights in their eyes slowly dim.

"Eonnie. You need to breathe; your eyes are dilating, and your scent is choking the air out of the room." Lili rubbed your upper arm, trying to calm you down. Her light hibiscus scent trying to wrangle your own but only managing to float along with it.

283

You weren't really hearing her. You were so lost in your thoughts, of anger, of sadness, but mostly of how much that must have hurt them all. How was Leo, the ball of sunshine he was now, after all that? And that was only what they deemed TV friendly. You can't imagine what went on off camera.

"Noona? Hey, sweetie. Can you take a deep breath for me?" The deep voice resonated within you, stroking along your turmoil and calming it down. It came from somewhere around you, but your omega couldn't smell it, him. Nonetheless you took in a deep lungful of air. It was shaky at first, but after a few breaths, and some praise from that deep lullaby voice, your head began to clear.

"Leo?" You looked at him through your phone screen. He smiled back at you, and it was like the world was righted again. That smile, those eyes, that glittering laugh.

"Yeah baby, it's me. Are you okay? Lili called me and said you were having a moment. What's going on? Do you want me to come get you?" His tone was light but tinged with worry. You're sure you were quite the sight, red puffy eyes and tear stained cheeks.

You waved him off, trying to give him a smile that probably came off looking more exhausted than reassuring. "I'm fine now, thanks Hun. I, uh, we were just watching the survival show and... I guess I just lost it."

Lili snorted from beside you. "Lost it would be an understatement. Murderous would be more accurate."

You glared at her, but there was no heat in it. Especially as Leo started cackling from his side of the phone. It looked like he was in a car, probably coming or going from schedules. "Hey! It's not funny. It was sad, and I was angry. I don't know how I'm going to look at your staff again, I want to claw their eyes out for everything you went through."

"I know, I'm sorry. We should have warned you. It wasn't that bad though, you'll see soon. And Damon really shielded us from most of it. He's the one who got hit the hardest. But seriously, everyone is okay now. So no more tears unless they're happy, yeah?"

You nodded, promising to text him or call him tonight if you needed him. The part he said about Damon swam around in your head though. You paid closer attention to him throughout the rest of the series. He really looked like it was sucking the life out of him. You could tell he wasn't sleeping or eating right by the way his cheeks hollowed and his eyes grew their own shadows. It didn't help the flaming embers in your heart, but it did solidify something else. Damon was always throwing himself in front of the flames for everyone, but who was shielding him? It wasn't even a conscious decision that you made, you just knew deep down that you would protect him, and them, at all costs.

You cheered for joy with Lili when they got the recognition that was so well deserved. You finally saw where the JuHan ship truly started as well. It warmed you, watching them bond so happily. By the end of their final showcase, you were on the edge of your seat. As the judge and MC announced they would debut at last you popped open the mini bottle of prosecco from your mini fridge. It was a rollercoaster of emotions and you felt completely wrung out.

Luckily Lili was there with the aftercare. She showed you clips of their other specials. You didn't realise how many shows they'd been on, it seemed like every year there was something. Honestly, you were wondering how it was humanly possible to do so much in a year. But it was good press, and when she showed you the video edits of some of the games they played you understood how that could draw someone in.

Currently you were watching a compilation of a game that loosely translated to shouting in silence. Two members would wear headphones while one had to get the other to guess a keyword. It was absolute chaos as they screamed at each other. Lili had to explain a few inside jokes, like why Hyunbin got so upset at Damon. The funniest you thought was the one where Damon and Hyunbin were paired together but neither of them could focus, instead dancing and singing along to the music in the headphones. It had you gripping your side, painful stitches ripping through you as you laughed at them.

You were starting to understand their dynamics more. You saw the competitiveness in their running man episode, the fierceness of the alphas coming out in spades. It was cute to watch how chaotic but adorable Hansung was. He was the loudest in front of the cameras, always quick to joke around. You saw how babied Leo was, which only made you want to pinch his cheeks and join in.

And then came the truly hilarious videos. You didn't understand the point of this edition, but oh boy was it funny. Watching them bounce on a trampoline like kids, or hunt each other down with pillows while looking spectacularly silly with party hats on their faces. The best part for you was the bubble suit game. You lost it watching Leo, who was clearly on a sugar high, bounce around joyfully in his giant bubble suit.

You watched a few more edits of their shows. Leo throwing himself into the water, giving up on the game. Damon looking stupidly hot in every outfit. Hyunbin being loud enough to not need a mic. Weekly idol episodes where they played questionable games that usually ended up in Minju being a savage. You lost count of how many times he called Damon old or made fun of someone's laugh. It was a different side to the guys you'd gotten to know. They were boisterous, witty, and competitive. Yet it still felt very authentic, like they were happy having fun in front of the cameras. Their fans clearly meant a lot to them.

What you weren't prepared for was the thirst edits. Video after video of the boys looking like walking sin. You felt like you were on a first name basis with Damon's abs, and while you were slightly flushed, the embarrassment he showed was well worth it. He covered his eyes watching their sexy choreography, and his less-than-clothed performances. A complete opposite reaction to Leo, your little sunshine, who flashed his abs with a shit eating grin and smoldering eyes. The duality of these men was something else.

"Oh, pause that! That's Bin's friend, what's he doing in these videos?"

Lili looked up at you sceptically. "You mean Wooyoung?" When you nodded her mouth dropped open. "You know who Wooyoung is but not that he's also an idol? We're going to be at this for a while. This is from their Empire time, Steez, another group that was also a competitor."

That was news to you. You hadn't asked who the two friends you'd met with Hyunbin were, because honestly you trusted him and his judgment and they'd both won you over by the end of the night. In fact, Wooyoung had texted you quite frequently since then. He was practicing his English, and you were practicing your Korean. Mostly through memes, the international language.

You pulled out your phone, again.

> **You: Wooyoung! Why didn't you tell me you were an idol too??**
> **You were in a whole show with them!**
> **Woo: I thought Hyunie tell you? No big important**
> **You: Yes big important!**
> **You wanted to drag me to that restaurant next week.**
> **I think I should know to watch out for paparazzi**
> **Woo: Nooonaaaaaa, I sorry.**
> **I really think you know.**
> **Want me beat up Hyunbin?**
> **You: He'd kill you, you know that.**
> **His biceps are the size of your head.**
> **Now I have to go watch the two of you act like idiots together so I can tease him.**
> **Woo: I help! I send you pictures**

You snorted as your phone blew up with incriminating photos of Hyunbin. You were definitely saving these for future blackmail.

"So, they're all friends then? I met Tae and Wooyoung and they seemed really close. Not like competitors at all. Are all idols friends or something?" You asked Lili, hoping she could fill you in.

And did she ever. She showed you a clip of Galaxy/Steez interactions during Empire. It made you really happy to see them all so friendly with another group, people who understood their lives and friendships that wouldn't feel the strain of their jobs. She told you many Stars were also Tinies, and that the fandoms often overlapped. You put Steez on your list to listen to, and found yourself already liking their vibe.

By then it was late into the evening, you'd spent the majority of the day shut in and binging videos. When you closed your eyes, you could see Hansung screaming, or Minju blinking slowly at the camera, a deer-in-headlights look on his face. Your brain was overloaded with information, and you knew there was still so much you hadn't seen. There were hundreds of lives you hadn't touched, only seen the fan edits. Most of them were Damon's, but Minju also had his own weekly live he did most of the time. On top of that, was their solo content. Minju's numerous TV show appearances, with the others having guest spots. Their guest MC episodes, or their appearances on reality talk shows. You were an inch away from kidnapping them and forcing them to take a month off.

What stopped you were the fans. Scrolling through tiktok you'd see just as many videos of fans saying how much the members meant to them or quoting them as their motivation to keep going. And the thing was, you could see how happy it made the boys. They genuinely wanted to help every single one of their fans. And that was beautiful. You cried, again, at an edit about Damon being someone's home. Because you could see it, see how easy it would be to call them home.

They could be your home.

Tired, and an emotional husk, you were left with some sense of clarity. You saw them through the eyes of their fans, and you found yourself enamoured. They weren't scary, nothing you'd seen today gave off any red flags, and fans were the best at finding and explosing red flags. The boys were beloved, and they made everyone feel safe. You'd always felt safe if you were being truly honest. Your biggest hold up was your fear that the past would repeat itself. But that wasn't fair to anyone involved.

You'd promised Mel to slow down, to have open communi-cation. And though it might feel rushed, you didn't feel like it was the wrong choice right now. It might even make it easier to spend time together unnoticed. Before you could talk yourself out of it you were on your phone.

> **Noona: If the offer is still on the table, I'd like**
> **to move in.**
> **On a trial basis.**

Leo: YES!!
  Sung: I CALL FIRST SNUGGLES!
  Damon: What they meant to say, was that of course we'd love to have you.
  Hyunbin: No, Hansung wants snuggles. He yelled it. Now he's fighting Leo for it
  Minju: I'm not cleaning if they break something
  Noona, are you sure you don't want to reconsider?
  Leo: Yah! Ho Minju! How dare you????
  Sung: Minju-Hyung is laughing at you
  Minju: Snitch
  Hansung is online shopping. Hyung, you need to take his phone
  Sung: DON'T YOU DARE!

You had the fleeting thought that maybe you should heed Minju's advice, the group chat devolving into a chaotic mess right in front of you. But that thought was quickly squashed by the overwhelming fondness that swelled and crashed like a wave on the beach of your soul. They were chaos, but you had always loved a bit of chaos.

After the emotional diarrhea from the day you decided that, despite it being past midnight, you wanted ice cream. You deserved ice cream. Not only did you spend the day learning and falling for your mates, you made the very adult decision to set your fears aside and move in with them. It still hadn't set in, or you're sure you would be panicking about now. Instead, you felt at peace with the decision. You told Lili, effectively cementing the deal by cancelling your realtor. Even that didn't bring down the impending sense of doom you were expecting. It would come eventually, that you were sure of.

But not tonight, no tonight you were enjoying the cool air blowing on your cheeks as you ate your ice cream, leisurely walking back to the hotel from the convenience store down the road. It was quiet, but not silent, the odd car driving by, or small groups of inebriated friends clutching to each other and laughing. This was going to be your future, that could be you with new friends, maybe even the boys.

That night you slept soundly, wrapped in the sweater you'd stolen from Hansung the other day, his cherries faint but enough to soothe you to sleep. Your dreams were empty, a peacefulness you craved most nights. You should have been more worried then, knowing from experience that nothing was ever this easy.

Fourteen

Blurry Pictures

⌁

"Wha?" You mumbled into your phone. Your eyes weren't open yet, in fact as far as your body was concerned you were still asleep, and this was all a dream. Sleep calling. Drunk dialing was a thing, so surely sleep answering was as well.

"The hell. Took you long enough to answer. Are you awake? I'll scream." Mel's voice was entirely too loud and energetic for you.

"Fuck off. I don't know what time it is but it's too early. You better be dying." You rolled over, the charger disconnecting from your phone as it pulled taut. Shit, you'd probably have to plug it back in. Your bed was so warm though, and the blankets so soft, you couldn't find it in you to be annoyed.

"I'm not, but you may be soon. Wake the fuck up and read the email I sent you." Mel had that no nonsense voice on, which meant you had no choice but to blink your eyes open.

It took a couple clicks to open the email and read the link that was attached. It was a Koreaboo article with a clickbait title, Galaxy's Minju in a secret relationship? You flicked down quickly skimming the article until you saw the picture. It was the two of you leaving the cafe. The image itself wasn't great quality and was taken from a bad angle, or a good one for you. You could see the back of Minju as he walked you to his car, his arm slung around your waist. There was a zoomed in picture in a bubble hovering over the picture, this one making your stomach drop.

"Fuck." You swore under your breath. You went back to your call, putting it on speaker phone.

"I feel like that's an understatement. Did you get marked without telling me?" Mel laughed hysterically under her breath. You understood, you were the last person on earth Mel, or anyone who knew you, would think to get marked and join a pack like that.

"Wow, these comments are..." You cringed, scrolling down the page to see what people were saying. That was mistake two of the day, the first being waking up at all.

"Vicious?" Mel supplied.

"I was going to say creative, but yeah, they aren't very nice. Although, them thinking I'm a model is a nice confidence boost."

"You should see the socials. It's trending everywhere. No one has even guessed close to you though, which is good. I've got one of my interns keeping an eye on it."

That was good at least. "How did you even see this so fast; it was posted like 3 hours ago."

Mel hummed. "Your assistant sent it to me. I like her, although I'm worried about her sleep schedule if she's up at 5 am."

You sighed at that. "Yeah, she's great. I think she said she goes on runs in the early morning. She's that person."

"Oh, you mean insane?" Mel teased. Neither of you were the early morning type unless it was for work, so the idea of willingly getting up at dawn to exercise was beyond you. The easy banter was helping the knot unfurl in your stomach.

"Well, she's got a great body, so she's probably on to something." Still wasn't enough motivation to get you up that early.

"What do you want to do about it? I'm guessing the boys' company will want to put a statement out." You could hear the clack of keys on her end. The question woke you up further.

"Well, they don't know who it is yet. So I'll have to talk to them and their managers and see what they want to do. Worst case I already have the press release drafted about me investing in the company. We can spin it that I met the boys there and I was out to dinner with one of them, platonically." It was an eventuality you'd planned ahead for. You had hoped it wouldn't come so soon. You also hadn't planned for there to be a mark on your body for the whole world to see.

Mel disagreed. "I don't know. If it was just the photo, that's one thing, they're touchy people. But babe, the mark… The company will protect the boys, but they hold no loyalty to you." Her words hit their mark, and unease settled in your stomach. There had been bigger scandals based on less, and they could easily dig your name up if they tried hard enough.

"Well fuck. Thanks so much, that makes me feel soooo much better." The sarcasm dripped like molasses from your lips.

"Sorry Hun, but you know I don't sugarcoat. I'm on a diet. Look, I have to go, but text if you need anything. I'm not above threatening anyone. And don't think we're not going to talk about that mark. I'm worried about you." You rolled your eyes but thanked her and let her go.

Well, that's surely one way to wake up. What were you getting yourself into? You'd avoided scandal your entire career, people barely knew your face and market research showed they associated your name with only your work. You lived a quiet life with only the occasional weird fan encounters at cons or expos.

Your phone buzzed in your hand, Damon's name popping up for an incoming call. You swiped numbly, putting the phone on speaker and letting it fall in your lap.

"Baby?" His voice echoed out.

"Hey." Words were hard.

He sighed. "I can see you're online. I won't ask why you didn't call me first because that's moot at this point. Are you okay? You don't sound okay."

Were you? You swiped open the app again, dazedly scrolling through posts and hashtags. It wasn't good, the press. But it wasn't awful. "I don't know actually." You decided on the truth. Your eyes pricked with tears, reading all the hateful comments as you scrolled. The numbness that had settled during your talk with Mel began to fade and in its place a wave of emotions rose and crashed over you. Something about Damon's soft voice broke a dam, whispers of safety and home and alpha flickering in your mind.

"We're on our way over. Sung and Leo have vowed to cuddle you better, and honestly, I'm not explaining how medicine works again. We'll be there in five." It was hard to hang up on him when you were suddenly feeling so vulnerable.

You needed to get a hold of yourself. No one knew it was you. Did the comments still hurt? Yes, no one knew it was you, but that was only a matter of time. You should have turned the phone off, should have waited for company, for support. Who cared what the internet said…?

For the second time that day you fell prey to your curiosity and the devil that was social media. Clicking on tags you plummeted down the rabbit hole. Certain words were like little stabs to your ego; ugly, fat, groupie, old hag. Kids on the internet who weren't old enough to see a rated R movie had a lot to say about an unnamed woman in a photo. They also narrowed in on your insecurities like they were sniffer dogs and your trauma was a drug.

That was how they found you, eyes red rimmed with silent tears flowing down your cheeks, still in your pyjamas huddled on your bed. You had forgotten you'd given them a key after your impromptu sleepover, that way Damon could let himself in instead of giving himself a minor stroke. So you startled, a yelp ripping from your throat as a body collided with yours, completely oblivious to the five men who had been watching you only a moment ago.

Three now; another body coming from the other side to scoop you and your assailant up. Once the panic cleared, helped by the familiar smell and feel of the two men, you looked up to see Hansung in your lap with Minju behind you both. The alpha smiled down at you, sadness in that small gesture of upturned lips, and unbridled rage in the deep brown of his eyes. Your gut dropped, you had been so focused on yourself, on the sharp words and brash comments, you hadn't spared a thought to how he must be feeling.

"I'm so sorry Min, I never wanted to cause you trouble." You looked around the room now, finding the eyes of the three others. Damon had his arms wrapped around a pouting Leo, whether in restraint or comfort you couldn't tell. While Hyunbin was sitting at the end of the bed, body turned to face you, hand on Hansung's leg. There was no anger or animosity, you didn't really expect any, but it was always an errand worry.

Minju spoke up from behind you, his grip becoming tighter. "You didn't do anything wrong, don't apologize." You turned to him, your rebuttal silenced as he glared at you. The look could curdle milk, yet you were somehow reminded of the heat of the other night and the predatory way he looked at you then. You wouldn't have thought it possible, but now you knew you could still be turned on amidst a life crisis. Good to know.

"Min is right. Baby, you have nothing to apologize for. None of us are upset, well not at you. At whoever leaked the photos, at the people commenting and blowing it up, and the shitty gossip rags for exploiting rumors for clicks. There's a lot of people to be angry at, and not one of them is you." Damon picked up, his voice steady while he rocked Leo and himself back and forth. It soothed a piece of your soul to hear it in words from them. You'd always had a hard time with your own self-worth, but years of therapy had taught you to listen to people you trust. You trusted them.

"I can't do this anymore!" Leo abruptly yelled, shocking the room. His eyes were wide, nostrils flared, and quicker than anyone could react he bit down on Damon's forearm. The elder shrieked, a look of horror and betrayal on his face as Leo took the opportunity and broke free from his hold. He immediately ran for the bed, clamouring up and over Hansung and Hyunbin (much to both of their dismay), wiggling his way into the pile of limbs now covering you. He stuck his head into the crook of your neck, inhaling deeply before settling down with a long sigh.

"Well." You said into the shocked silence. "That was a dramatic way to ask for a hug but sure, come on in. Might as well have everyone in the bed. C'mon big scary leader, I know you want in on this too." You wiggled your brows, a laugh bubbling out at his eager waddle over. After some shuffling, and complaining, the six of you were settled on the bed. It wasn't conventional, there were a lot of overlapping body parts, and everyone had some contact with you, but it was comfortable.

It stayed that way for the next hour, the air filled with contentedness, and idle chit chat going back and forth. You stayed mostly quiet, soaking in their presence. They fit so well together, the way they read each other's minds, the way their bodies instinctively knew where the others were. You knew they were keeping it light on your behalf, and you appreciated the time to sort your thoughts.

Your emotions levelled, the sadness and anxiety not quite so prominent, and the numbness fading into the background. Now that your head was clear you could think about the facts.

Fact 1: Your identity was still secret for now, all these comments had nothing to do with you.

Fact 2: The photos were poor quality. Which meant the mark was poor quality and could be written off, or hopefully forgotten about with proper distraction.

Fact 3: 90% of the negative comments were geared towards you, not the boys or the band. Which hopefully meant the backlash would be minimal.

Thinking it out made you feel better, and once you had made up your mind you talked to the guys. Their headspace was in a similar position, even though they were mostly concerned with your feelings. Sweet, naive but sweet. You told them of the ideas you had, asking their opinions.

"I, no we, will support whatever you want to do love. If you want to come out as our mate, or if you want to continue keeping it on the down low. We care about you, not what anyone thinks about our relationship." Leo was the first to respond, earning agreement from the others.

"Jagi, if you choose the press release… You'll be watched all the time. They'll know about you." Hyunbin brought up. It was a valid point, but it was bound to happen eventually.

You told them as much. "But it's okay. I may not be ready to be out with you, but I don't care if people know we're friends, that we're in each other's lives."

"This can be the trial run for our marriage announcement. I looked it up, I think a spring wedding with a three-page spread in the daily news. Maybe we can get Balmain to make my suit." Hansung stopped when a pillow flew into his face, his shit eating grin never leaving his face.

"Yah!" Damon yelled, his face beet red.

Any other day the idea of marriage would send you into a champagne fuelled coma, but today you appreciated the younger's teasing. "What? You don't want a spring wedding? Or you don't want to marry me?" You joined in, face turned in mock offense. Hansung laughed loudly from beside you, high fiving you.

Damon sputtered, still red and speechless. "That's not- I didn't- fuck you both." He gave up, face hidden in his hands, red ears still on display under his brown curls.

"What about a summer wedding then?" Leo posited.

You hummed, considering. "I think that would be too warm. Destination then?"

"Is Noona paying?" Hyunbin winked, the thrill of teasing his pack alpha all too obvious in his grin.

"For you baby, anything." You winked back, sending him a finger heart. The ribbing continued back and forth, everyone joining in to pile on their pack leader's embarrassment. By the time you called it, afraid Damon might literally combust, all six of you were breathless from laughter. The air felt lighter, it felt like life had been breathed back into you, and all it had taken was some reassurance and support, and a really awful joke. You felt ready to tackle the rest of the day.

* * *

DAMON

The drive to the office was quiet, but comfortable. You let him hold your hand the entire time. The two of you didn't speak much, since you were being driven by a staff member, but he subtly kept an eye on your pulse point. You seemed calm now. Which was more than he could say for himself. He was a ball of tied up emotions, nervous energy thrumming through him.

Damon was bouncing on his feet as he showed you to the conference room. Luckily for him you were too lost in thought, a sober look on your face. There were already some staff seated once he'd arrived, and he instinctively held you closer. He didn't miss the way they scrunched their noses as you two settled into seats.

One of his managers, Dokyung, smiled and greeted them, going so far as to stand and bow to you. Damon snickered as everyone else rushed to do the same, some of them confused as to why his manager, older than both of you, was using such formal language with you, his mate.

"Nice to meet you. Please, let's speak informally." He was again surprised by your use of Korean. Your pronunciation was already good for a foreigner. Better than Leo's when he got here. He could tell your efforts went a long way as his staff smiled at you.

"Do you want to speak in English, or can Dae translate?" Dokyung asked you. He watched you consider, but you smiled and looked over at him. Nodding an understanding that he could translate for you. His heart swelled with pride.

"I'll translate. We already spoke about the article as a group, so let's get to it. What are your thoughts?"

"Well, as far as the company goes, they have given us their support in whatever we decide. And, in deference to your mate, we don't want to offend anyone."

"Hyung, just speak plainly, you've never pulled punches with us. She's not fragile, her feelings aren't going to be hurt that easily."

"In that case, it's not great. It's still trending, and the reaction is mixed. A lot of the attention isn't coming from Stay, but antis as well as locals. A lot think she looks like a foreigner, which they aren't happy about. Analytics are still going to see if this will turn into something bigger. But…"

"But?"

"I don't think they'll let it go. It's the first real leak about your personal lives, so they're latching onto it like leeches. I think it's very likely they'll dig into it until they find her. And... the comments are... not pretty. Again, analytics is going to go over all the trends. But we should prepare for the inevitable, since you're, uh, serious with staying together."

"Hyung, watch it."

He was getting agitated, his eyes twitching. A hand landed on his thigh, squeezing reassuringly and pulling him out of his head. He looked over at you and smiled gratefully.

"I'm aware of the risks. I've had my assistant contact my hotel to stress security and secrecy. As far as the mark is concerned, it's not permanent, but we do plan to keep seeing each other."

Damon hummed his agreement. "We have two options that we talked about. Ignoring, which seems no longer be an option, or she has a press statement prepared about her investment in the company with a story about how she met us through her friendship with the CEO and that we're friends now. Not a lie, but it gives us more time." You squeezed his thigh again.

"That still doesn't address the mark. It's the highest trending point. Not more than a couple weeks ago you went live and told the entire world you found your fated mate. Then these pictures surface, with Minju not you, and a marked woman.

The rumour mill is going crazy. Some of them are getting close to the truth."

Damon felt the unease rise in his gut. He'd already had it out with Minju, had ranted about how badly he crossed the line. He hadn't had it in him to reprimand him, again, because of the new danger it posed: exposing them. The guilt was written all over his face since this morning. It didn't make Damon any less angry over the whole situation. However, now wasn't the time for pack laundry to be aired. You two had come in with a plan and the agreement to be a united front. A wall of solid iron.

You tapped your fingers on the table, your brows wrinkling as you thought. "Why do we have to address the mark? It's not permanent, in fact it's healed over for the most part already. We can address the rumour with the press release. Do a few targeted outings with each member separately to make it seem normal and ignore any questions of the mark."

The staff broke into conversation amongst themselves. They argued over the pros and cons of both options, and he let them. He knew it was better to observe and let someone else be the first to speak in these situations. He was glad your Korean wasn't good when one of the assistants brought up the comments, reading some aloud.

"They're saying she's 'unfit', 'too fat for idols', and more. There's more too, some saying if she's dating them, she should be ashamed, how she's not good enough and too many telling her to kill herself and save the boys the scandal. It'll get worse

307

if they find out who she is."

"I agree, it'll be a war. Her fans outnumber ours, and she has serious social currency. What if they turn against the band?"

"Yeah, but her show is super popular right now here. Plus, the buzz wouldn't be bad for our international numbers. If they come for her, I'm sure her celebrity friends will come to her defence."

"Enough!" He growled, completely done with hearing them talk about you like you weren't in the room. "Babe, what do you want to do?"

Throughout the entire meeting you stayed calm and collected, not a hair out of place and giving nothing away. He was impressed, he needed to remember to ask you how you managed it. Now you looked at him, completely focused as if only he were in the room. "Put out the press release. It'll ease their worries. And tell them that if they want me to not understand they shouldn't use konglish words." He cringed, knowing she'd caught the part about the comments online. You didn't seem phased though, so he hoped you weren't too upset. He would still be keeping a close eye on you.

He relayed the message, and they all got to work. He texted the group chat, letting the boys know what was going to happen, while you sent the necessary files and updated your own team.

The rest of the meeting was wrapped up quickly. He knew he wasn't hiding his stress or animosity well, but he didn't think it was that bad until they were all giving him a wide berth as they left. Not a single one looked at his mate, all averting their gazes when he looked at them.

Once they were alone you started to giggle, still typing away on your laptop. He turned to you, confused. "What?" He asked.

"You realize you basically pumped out 'fuck off' pheromones the entire meeting, right? Especially towards the end. I'm shocked they didn't cover their noses and make a run for it." You chuckled to yourself.

"No, I didn't do that did I?" Sure enough, when he sniffed around in the air, he could smell the possessive warning that was fading in the air. Well, fuck. He ran a hand through his hair dejectedly. He thought he'd been doing so well too.

"It's okay honey, I'm sure they understand. We'll buy them all lunch today as an apology. I already texted Lili to come by this afternoon with enough bubble teas to drown in. If you know what they like, text me and I'll forward it on." You hadn't looked up at him once yet, the words coming from you so sure and easy.

He marvelled at you again. You took everything with so much grace, he felt like a child in comparison. He felt an overwhelming need to hold you, so he did. He picked you up unceremoniously, smiling as you screamed at him. He sat in your chair, repositioning you so you were sitting on his lap comfortably. When you glared at him, he poked your cheek, making you gasp in contempt. You looked so cute like this.

He cuddled into you, face pressed into your shoulder as you worked. Breathing in the scents of his pack on you calmed his racing heart, and soon the room was rid of any threatening scents. Instead, if someone walked in, they would be enveloped in a soft cocoon of contentment and pride.

* * *

Notice regarding recent photo leak

Hello, this is KC Entertainment

Firstly, we apologize for causing concern to Stars. Recently there was a photo leaked of Ho Minju with an unnamed female. We want to clear up the speculation. The woman with them is the author of the book series and hit TV show Finding Asgard. She has decided to make an investment in KC and its affiliates, and become an active voting stockholder. She met the boys through an event with the chairman, whom she has been friends with for years. After meeting, the boys and her became close and are now friends.

Please respect both Galaxy members' privacy and hers in this matter.

Thank you.

Fifteen

Red Paint Stains

You blinked awake only to be momentarily blinded by sunlight. The ray of sun, so cheeky and bright, danced along your bed mocking you. You supposed it was your fault for forgetting to close the blinds, which meant you were rudely awoken by the warmth and brightness of the sunrise instead of your alarm.

Trying to kill time getting ready didn't work out so well. You ended up standing in your living area fully dressed, only twenty minutes later. You'd gotten so used to having the guys around that without them it was eerily quiet, almost unsettling. You decided to depend on old routines, making yourself a coffee and sitting outside. It only took three tries and fourteen curse words, but you triumphantly carried your coffee out to the balcony off the dining room. Today was pushing you already.

The streets were quiet, but slowly waking up. You indulged in the cool breeze and noises of familiar life starting up around you. It wasn't the birdsong you were used to at home, but there was a certain fulfilling quality to listening to a city come alive. Your nerves settled as you soaked it in.

At least, they were settled until you opened your phone and made the mistake of browsing through socials. Your press release had come out yesterday evening, and under Damon's authoritarian regime you'd all been banned from checking your phones the rest of the night. He even had Lili in on it, which you still couldn't get the girl to tell you how he'd contacted her. You didn't entirely mind it, you had so much work piling up now that a break from your screen was a small blessing.

As expected, you were all trending. It was a clusterfuck honestly, posts ranging from confused, to rabid to the conspiracy theorists. You had your own fans to blame for that one, there was now an abundance of theories about your next work having something to do with Kpop or the boys. It wasn't a bad idea though, you filed it away in your notes to think about. A few comments hit a little harder than others.

> **@minniespillow**
> **Why is this old hag hanging around?**
> **Ouch, I'm the same age as Damon. That's uncalled for.**
> **@hyunoneeek**

The guys become world famous and this wannabe latches on. Get a grip, your not at their level.

   @diebellaswan: Uhh, do you even read? Your little Kpop group is the wannabe here. She was in Forbes, Times and on the bestseller's list more times than any other author her age. Her show has won more awards than you have brain cells.

   @diebellaswan: also it's *you're

@Leeeeoshine

   I want the boys to be happy, really I do. But... they can do soooo much better. This feels gross and creepy. Is she their boss now? And shes friends with their chairman?🫠

   @cherry*streamingglxy*: OMG RIGHT?!! If this was a girl group and a guy everyone would hate him. Just cuz shes a woman doesnt mean shes not a creep for this

   @Leeeoshine: exactly shes just using her money to buy her way in the door. Wat does she even know about kpop??

@g@laxyfighting

   Soooo... are we not going to talk about how out of their league she is? She should go back to america where everyone is fat like her #notakoreanbeauty

   @koalen03: idt she knows what a diet is, maybe someone should show her ☻

Your fingers moved mindlessly, scrolling through thread after thread. There were even tiktoks. It's not like you've never been made fun of, you grew up being bullied and pushed around by other people as well as your own pack. Your 'father' pointed out your flaws every chance he got; you'd ruined many pillowcases from crying yourself to sleep. But you'd gotten away from it, survived through it, and came out only slightly traumatised. You liked to think it added a little bit of personality and spice.

The traffic was increasing and the sounds of the city with it, but you heard none of it. You were trapped in your own mind, reliving memories you wish would wash away like your lessons in math. Why could you remember every tragic insult, every hated look in the mirror, but you couldn't remember the Pythagorean theorem? The memories started to pass and fade, leaving you feeling cold and empty. You glanced down at your phone and saw it was peppered in drops of water. You looked out at the light blue grey sky, no rain in sight. Ah, it was your crying, you noted as you passed a hand across your cheek.

You couldn't stay out here any longer, even the open air felt suffocating. Going back to bed, though appealing, wouldn't work either and would only leave you alone with your thoughts. You wished you knew the area well enough to go for a jog, but Damon would murder you with his eyes if he found out you ran around and got yourself lost. Again.

You settled for a walk to the coffee shop down the block. Straight line, you would probably not get lost, and if you did well... you probably deserved the scolding at that point. Maybe even a tracker chip. You grabbed your purse from the counter, the perfectly good coffee machine you'd just used staring at you in judgment, and headed out.

The weather was even nicer down on the street. You closed your eyes and breathed in the, sort of, fresh air. It smelled like gasoline and pavement, but it was better than the self-loathing that coated your room currently. You turned to the left, checking Naver Maps quickly, and started walking in the right direction.

You weren't more than a foot away from the boundaries of the hotel, when you were roughly pulled into the adjoining alleyway. A clammy hand covered your mouth before you were able to scream. You looked around frantically, trying to wiggle out of their grip but too soon you were pushed forward and kicked to the ground. Your hands barely came up in time to save you from falling face first into the grimy concrete.

Three girls surrounded you, sporting matching black windbreakers and masks. You couldn't see half their faces, but from what you could they were furious. Which didn't make sense, shouldn't you be the one angry right now? What stick did they have up their asses?

You soon found out as they started yelling at you. Most of it was in Korean, too fast and accented to understand. You did understand when they started throwing things at you. It took you a moment to figure out what it was, your first instinct was to curl into a ball and protect your face. You felt a warm

315

liquid splash you with each hit, opening one eye and seeing your arms coated in red paint. You looked up, sure enough they were throwing water balloons filled with paint at you.

"Whore!" One yelled in heavily accented English.

The middle one threw the last balloon, whipping it hard and directly at your face. You were frozen in shock, the hit landing square on your nose. The pain bloomed as you choked on the vile tasting paint.

"Stay away. Or you blood next." Wannabe baseball pitcher spat at you with venom. The pieces were connecting, but your body was too slow and confused to do anything but stare as the girls ran away.

Everything after that was a blur. At some point some stranger must have noticed you lying curled up because there were people talking, lights flashing and then you were in the emergency room. It felt like when you were driving somewhere and found yourself at your destination, or halfway there, having no recollection of driving. It was terrifying, but at the same time you were thankful because it left you numb, able to get through it without having a breakdown.

You were alone now in a sterile smelling room, hospital machines asleep behind you, fluorescent lights beating down from overhead. A curtain closed you off from the other beds and patients, but not the noises. You stared at your phone. It was covered in dried red paint, but it looked like someone had already tried to wipe it off. You? A nurse? Someone who found you? You had no clue but it kept your mind occupied until the doctor came in.

"Hello, I'm Dr. Ahng. How are you feeling?" He was a kind-faced man in his early forties, you guessed by the laugh lines and streaks of peppered gray in his hair.

You shrugged. "About as good as I can be after being assaulted with paint balloons I guess." Dr. Ahng grimaced, your joke not hitting as well as you'd hoped. "Physically I'm fine, the only thing that really hurts is my nose."

The doctor nodded, explaining that you hadn't broken it, but it would be bruised and swollen. They'd given you a cortisone shot to help the swelling and cleaned the shallow cuts on your forearms. After a quick talk about icing it and taking the antibiotics in case of infection he had a nurse bring you in a change of clothes and help you take a quick shower. You didn't look half bad in the teal scrubs. Maybe you should have been a doctor. No, that was a terrible idea, you would definitely kill a lot of people accidentally mixing up prescription names. You couldn't even remember the right name of the kind of ramen you liked.

"Okay, you go. Have pack? Family?" The nurse asked. She'd been looking at you with so much pity all morning, it was driving you insane.

You shook your head automatically. She furrowed her brows, obviously thinking of how to say what she wanted in English. "Pack? Galaxy boy. I see photo. He not mate? You call, he come." Shit, of course that's what all the pity was from, not just the fact that you were rushed in here covered in paint with a bum nose, but why.

Could you call them? Yes. Should you call them? Damon's hurt face flashed in your mind. Yes. Did you want them to see you like this? Hell no. They'd been blowing up your phone, and from the texts you were also getting from Mel and Lili, you guessed your assault was front page news. Which meant reporters would be staked outside, waiting. If the boys came, and they all would, it would only add fuel to the fire. No, that was not an option. You wanted them far away from all this. In fact, you wanted yourself far away from all this.

Consequently you denied, and the nurse left it alone. She did do you a solid though, helping you call a taxi to one of the service entrances, letting you bypass the paparazzi. You snuck up to your room from the underground parking lot, breathing a lot easier once you closed your door, your back leaning against it. You closed your eyes and slumped down, sliding to the ground.

A throat clearing had your eyes opening and pulse racing, the trauma from earlier rearing up until you saw who was in front of you.

"Oh, hey everyone. What's up?" You tried to sound casual, looking at each of your mates. Who were standing in your hotel room, furious looks on their faces.

Well, fuck.

Multiple things happened at once, and your still lagging and overwhelmed brain tried to process them in order. Damon was speaking, Hyunbin was glowering, Hansung was crying, Leo was walking towards you and Minju was shifting on his feet, hands clenching and unclenching with a dangerous look on his face. The room exploded in scents, your olfactory nerve almost shutting down from the barrage and force of them. Tears started welling in your eyes, but you weren't sure if you were upset, or whether the anger, disappointment, fear and guilt in the air was to blame.

"-and how did you think that would make us feel?" You caught the end of Damon's tirade, his eyes softening a fraction when they met your tear-filled ones. Leo was crouched down in front of you now, hesitantly reaching for your arm. His face was pinched as he took in your scrapes and bruised face.

"I'm sorry." It came out more monotone and quiet than you meant. You were sorry for causing them to worry. But you weren't sorry for not telling them. You stood by your decision.

Minju's eye twitched and he moved into your sight line. "Are you? You don't seem sorry. When were you going to call us? When you got back?" He paused, tilting his head. "Were you going to tell us at all?"

The air felt electrified in your silence. You hadn't thought that far, surely you would have told them. At some point. Minju read into your reticence. "You weren't, were you?" It wasn't a question, you all knew it. Not by the deadened tone he used.

"I-I don't know. Probably. I'm not even fully myself yet." You felt your temperature rising, the panic and exhaustion of the day raising your defences and flustering you. "I just got home after a fucking hell of a morning. I haven't eaten, I have paint in places I don't want to think of, and I just wanted to go the fuck to sleep. I didn't think about when I would call you, but I would have when I was ready." You were shaking now, the anger spurring words out of your mouth you both meant and didn't.

Leo's hand gently cupped yours. He held it like it was broken, like you were something broken and fragile. Somewhere you knew he meant well, but right now it felt like you were being coddled, pitied. And you hated it.

"Baby, we didn't mean anything-" Damon's soft voice was cut off by your glare.

"No. You didn't. You probably all meant well, but did you think for a second about what I needed? YOU needed to see me. But what did I need? I needed to not come into my safe space, after being assaulted, to be surprised by five people. I needed to rest, time to process everything that happened by myself." You were being petulant at this point, your tone whiny and rude. But you had no mental capacity to care. If there was a limit for what you could endure in one day, it had been met. You were now closed for business. Anyone who chose to disrespect that came at their own risk.

You got to your feet, shakily, but with the help of Leo and his still gentle hold. You didn't want to hurt him, instead squeezing his hand and looking at him intently before pulling away. Even the small sad smile shrivelled your heart just a little. The others were quiet, looking at you in shock underlined with hurt. The cogs were working though, and it didn't take long for them to unfreeze.

"We're sorry we didn't... You're right we didn't think about what you wanted." Damon said as you walked towards him. You ignored him, moving to walk past him and towards the bedroom. His arm reached out, large hand circling your wrist. "But," his voice was louder now and you stopped walking. Not that you had much choice. "But, you should have called us right away. We would have been there at the hospital with you."

"We should have been the first people you thought of." Hyun-bin muttered under his breath.

That comment was like a spark on dry pine needles, a flame roaring to life. You whirled on him, glaring daggers. "Excuse me?" You spat. "All I did was think of you!" You ripped your hand from Damon, turning to look at each of them. They cringed at the fire and rage in your gaze. "From the first second I was pushed to the ground, to when the nurse asked if I wanted to call my family. I went through this all alone because I was thinking about you!" You screamed. It was rare for you, this burst of emotion, even more so the raised voice. You preferred cold and icy over hot and fiery. Because as quick as a pine needle fire ignites, it also burns out, leaving nothing but ashes and smoke in its wake.

Your insides were nothing but ashes now, your voice hoarse and catching on the tears now flowing down your cheeks. "If I called you all would have run to me, without a second thought. Without caring about the paparazzi. Or the rumors, or your careers. Your lives."

"We don't give a shi-" Hansung started but you silenced him with a watery look.

"I know. That's exactly the point. You don't care about any of it. It's one of the things I love about you. But it's also exactly why I'm in this situation." You sniffled as you spoke, looking into the beautiful brown boba eyes of your mate. He looked as heartbroken as you were beginning to feel. Reality sinking in as you spoke. "All of this over a blurry picture and a press release. What happens when all five of you suddenly rush to my bedside?"

"Who cares? We can deal with it." Minju sounded exasperated, annoyed at the thought of bothering with anyone else's opinions. You wished you could be so carefree.

"We can protect you. Move in with us, we'll never leave you alone again." Hyunbin offered, clinging on to the other side of the molten coin. Like there was a good side to be had.

You took in the faces of each man. Heartbroken guilt eating away at them, but joined by hope, naive thoughts of an easy fix. Ever since you'd joined their rag tag little group, as rag tag as immensely popular artists can be, you'd been dancing around the giant volcano in the room. That's right, volcano, because elephants were wise and amazing, not prepped to go off and destroy entire cities. And now the fissures were opening, seeping hot lava scalding your feet. It was only a matter of time before an eruption began. You'd do whatever you needed to save your city, your little pack.

You memorized their faces. Their sharp jaws, sparkling eyes, the memory of radiating smiles, warm hugs and safety. You smiled, genuine and tinged with the sadness seeping into your bones. "I'm tired, I don't want to talk anymore. I'm sorry for worrying you, we'll talk when I wake up okay?"

They all nodded, clearly having more to say but respecting your wish. You didn't expect them to leave as easily as they did, owed in part to Leo who started herding them out complaining about being hungry. You gave him a grateful smile when he paused at the door. He looked uncertain, as if there was something he wanted to say. He seemed to rethink it though and simply smiled back and waved goodbye.

The door clicking closed felt so final, the last notes in a song, the ending scene in a movie. The last pages in a book where the protagonist sits alone on a bench and reminisces about things lost and found. If you stayed too long, thought too long, you wouldn't be able to do what was needed.

You showered again, your movements robotic and stiff, the hot water barely registering. Changing into sweats went much the same, your body working on autopilot. After you crawled in bed, exhaustion pulling on your muscles, and before letting yourself fall asleep you tapped away on your phone. You only had to send one message, which was a relief as sleep took you moments after you hit send.

(1) New Message

Mel: (airkticket.pdf)
   I'll be there to pick you up. I've got you.

Sixteen

And Then There Were Five

HANSUNG

His days off were all pretty similar; he'd sleep in, roll out of bed to make himself food and coffee, check to see if anyone was around and then head back to his room. He'd watch anime or dramas, occasionally turn on a game Leo had gotten him into or finish one of the many ongoing books he had strewn about the house. The key element was relaxation. Anything he could do by exerting the least amount of effort possible. Minju and Damon liked to call him 'an inside cat', and he didn't disagree.

Lately he hadn't been able to indulge in his relaxing days off. He wasn't upset, spending time with you was so much better. But he was looking forward to a nice sleep in. Theoretically he could have had it today. After yesterday's shitshow they had had an impromptu pack meeting and decided to give you space until you were ready to talk. It wasn't exactly easy, and although he could have caught up on sleep since they'd cleared their schedule, he was plagued by unease every time he closed his eyes.

He'd see the pictures spreading online, ones of you covered in red and looking dead to the world, ones of you being put on a stretcher and loaded into an ambulance. His imagination ran wild, suddenly the paint was dark red blood and the figure on the stretcher was covered in a spattered sheet, lying still. He conjured images of knives and poison, all kinds of ways you could have been hurt. It's not out of the realm of possibility after all; Sasaengs have poisoned idols, they could do so much worse to civilians.

He felt like a zombie on Adderall. He was slumped against the breakfast bar at their apartment. It was midmorning, but there were no signs of life. His stomach was in knots, too upset to force food in it. His leg bounced while his head rested on the cool stone of the countertop. Something was wrong. He felt… off. Yet he couldn't pinpoint what it was. The best he could come up with was that his spirit felt disconnected from his body. It was straining and searching for something.

He could have sat like that for hours, time passed simultaneously in a blink and like it was stuck in molasses. He blinked his eyes open when a warm hand began rubbing his back. "Mmm. Nice." He mumbled out, a little bit of drool dripping from the corner of his mouth.

A deep huff of laughter followed another hand joining in the rubs, gently massaging his tense muscles. "Wanna get up baby? You're going to hurt your back like that." Hyunbin coaxed.

"Nope." Hansung muttered. He didn't want to move, but his packmate was right. He groaned as he straightened, one hundred percent regretting his place of rest. There was a couch ten feet away.

He was guided over to said couch, gratefully plopping himself face first into the cushions. Hyunbin chuckled at his antics. "Not exactly what I meant but sure. You okay Sung? You seem off."

Hansung shrugged his shoulders. "Are any of us okay?"

Hyunbin sighed before picking the younger up and sliding underneath him. He settled his head to lay in his lap, Hansung happily cuddling into the thick thighs. "No, I guess we're not. But we will be, it's just the first bump in the road. We'll figure it out. She'll move in here and we can figure out a way to protect her better. Maybe set her up with an office at work."

"Hyung, I don't think that's the solution. Did you see the way she looked when you brought it up? Look, I want her here as much as the rest of you, but I think saying that might have been a mistake."

Hyunbin frowned down at him, his hand idly playing with the silky brown strands of his hair. "What do you mean? I know I shouldn't have said it at the time, but it makes sense. Once she's calmed down we can talk about it again."

Hansung sighed. His hyung, as lovely as he was, could be dense sometimes. He knew in his gut you wouldn't be taking that offer. Even without the assault and security threat, you were too independent. He loved it, he loved that you said 'fuck you' to the world and did things your own way. You could protect yourself, omega or not, and he admired it. He strived to put out the same image, strength despite nature.

It wasn't the only reason though, there was an underlying ominous feeling. It churned again at the mention of working things out, at an easy solution. "Hyung. It's not going to be that easy. Not this time." He thought for a moment. "I'm really scared." He confessed. That about summed up his messy feelings.

"Oh baby, it's okay. I think we're all worried but there's nothing to be scared of. Have you ever known Damon to not get what he wants? Remember when they didn't want you to produce on our third album? We were finally getting bigger, and they thought you should take a more submissive role, play up the helpless baby girl role."

Hansung grimaced at the memory. God, the fittings alone for the potential 'new look' were a nightmare. So many skirts and netting. He wasn't against it, but it wasn't his thing, give him a cozy hoodie and pair of jeans any day. They passed him around the art department, playing dress up for a week before Damon caught him mid breakdown, crying his eyes out as he tore at some forsaken pink frilly clothing item. The eldest had gone on a rampage for two weeks. He refused to work, throwing potential collaboration meetings, and threatening to get the Omega Welfare Society involved. He even started printing out articles on omega mistreatment and tapping them up in the halls throughout the building. He was a one-man revolution.

"Don't remind me, I still get emails from the Omega Daily asking for interviews about my 'position as an omega role model'. It's all his fault. But I love him and wouldn't be here without him." He acquiesced, a fond smile working its way out as he thought of their pack leader.

He let himself be talked into believing his hyung, that they would get through this, and you would be okay. It probably was naive of him, of all of them, to think that way. That only their determination would win the day. It was definitely naive of them.

Because as the day wore on, they continued to hear nothing from you. It was radio silence. It unnerved him, the tight ball inside him becoming more and more compact, quickly nearing panic attack territory. Where were you? Why weren't you answering them? They'd all left texts, limited to two each by Minju who scowled at them until they acquiesced. No one had called. Partially because they still held out hope that you were sleeping.

"She could be blacked out, you know how you get when you don't sleep for days." Leo tried reasoning.

It didn't take much longer for Damon to lose it. He was tense, they all were. But they wore it differently. Hyunbin let himself feel his emotions as they came on, stress, anger, sadness, contemplation. In between he tried to distract the others with jokes or light-hearted banter. Minju stress cooked, letting his temper and angst out on poor unsuspecting noodles. Leo nested, weird for a beta but on par for their team. Damon, well he paced a hole in the floorboards, anxious energy turning into random spurts of 'fix-it-Dae'. No wobbly leg or squeaking door was safe.

"I'm calling." He announced, phone already to his ear. They

collectively held their breath, eyes focused on their leader. His frown was like a domino effect, their own frowns appearing one after the other. "She isn't answering, her phone is off."

"Maybe she forgot to plug it in, that happens to me all the time." Leo; Mr. Brightside at every wrong turn. Hansung would coo at him if he wasn't fighting to breathe in properly.

"I'll try, maybe it was a fluke." Hyunbin offered, getting the same dial tone. One by one they each tried, each getting the same wretched dead tone. What was that saying about insanity? Because they continued calling. On and off for hours, even going so far as calling her assistant.

"Lili-ssi, please. I'm begging you." Damon pleaded into his phone. He was sitting on the sofa, Hansung on one side and Leo on the other. His free hand was gripping his knee tightly, the knuckles going translucent.

Minju grabbed the phone hastily from his perch hovering behind the back of the couch. They listened in to the one-sided conversation.

> *"Lili-yah. I'm your bias, right?*
> *Good, good.*
> *I know she's your boss, but I'll give you anything you want. A one-on-one date with me.*

Yah! I should be offended at that!

Okay, okay I'm sorry.

What about a date with any idol? I know a lot of people.

...No... No I understand. We're worried. Please just call us or tell her to call us when you see her."

Minju threw the now darkened phone back to Damon. "She says she can't say, that she doesn't know anything and what she does know it's not her place. Hyung, I know we said we'd give her space, but this doesn't sound good."

"It sounds like she's ignoring us." Hyunbin sounded defeated and scared.

"She wouldn't-" Leo started, on his way to saying yet another comforting thought.

"Stop!" Hansung yelled, surprising everyone. His face was red with anger, his breathing coming in quick bursts and tears welling in his eyes. It was all too much. "There's no positive spin to this Leo, just fucking stop."

"Choi Hansung..." Minju warned. Leo's face began to crumple, his lip quivering. Hansung felt like a piece of shit for making his packmate upset, but it was a later-him problem because currently he was spiralling.

"No! I told you, I told all of you since this morning something felt off." He gripped himself tightly before standing abruptly. "I'm going to the hotel. You can come, or you can fuck around here and keep pretending it doesn't feel like your soul is being ripped to shreds." If he'd spared a look back as he grabbed his coat and keys he would have seen the bewildered look on their faces, or caught Damon questioning what he meant. It probably wouldn't have made him feel any less crazy to know they didn't feel such an intense physical pain as him.

In fact, it was a good thing they didn't because the pain became unbearable as he stood at the concierge desk of your hotel. He wasn't listening anymore, he'd stopped after hearing you'd checked out earlier today. Time stopped, people around him stopped existing. It was only him and his soul ripped from his body and floating in the wind, a new sense of wrongness settling where he thinks his heart might have been before.

And his inner omega howled. It howled as if it was a sentient being inside him, a corporeal wolf living under his skin instead of DNA and hormones floating in his cells. Its howl was dark, full of pain and broken promises. He felt something reach out to him, to it, but the pain only increased until it ceased altogether. His omega quieted, burying itself so deeply inside him he couldn't feel it anymore.

You were gone. And you'd taken the piece of life, tranquillity and future you'd given them with you. They may not have noticed it was missing before you, but they surely felt it missing now, like a gaping hole in the side of a building.

You were **gone**.

About the Author

R.L. Carroll wishes to stay anonymous. She believes that who the author is doesn't matter, especially with her story. She wants you to be the author of your own story, bring to life your own desires and daydreams.

But, as far as anyone knows, she lives in a cabin in the woods in a cold country with her small family. She has two dogs and a black cat who may, or may not, be a demon in disguise. She feeds him a lot of tuna just in case. Her love of KPop began during the pandemic, much like a lot of others', and she has been lost in the fandom ever since. She refuses to call herself a multi, but her friends all know that for the lie it is, because how can you only love one?

You can connect with me on:

🌐 https://lukowskicarroll.wixsite.com/r-l-carroll-books

✎ https://www.instagram.com/rlcarrollbooks

Subscribe to my newsletter:

✉ https://lukowskicarroll.wixsite.com/r-l-carroll-books

www.ingramcontent.com/pod-product-compliance
Lightning Source LLC
Chambersburg PA
CBHW072026020726
47501CB00006B/1980